———————— ★ ————————

She heaved a sigh of relief when she reached the inlet box. Unfortunately, entering this inlet box gave Tory no relief from the cramped space of the pipe she had just exited, because it was now holding two bodies: hers and another lifeless, staring one, hanging upside down, stuffed down into the access hole to the box, with a face suspended at roughly Tory's eye level.

Instead of giving in to the panic, she concentrated on taking slow, deep breaths. To immediately exit the storm-sewer system, she would have to somehow remove the body that was blocking her way. The very next feeling that hit was an overwhelming fear that she was trapped, and that the person who had killed this woman was standing over the inlet box, ready to kill her, too....

———————— ★ ————————

"...a talented author who has cross appeal to romantic suspense fans as well as who-done-it readers. She is a rising star in both genres."
—Harriet Klausner Internet reviews

Previously published Worldwide Mystery titles by
AILEEN SCHUMACHER

FRAMEWORK FOR DEATH

AILEEN SCHUMACHER

AFFIRMATIVE REACTION

WORLDWIDE.

TORONTO • NEW YORK • LONDON
AMSTERDAM • PARIS • SYDNEY • HAMBURG
STOCKHOLM • ATHENS • TOKYO • MILAN
MADRID • WARSAW • BUDAPEST • AUCKLAND

To my son Kevin, travel companion above and beyond the call of duty, who waited patiently, for the most part; you are my sunshine. (But you are not taller than I am. Especially when I'm wearing heels.)

AFFIRMATIVE REACTION

A Worldwide Mystery/July 2000

First published by Write Way Publishing, Inc.

ISBN 0-373-26355-4

Printed in U.S.A.

Acknowledgments

I would like to acknowledge the following people:

My husband, Richard R. Blum. All the books are dedicated to you, even when they're not. My daughter, Dominque Raye Blum-Schumacher, for always liking the mushy stuff. Bobbye Straight, JoAnne Bowers and Janne Kafka Skipper, for being there from the beginning to provide champion-class hand-holding. Sandie and Bill Herron, for doing a pretty good job as latecomers. Tim Merrill, for saving me from stupid errors, and his wife, Alison, for losing the second book so I could know how well this one stood alone. David Eckel for medical advice, and Donna Eckel for being gracious about it; Jim Skiles for insurance advice; Bruce Hoffman for legal advice; and Ana Reyes, for keeping my Spanish profanity correct, as usual. Alison Hendon for tracking down the poem. Robert Boyd, for being my El Paso engineering contact, and Ivonne Peralta, for showing me what Tory looks like. Elaine Reed for knowing the real story behind Kiki Stearns. Andi Shechter, for her support and always being ready to provide a hyphen. Ann Boyd for finding those last devious little camouflaged errors. Paul Cakmis, Terri Cakmis, Lori Hilman and the gang at the 43rd Street Deli, for furnishing all the iced tea that made this book possible. My parents and father-in-law, for their support. Jake Elwell, for letting me pursue him until he agreed to be my agent. Dorrie O'Brien, for making this series possible. Pat and Rollie Steele, for always taking my phone calls. The USAir Pilots who landed our disabled plane on the way home from Bouchercon; obviously, without you, there wouldn't be a book. Jane Rubino, for always being there for me. Lorena Haldeman, for everything from setting up signings to providing a standing New Years Eve invitation. Jeff Buckholz, for the title of Chapter 27. To every single person who has reviewed my books, recommended them to others, or shared words of encouragement, my sincere thanks. To the subscribers of DorothyL Mystery Digest—keep on posting. To anyone I've inadvertently left out, my sincere apologies and my assurances that I probably remembered that I needed to thank you about ten minutes after this book went to press.

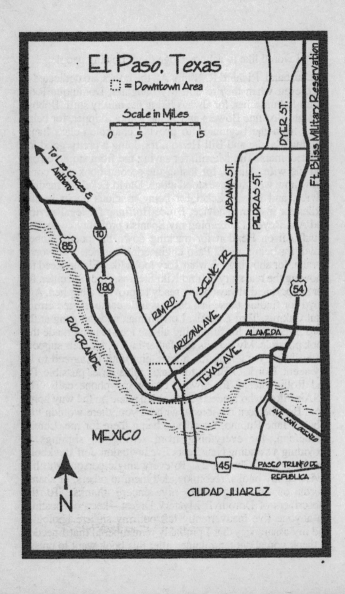

El Paso, Texas

▢ = Downtown Area

Scale in Miles

0   5   1   15

To Las Cruces & Anthony

10

85

180

RIM RD.

SCENIC DR.

ALABAMA ST.

PIEDRAS ST.

DYER ST.

Ft. Bliss Military Reservation

54

ARIZONA AVE.

ALAMEDA

TEXAS AVE.

RIO GRANDE

AVE. SAN LORENZO

MEXICO

45

PASEO TRIUNFO DE
REPUBLICA

CIUDAD JUAREZ

N

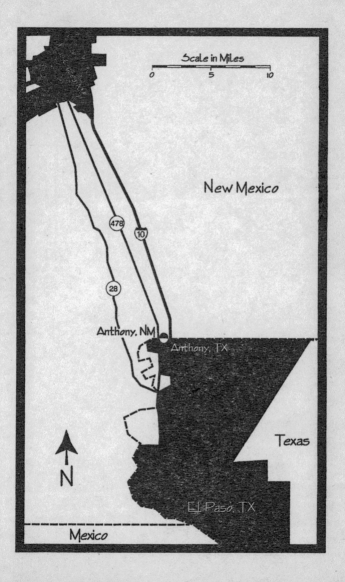

PROLOGUE

SHE FIGURED it came down to a choice between going to work or committing murder.

Thoughts of homicide might seem discordant on such a clear, sunny day, unseasonably mild for mid-January in the Southwest, but the beautiful weather was no match for the unbearable claustrophobic domestic situation unfolding before her.

Did he really think he could replace her, she, who had come first in his life for all these years? Did he expect her to passively stand by and watch as he focused all his attention on the girl now constantly in their midst? He tried to act as though nothing had changed, but the palpable attraction between him and the girl was almost tangible in the charged air of a house suddenly much too small for four people.

For there was the other one, too, the one who was older and wiser, and should have been loyal to her, considering the length and ties of their relationship. But he was worse than useless. If anything, he was enchanted with the girl himself.

She heard their voices rising and falling in the next room, no doubt planning some type of Sunday afternoon entertainment. She would be invited to join in their plans, of course, but simply to maintain appearances, not out of any real desire for her company. Being with the three of them, watching him and the girl, and the other one, looking on with benevolent approval, was more than she could bear.

It was a relief to decide to take an action. Making up her mind, she gathered the necessary equipment—a hardhat, camera, clipboard, flashlight, cellular phone. Tory Travers would not spend one more weekend afternoon watching her besotted fifteen-year-old son, the elfin girl who was now the center of his attention, and his dotingly approving grandfather. If she couldn't

control the relationships developing before her very eyes, she
could at least investigate the technical questions plaguing her
latest engineering project.

Later, she would remember the irony in her conviction that
whatever she found at work that Sunday afternoon, it would be
better than remaining at home.

ONE

SUBSURFACE CONDITIONS

TORY WASN'T particularly concerned that someone had met a violent death out on the isolated tract of land that was her destination. Instead, her misgivings had to do with the fact that solitary inspections of enclosed spaces were not considered good practice, but like every other person who ever decided to ignore a safety guideline, she told herself that she knew what she was doing. There certainly wasn't anyone in sight to argue with her, for Monte Vista Heights was the opposite of a ghost town—it was haunted by the people who had never lived there.

A development of over a hundred acres, planned to accommodate three hundred and fifty suburban homes, it was visually isolated from neighboring subdivisions by the hilly terrain from which it had taken its name—Mountain View. The partially developed, deserted subdivision boasted neatly laid-out roads, now cracked and overgrown with weeds, cul-de-sacs lined with no houses, and curbs intended to complement nonexistent sidewalks and driveways. And then there were storm drains. Yes, there were definitely storm drains.

It was the malfunction of these drains that had brought the development of Monte Vista Heights to a halt over fifteen years ago, and for the life of her, Tory Travers couldn't understand why.

Before the regulation of subdivision development in the United States, various unethical speculators got rich serving the needs of the ever-expanding suburban population. These individuals acquired tracts of land, subdivided them, put in roads and utilities as cheaply as possible, sold the lots and then moved on, usually dissolving their corporate structure as soon as the last lot was sold.

All across the country, cities and counties found themselves inheriting the problems of substandard construction practices, suddenly held responsible for maintaining roads and utilities that had to be immediately repaired, renovated, and upgraded. Frustrated with the economic burden caused by the developers who were no longer around to be held financially responsible, local governments began to enact codes and ordinances that had to be met before subdivision lots could be sold.

Failure to meet such standards had halted the development of Monte Vista Heights, and Tory's engineering firm had been hired by the City of El Paso to determine how to rectify the situation. The problem was, the city's project manager didn't choose to believe what Tory had to tell him. She could see tangible evidence of the results of their last conversation even before she stepped out of her car, manifest in opened manhole covers at every storm drain inlet.

Cal Cortez was a good guy, and a decent engineer; he obviously hadn't liked what he'd had to tell Tory a week ago. He had sat across his desk from her and frowned at his copy of her company's engineering report like he'd hoped it would change the words written there. It hadn't.

"Well," he said finally, nervously running his hand over his head as though he still had a full head of hair to straighten, "we just can't accept this report."

Tory envisioned her company's invoice to the city, the invoice that would now be in contention, the money that would not be forthcoming, and all the paychecks that would have to be cut between now and resolving whatever bureaucratic mess was evolving before her very eyes. "What's wrong with the report?" she asked, going to some effort to maintain a reasonable tone of voice.

Like most people stuck with conveying bad news, Cal chose to address her question via a circuitous route. "This tract of land has been sitting vacant for fifteen years, ever since the project was taken over by the city," he said.

"That's right," she replied, figuring it would be good to agree while she could.

"Then the Housing Board got a grant for low-income assisted housing. It's a nice fat grant, a chance for some good PR for the city. We don't have to purchase land if we bring Monte Vista Heights up to code and use it for the housing project. No more eyesore of deserted property out there, and deserving low-income families get a chance to have decent homes."

"That's right," Tory said again. Actually, it was mainly the City Engineering Department, and specifically Cal's supervisor, who would reap the good PR for this particular plan, but it didn't seem appropriate to point this out.

"So we went looking for an engineering firm that could tell us what we needed to do to make this land useable for the housing grant," continued Cal, with the unmistakable determination of a man who has a verbal destination in mind and only one way to get there. "We advertised the job, evaluated the responding proposals, and your firm was selected to do the study and give the city a report with your findings."

"And that's just what we did," said Tory brightly, in case the problem was that Cal had forgotten the thick document he held in his hands.

"But your report says that it won't take a lot of work to bring Monte Vista Heights up to code," said Cal, sounding like his best friend had failed the Professional Engineer examination.

"That's right," said Tory yet one more time, still trying to maintain her bright tone. "And we thought that would be good news, since it helps you stretch your grant dollars even further. You'll have to do some work, of course, because the original construction is fifteen years old. It's not the best I've seen, but it's not the worst, either."

"Then why the hell did the city condemn the project fifteen years ago?" asked Cal. He leaned forward, peering at her intently. He had obviously gotten around to the point he wanted to make.

Tory was stumped. "I didn't know it was condemned," she said. "We were hired to do a visual inspection and report the findings, that's all. I don't know how the city came to own the property."

Cal looked dismal. "The property improvements were bonded to the city. When the developer defaulted on the bond, the city took possession."

"Well, that's interesting, but it wasn't part of our study. It's not my problem."

"Well, it's my problem," replied Cal. "And so it's your problem, too. This project is politically sensitive," he added, using two words that strike fear into any engineer's heart. "It has quite a history, one that we're not anxious to revisit."

"What history?"

"You don't remember Craig Diaz and his campaign for city commissioner?"

Tory shook her head. Fifteen years ago she was an engineering student at New Mexico State University, forty-five miles north of El Paso, a relatively new wife, and a very new mother. El Paso, its engineering projects, and its politics, had held no interest for her.

"Craig was one of the first Hispanic contractors to really hit the big time," said Cal reflectively, "right after affirmative action programs really got rolling. That was back when establishing some kind of minority program at the local level was the trendy thing to do. There was a big move from some quarters to adopt a local program here; meanwhile, Craig had the golden touch. For a while he couldn't do anything wrong; he went from a one-man outfit to a major player in just a couple years. Of course, there was a big backlash, there always is, and lots of people attributed his success to being the token Hispanic profiting from a liberal political climate. But I remember Craig; he wasn't a bad guy. I think he just tried to go too far too fast, and got stretched too thin."

"What does this have to do with Monte Vista Heights?"

"It has to do with justifying the fact that the city condemned the project fifteen years ago, with fatal results."

"You mean fatal to the project, right?" It might be bad news for a contractor to end up on the wrong side of the Permitting

Department, but Tory hadn't heard of any executions for failing to meet codes. Yet. The concept gave a whole new meaning to the city's new buzzword, "One Step Permitting."

"No, I mean fatal to Craig Diaz," replied Cal soberly. "Monte Vista Heights was his landmark project, larger than anything he'd done before. Craig got the financing for the development at the same time he decided to run for city commissioner. I have to say this for him, he certainly appeared to practice what he preached. He wanted to establish an independent city program of minority business set-asides. The whole affirmative action thing was like a religion to him. He was so busy campaigning that he got overextended, and his work started failing inspections."

"What's fatal about that?" asked Tory. "It can be a nasty wake-up call, but it happens all the time."

"Craig kept telling us he was taking care of the problems, but nothing changed. The Permitting Department decided that the situation warranted extra attention, so they made him run a water-tightness test on his storm-sewer system."

"Bummer," said Tory. A water-tightness test was a major undertaking. It involved plugging the outfall of a sewer system, filling the drains with water, and recording the water level twenty-four hours later. If too much water leaked out during the test period, the system was declared unacceptable. The contractor not only had to fix the problem, he had to find it first.

"His storm drains failed the test," Cal continued. "Craig was blown away by the results. He swore up and down that he'd supervised that part of the construction himself, but I know for a fact that he had his son in charge of the storm-sewer construction. Just out of high school, poor kid. Craig was so sure there had been a problem with the test that he got the city to agree to run it again."

"What happened?" Tory could commiserate with a contractor who had to make payroll week after week, no matter what else was going on.

"It failed again. The second set of test results were even worse than the first, if I remember correctly. The rest of the project was so marginal that the city condemned it, the bank pulled his financing, and Craig went belly-up. Transformed from successful contractor and commissioner candidate to bankrupt nobody overnight. A few weeks later he drove out there in his pickup, drank half a bottle of tequila, and put a bullet in his head. They didn't find him 'til the next day.''

Tory stared at Cal, trying to keep her mouth from dropping open.

"Find that story hard to believe, do you?" he asked. "It's the truth, every word of it.''

"Cal," said Tory slowly, "we didn't see a single significant thing wrong with the storm drains.''

Drains might not be an exciting topic to the general public, but let them malfunction, and the consequences were both significant and detrimental. Subdivisions had two types of drain systems: storm water and sanitary sewer. The purpose of storm drains was to convey storm water out of a developed area to prevent flooding, while sanitary sewers collected domestic waste water and transported it to a sewage treatment facility.

Both systems were expected, within reasonable limits, to be water-tight. Leaking sanitary sewer lines could result in the discharge of raw sewage, an aesthetic problem at best and a significant health hazard at worst. A poorly constructed storm-drain system could also have catastrophic results; leaking storm water could erode subsurface soils, leading to the sudden collapse of any roads or structures located above the drains.

Like any collection system, storm-sewer pipes started out small in the areas where water was first collected, graduating to larger and larger diameter pipe until reaching the discharge point. Only the portions of the system with pipe large enough to accommodate an inspector could be observed directly; the inspection of smaller diameter portions of a drain system had to be accomplished via television cameras traveling the lines, a relatively sophisticated, costly procedure, and definitely outside the scope of the study Tory's firm had been contracted to perform.

The most common causes of leaks in a drain system were

cracked pipes, leaky joints, or faulty connections where the pipe direction or diameter changed. Tory's inspectors had not seen anything that would explain why this particular storm-drain system had failed the water-tightness test so dismally not once, but two times. She had spent the past week studying the original permit applications, previous test results, and her inspectors' notes and photographs, but nothing corroborated what Cal was telling her.

However, in spite of her firm's conclusions, the City Engineering Department decided to go looking for their own answers, or justifications, depending on how you looked at it. They decided to run yet another water-tightness test. On Monday, the discharge points of the storm drains would be plugged and the drains would be pumped full of water. In twenty-four hours, the field technicians would return, measure the water level, and calculate from the volume of the drains the amount of water that had leaked out. If this volume exceeded the guidelines, the storm-drain system would once more be declared unacceptable, and Travers Testing and Engineering Company would be put on the spot to explain how they had missed the problem.

It was a touch of arrogance, perhaps, that had Tory out here alone on a Sunday afternoon, thinking she could find something that had escaped the attention of others. But she had an engineer's curiosity about things that didn't appear to make sense, she had a fifteen-year-old son at home with an intense interest in a fifteen-year-old neighbor girl, and she had her father as a house guest. The same father she hadn't seen for the previous seventeen years. All that put together made her decision to do some lone storm drain inspection out at Monte Vista Heights seem inspired.

And the city had made her job easier by removing all the manhole covers to the drain inlets, obviously in preparation for Monday's water-tightness test. As far as Tory was concerned, that was sloppy work, but the city workers probably reasoned that the subdivision was isolated enough that there wouldn't be a problem with people falling down opened manholes. And besides, she was going to be breaking safety rules herself, so she wasn't in a position to quibble.

It was a bright, sunny day, no clouds in sight, and it wasn't like she was planning to crawl into a space that could be full of deadly fumes. This was a storm-water system, not sanitary pipes with the potential hazard of lethal sewer gas, and not industrial lines conveying chemicals. About the worst that could happen would be to run into unsavory creepy-crawly creatures, but it was too cold for rattlesnakes to be out, and she was dressed appropriately in boots, blue jeans, and a long-sleeved shirt.

Tory resolutely shook off her last misgivings. She only planned to take a look at some random parts of the system, not go too far, and certainly not try to make her way through any pipes smaller than what was comfortable, with a hefty safety margin to spare. She would wear her hardhat and she would take her cellular phone with her. Piece of cake.

Tory located the manhole where she was going to enter the system on her site plan of the subdivision. No use being the Lone Ranger of inspection, finding a problem, and then not being able to describe its location. She flipped on her flashlight and her cellular phone, and lowered herself slowly and carefully through the opening into the drain inlet below.

Although she was not claustrophobic, she had to admit to a healthy dislike of dark, enclosed spaces. As she climbed down the metal rungs into the inlet box, she recalled the rejected engineering report and the invoice for services rendered, now in contention. "It's a dirty job, but someone's got to do it," she muttered to herself.

Tory took a moment to get her bearings and take a look at the inlet box itself. Stamped on the concrete wall of the six-foot-by-four-foot box was the name of the manufacturer—El Paso Precast Concrete Company—in large, black block letters. Now there was a blast from the past.

Memories of someone trying to smash a trailer with a wrecking ball while she was in it came back unbidden. Tory took a deep breath and forced herself to think about the matter at hand. "Makes this inlet box a collector's item," she told herself. El

Paso Precast Concrete Company had long been sold to another firm, one whose name didn't immediately come to mind.

Tory turned her attention from the inlet box to the pipe segments that fed into it. Two sections of pipe, at right angles to each other, took off into the darkness away from the box. One segment was a forty-eight-inch diameter pipe, the other was a thirty-six. Easy choice. Hunched over, Tory began slowly duck-walking the dark length of the larger pipe, shining her flashlight over every inch of the surface, looking for something that could account for the system's water loss. It was slow, uncomfortable going.

After about fifteen minutes, Tory could see a light at the end of the tunnel, so to speak. The light had to be coming from an opened manhole cover in another inlet box. She told herself that if the pipe diameter stayed the same and this was simply an inlet for a change of direction, she would walk another length of pipe. But if it necked down to a thirty-six-inch segment, she was out of there. Smaller diameter pipe would necessitate a mechanic's creeper to roll on, and she hadn't come prepared for that.

She heaved a sigh of relief when she reached the inlet box. It was nice to have some reassurance that the sun was still shining brightly overhead, not to mention the welcome sensation of fresh air as she approached the light. Unfortunately, entering this inlet box gave Tory no relief from the cramped space of the pipe she had just exited, because it was now holding two bodies: hers, and another lifeless staring one, hanging upside down, stuffed down into the access hole to the box, with a face suspended at roughly Tory's eye level.

Never had Tory understood so well what it must be like to be in a claustrophobic panic. She could hear her own ragged breath, knowing it must be her imagination that she couldn't get enough air into her lungs. All she wanted to do was to get out of the enclosed space, and to get out immediately. Instead of giving in to the panic, she concentrated on taking slow, deep breaths. To immediately exit the storm-sewer system, she would have to somehow remove the body that was blocking her way. She knew it would be better if she didn't disturb anything, and the body looked so firmly wedged into position that she was not sure if she could budge it. And, as much as she wanted to get out, she didn't want to try moving that horrible dead thing suspended in front of her.

She sank slowly into a sitting position, all thoughts of scorpions and spiders a thing of the past, her back sliding down against the concrete box wall. At least now she didn't have to look the corpse in the face. It was a woman, with a bullet hole in her forehead and black, shoulder-length hair similar to Tory's own, hanging down and waving gently in the inlet box with every movement Tory made.

After the urge to somehow claw her way to the ground surface subsided, the very next feeling that hit was an overwhelming fear that she was trapped, and that the person who had killed this woman was standing over the inlet box, ready to kill her, too. She told herself that there had been no one within sight when she had first, eons ago, entered the drain system. Herself answered right back that didn't mean there wasn't someone up there right now, standing over the drain inlet, pointing a gun in Tory's direction.

She kept as quiet as she possibly could, switched off her flashlight, and forced herself to look up at the woman's face, partially visible in the light shining in from the opened manhole cover. There was some blood, but not much; it was dark and dried, and it ran a course from the hole in the forehead over both sides of the face, disappearing into a navy blue sweatshirt with yellow flowers embroidered around the neck.

This has to tell me something, thought Tory, if I can calm down enough to figure it out. The blood doesn't look red, it looks dark and dried, so this woman didn't die recently. And, I'm an engineer, I understand drains, which depend on the fact that water flows downhill, so should blood. This woman was killed while she was standing or sitting upright. She was dead before she was put into the inlet box. Tory found this line of logic comforting, and began to feel as though she could think again.

The thought that immediately came to mind was that someone

else should deal with this, and that her place was at home, no matter what company she had to keep. She kept her eyes glued to the opening overhead, or what she could see of it around the body wedged in there, just in case someone should lean over and start shooting into the box. She reached in her hip pocket for her cell phone, thanking the gods of all technology that this was not one of the times the battery had unexpectedly run out. She further thanked the gods of serendipity that the number she was going to call was one she had committed to memory.

She wasn't going to dial 911. She didn't want to explain to a uniformed police officer how she came to be in a storm-sewer inlet box containing a dead body. She planned to call Detective David Alvarez of the El Paso Police Department Special Case Force. He had been complaining loudly about being on restricted duty while recovering from an injury. Well, this should certainly give him something to do, and if a corpse in a storm-sewer inlet box wasn't special, Tory didn't know what was.

TWO

ILLUMINATION

TORY SCOOTED BACK a little way into the pipe she'd exited a few minutes earlier, just in case there really was someone standing above her. Someone responsible for the dead body hanging suspended in the inlet box with her.

She punched in Alvarez's phone number, regretting that she'd never programmed it into her phone as an automatic dial; at the time, it had seemed like too much of a commitment. Then she regretted the fact that his phone kept ringing. He had always picked up by at least the second ring. Always. The thought that he might not be there was too horrible to contemplate.

Then he picked up the phone and said "Alvarez," just like he always did.

"It's Tory," she said urgently.

"Tory," he repeated. He sounded pleased. And surprised. And like he thought this was a social call.

"Yes, Tory." Surely by now they'd dispensed with the identification-of-caller routine. "Listen, I need your help. I'm in a storm-sewer inlet box, and there's a body." There was no response on the other end. "A dead body," she added, just in case he didn't understand.

"You're kidding," he replied.

She couldn't exactly start shouting when there was just the tiniest chance that a killer was standing overhead. "No, I'm not kidding," she hissed. "Have I ever kidded about something like that?"

"Got a point there," he conceded. She heard the muffled sound of a hand going over the receiver to silence a conversation on the other end. Then he was back. "Okay, what's going on?"

"Is someone else there?" She immediately regretted asking the question. There were more pressing matters at hand.

"Yeah, but it's not a problem. Where are you?"

"Monte Vista Heights."

"Never heard of it. Give me an address."

"I don't have an address."

"A street name, then."

"The streets aren't named yet. Well, they are, but they're named A, B, C, and D, and so on."

Alvarez obviously had no constraints on his end regarding raising his voice. "Where the hell are you, Tory?"

"I'm in the storm-sewer system at an abandoned subdivision, northeast of Ascarate Park."

"You're what?" Tory had to hold the phone away from her ear.

"In the storm-sewer system," she repeated.

"By yourself?"

"Yes."

"Why the hell do I even bother asking? Let me get this straight. You're in a storm sewer, by yourself, on a Sunday afternoon, on some abandoned piece of property. And you've discovered a body."

"Yes," she said again.

"I could ask what the hell you're doing, but I'd be happier not knowing, right?" Tory couldn't think of an appropriate answer to that, and it didn't matter, since Alvarez didn't wait for a reply. "Are you sure there's no one else out there?"

"No one was here when I arrived. But I've been in the pipes for the last twenty minutes or so, and my X-ray vision that enables me to see up through three feet of soil isn't working too great, so no, I'm not absolutely sure."

Alvarez swore creatively in both Spanish and English. "Tell me how to get there," he said, and she told him as best she could. "Keep your phone on in case I have problems finding you. And stay where you are until you hear me drive up."

"How will I know it's you?"

"Give me your cell phone number. I'll call you when I get there."

She gave him the number. "You've finally got a cell phone of your own?" she asked. She didn't want to admit it, but she was hesitant to have him hang up.

"New year, new budget, new departmental issue. Why are we discussing this? You have a sudden urge to chat or something?"

"How long do you think it will take you to get here?" she asked, hoping that didn't sound as wimpy as she thought it did.

"Thirty minutes, tops." He sounded like there was no doubt that he knew exactly where he was going.

"And if you think you're lost, you'll call back and ask for directions, right? Tell me that you won't do that guy thing where you just drive around for hours if you get lost." She was blithering, but she couldn't stop herself.

"Tory, I'm out of here. Hang tight, I'm on my way."

"Okay. Thanks," she added as an afterthought.

"No problem. And Tory..."

"What?"

"You really don't have to keep finding dead bodies to keep me interested."

Before she could think of an appropriate reply, the line was dead.

ALVAREZ PULLED his bronze Corvette up next to Tory's white Mazda RX. He didn't have to go looking for her; she was perched, waiting, on the hood of her car. The sling on his left arm didn't slow him down much as he got out of the car and closed the space between them. Alvarez didn't have to take off his sunglasses to see that Tory was pale in addition to being grimy. He used his good hand to pat her shoulder. "Are you all right?" he asked.

He was standing with his back to the sun, so she had to squint to look up at him. "I'm okay. I thought you'd be pissed because I didn't wait in the storm sewer."

"That's our next topic. Are you sure you're okay?"

"I thought you weren't supposed to be driving."

"Minor detail. I've gotten really good at steering with my elbow while I shift. What the hell are you doing out here like a sitting duck?"

"I didn't want to hang out in a storm sewer for another half hour. I went back to where I started, climbed up, stuck my head out real slow, and no one was here."

"And what if there had been?" he asked. She shrugged and looked away. "Move over," he said.

That earned a surprised look. "There's a woman's body in that inlet box over there," Tory reminded him.

"She's dead, right?" Tory nodded. "Then she can wait for ten minutes while you tell me what you're doing here. You can tell me in ten minutes, can't you?" Tory nodded again. "Then move over," he repeated. She did, and he joined her on the hood of her car, where they could both look out over the abandoned subdivision dotted with opened manhole covers at regular intervals. He put his good arm around her; she didn't move away. "Don't tell me you pulled off all those manhole covers by yourself," he said to get the conversation going, "because I'm in no shape to help you put them all back."

"What's wrong with you?" she asked, not looking at him. "You're supposed to think this is all my fault, talk to me in that cop voice you use when you're really mad, and then threaten to shoot me yourself."

"A close brush with death changes your perspective on things," he told her. "This is the kinder, gentler me, but be patient, I'm sure it will pass. Besides, I've been trying to get you to go out with me for the past two weeks."

"I have a house guest."

"From what I understand, he's old enough to take care of himself."

"You're injured."

"Not anywhere it counts."

"I don't want to remind you of any moral dilemmas."

"I'll handle my moral dilemmas and you handle yours." He considered what he'd just said. "I might want to re-think that. What the hell are you doing out here, Tory?"

"Cody likes this girl."

Alvarez made an effort to remember his kinder, gentler self. "The one who had the sex-change operation," he said, to keep up his end of the conversation.

"A makeover," said Tory firmly, "not a sex-change operation. I thought she was a boy named Cole, but then Sylvia gave her a makeover, and she turned into this elfin girl named Kohli. Right before our eyes. Cody took one look at her and he hasn't been the same since."

Alvarez felt sure that Cody Travers would have gotten around to taking a good look at Kohli with or without the help of Tory's flamboyant secretary Sylvia, but he didn't voice the thought.

"It's not like they're doing anything awful," Tory continued. "They're not kissing every minute or groping each other in front of me or anything like that. But she's over at our house all the time, or he's over there. It's not like it used to be," she concluded dismally.

"Cody's almost sixteen," said Alvarez. "He's growing up. It's a good thing, Tory—believe me, it's better than the alternatives."

If Tory remembered that Alvarez's sister would never progress beyond the mental age of a third-grader, it didn't seem to make her feel any better. "And my father thinks it's all wonderful," she added dismally.

"Just how long is your father staying?" asked Alvarez. "Don't tell me he's decided to make up for the last seventeen years by visiting for the next seventeen."

"He's staying 'til the end of the month. Cody's in some big debate competition called Lydia Patterson; he wants to stay for that."

"I know about Lydia Patterson," said Alvarez, surprised that he did. It was amazing, the extraneous things one learned in the course of various homicide investigations. "It's held at Austin High."

Tory looked at him blankly, distracted from her thoughts of Cody for the moment. "Were you in debate in high school?"

"Not unless you count discussions with the assistant principal in charge of discipline—" He stopped himself, shook his head. "You know, I still have no idea what the hell you're doing out here."

"He hasn't said he's sorry," said Tory miserably, and Alvarez was taken aback to see a tear slide down her cheek.

He had to let go of her to use his good hand to fish out a handkerchief. She wiped her eyes and blew her nose and crumpled his handkerchief into a smaller and smaller bundle of cloth. "Do you really expect Cody to apologize for being interested in a girl?" he asked.

"Not Cody, my father," said Tory, thrusting the handkerchief back at him as though it had fallen out of favor along with its owner. "He's never apologized for what went on, all those years ago, when I left home." She took a deep breath. "And Cody even told him. Cody told him what really happened."

The conversation was finally starting to make some sort of sense, at least in terms of why Tory was so upset and had gone looking for solitude on this clear winter afternoon, although why she had been crawling around in a storm sewer was still beyond him. "I didn't know that Cody knew," said Alvarez treading carefully. He'd never heard anyone else refer to her parents as "those people." But then, he'd never known anyone set up to take a fall by her own mother, a fall resulting in a seventeen-year estrangement.

"I told Cody last summer, after you found out about all of it." Tory sounded as though she were going to some effort to keep her voice steady. "Then, when he was visiting my father in Florida, while we were occupied here with that maniac drug lord from Nebraska on the loose, Cody decided to tell him."

Alvarez thought this over. "Sounds like Cody is growing up in more ways than one."

"But it hasn't made a difference," Tory said, and two more tears slid down her cheeks. Alvarez pushed the crumpled handkerchief back into her hand.

"Sometimes, I think we get caught up in our own frame of reference," he said, looking straight ahead. "Maybe sometimes we need to try to see things in a different light. Your father came to visit you. Maybe that's his way of saying he's sorry.'' He waited to see if he would get any response. When he didn't, he added, ''Maybe that's as good as it's going to get.''

Tory dabbed at her eyes with his handkerchief again, then resumed compressing it into its minimum volume. ''So that's why I'm here,'' she said.

Alvarez took a deep breath. ''Let me make sure I have this straight. Your son is growing up and your father refuses to apologize for all the years he hasn't been a part of your life, so you decide to drive around and look for some subterranean drains to crawl into. And, on top of that, you pick the one drain in the state of Texas that has a dead body in it. Am I missing anything?''

''I'm not sure that's right,'' she said. ''About this being the only drain in the state of Texas with a dead body in it. Statistically, that may be doubtful.''

The kinder, gentler version of Detective David Alvarez was fading fast. ''This is where I say 'we can have this conversation down at the station.'''

Tory didn't seem intimidated. ''You're starting to sound like yourself again. You told me a long time ago that's just a threat. You can't take me down to the station unless you're ready to charge me with something.''

''Tory, don't make me ask again. What the hell are you doing here?''

This time she told him, and he listened with a detective's mindset, sifting and sorting through the information she related, thinking like the cop who would write up the report, evaluating how her story would hold up in clearing her of any involvement with whatever she had stumbled into. Tory was just finishing her explanation of what she'd been looking for and why, and what she'd found instead, when a third car pulled up and Alvarez's partner, Scott Faulkner, stepped out.

''Here comes the cavalry,'' said Alvarez. ''Late as usual.''

''You called Scott?'' Alvarez couldn't tell from Tory's tone of voice whether she was making an accusation or surprised that he'd called for help.

"Had to call someone to make this kosher," he answered. "I'm on restricted duty, remember? But don't worry, Scott does everything I tell him to, *tu crees, hombre?*"

Scott took in Tory's pallor and Alvarez's arm around her and frowned. "Are you okay?" he asked Tory.

"I'm fine," she told him.

"How come you don't ask about my health?" Alvarez inquired.

"B-b-because you look just fine to me," said Scott. "What's going on?" He turned his attention back to Tory. "Don't t-tell me you're being harassed by someone who won't take no for an answer."

Alvarez snorted in disgust. "Tory's firm inspected this abandoned project, and decided everything looked pretty good. Then the city told her that it was condemned fifteen years ago and that leaky storm sewers were a major problem. Tory, who, as we well know, never takes anyone's word for anything, couldn't figure out why the city thought the storm sewers leaked, so she came out here to take one last look for herself, before the city pumps the pipes full of water tomorrow, runs a water-tightness test, and potentially proves our favorite engineer wrong." He paused and looked at Tory. "How'm I doing so far?"

"All right for government work."

"Anything more would be exceeding my job description." He looked at Scott. "You with me so far?" Scott nodded. "So, when other people would be home reading a book, spending quality time with their family, or fooling around with someone of the opposite sex, Girl Engineer here decides to go inspect storm sewers. By herself." He stopped and looked at Tory. "Wonder what Jesus Alfonso Rodriguez would have to say about that?" She didn't answer, apparently not willing to hypothesize what her outspoken foreman might have to say about her solo inspection activities. "So, Tory climbs into one of these," he pointed to the nearest opened manhole. "They open into big concrete boxes called drain inlets. Tory walks a length of pipe, gets to another drain inlet, and discovers a body stuffed in there, hanging upside down. A woman, shot in the forehead, dried blood on the face, obviously dead for a while. She calls me, I call you, and here we are.''

Scott considered what he had just been told. He looked at Tory. "I don't know what's going on between the two of you," he said, "b-b-but let me tell you something. You don't need to keep finding b-b-bodies to keep him interested."

There was a long silence while Tory gave Scott the type of look she usually reserved for Alvarez. "I don't get it," she said finally. "You're partners. Isn't one of you supposed to be the good cop?"

"See anyone else here?" Scott asked Tory.

"Not from the time she got here 'til I arrived," Alvarez answered for her. "Obviously whoever did the deed wasn't considerate enough to stick around. A disappointment to be sure, but it's also job security, right, *cabrón?*"

Scott had lots of experience ignoring his partner's extraneous remarks. "What does it look like?" he asked Alvarez.

"How should I know? I've been busy comforting Tory here." Tory turned and glared at him. "What do you say we go take a look?"

Tory climbed off the hood of her car, produced a large industrial flashlight, and walked off. The two men followed her to an opened manhole about two hundred feet from where the cars were parked. Alvarez noticed she didn't look down; she just handed him the torch. He and Scott both squatted at the opening, Alvarez trying to angle the light from the torch to get a good look.

"It's a body, all right," he said.

"A dead body," Scott concurred helpfully.

"A woman, but I can't tell much of anything else from here." Alvarez pulled off his sunglasses, and he and Scott spent some time jockeying for position around the opened manhole, trying unsuccessfully to illuminate the body better. Scott stood up next to Tory. Alvarez stayed where he was and looked up at them. "Why don't you go ahead and call it in," he told Scott. "While we wait for the Crime Scene Unit and the ME to get here, I'm going to try to get a better look."

"I'll wait in the car," said Tory. She turned and abruptly headed back toward the parked cars.

Alvarez shook his head. "Why is she acting like a civilian all of a sudden? She's pretty observant, and that could help."

Scott looked at his partner. "She's observant all right," he said stutter-free. "That's the problem."

Alvarez always got suspicious when Scott's stutter disappeared. "What are you trying to tell me?"

"She observed the lipstick on your cheek when you took off your sunglasses," said the ever-factual Scott Faulkner.

THREE

IDENTIFICATION

ALVAREZ MADE a perfunctory swipe at his cheek, put his sunglasses back on, and headed after Tory. By the time he caught up with her, she had climbed up on the hood of her car again. He climbed up beside her without waiting for an invitation, but he didn't try putting his arm around her this time.

"Scott told me about the lipstick," he said without preamble. "Keaton was over at my house when you called. She needed a shoulder to cry on, and when I hustled her out of the house to come meet you, she kissed me goodbye."

"It's none of my business," said Tory. She didn't ask who Keaton was; Tory obviously remembered Keaton as the heiress involved in his last case, in which he and Scott had asked Tory to determine the cause of a residential collapse. During the investigation, it came to light that Keaton's seven-year-old daughter was not her husband's child, but was instead the offspring of a former boyfriend, one whom a younger Keaton had abandoned under duress. The child's paternity had come as a total surprise to both the husband and the former boyfriend, and the fact that a huge trust fund was at stake didn't simplify things.

"Keaton may have some other things in mind," Alvarez continued, "but that's all she's getting from me, a shoulder to cry on."

"Scott says she's drop-dead gorgeous," said Tory, watching his partner stand guard over the inlet box two hundred feet away.

"She is," he agreed, "and she's drop-dead rich to boot. But Keaton doesn't have the slightest idea how to stand on her own two feet. She was brainwashed by her family from the beginning."

"Bet that didn't require a lot of detergent."

Alvarez grinned. "I need to tell you something; I want you to listen to me."

Tory gave him a hard look. "This thing here is not my fault," she said firmly. "I'm not involved. If you start to Mirandize me, I'm out of here."

Alvarez ignored her. "You told me once that you don't like surprises, so I'm telling you this straight up. I've got you stuck in my head, and I'm tired of dancing around it." He stopped, trying to think of what he was going to say next.

"You know," said Tory, suddenly intent on watching Scott again, "this has been a stressful afternoon. You may be used to things like this, but I'm not. I'm so much better at conversations if I know what the topic is."

Well, if that wasn't a lead-in, he didn't know what was. Alvarez took a deep breath and plunged ahead. "I want to be very plain about this. I want you in my life. Hell, I want you in my bed. You, not Keaton, not anyone else, you." Tory was watching Scott like her life depended on it. Alvarez thought his partner looked like a man running out of things to do but without the nerve to abandon his post.

"I should have stayed home this afternoon," Tory said. Alvarez didn't think she wanted to hear his reply to that.

"How can you just come out and say stuff like that?" she asked in a rush, still watching Scott.

"I figure the direct approach is the only way to go. Otherwise we'll just keep meeting over dead bodies, and the only time you'll spend the night with me is when I'm injured in the line of duty."

Tory's booted foot was beating an impatient tattoo against her car. She still wouldn't look at him. "The cheekbone is a funny place to kiss someone," she said. "What was she aiming for?"

"My eye?" he asked tentatively. Getting no response, he decided it was safe to continue. "Keaton's under a lot of stress. Her husband moved out, and her former boyfriend, the spurned Dr. Cabrioni, is supposedly considering suing for custody of the kid. It's no wonder Keaton's aim is off. I should be grateful she didn't have a gun."

"Forget it," said Tory. "I'm sorry I asked. Next thing I know, I'll be feeling sorry for her. Let's talk about something else, like when I can go home."

"Not quite yet. I'm not done telling you what I want."

He succeeded in wresting her attention away from watching Scott. Tory turned to look at him in exasperation. "After everything you've said, what else is there?"

"I want you to show me how to get into that inlet box so I can take a better look."

IT WASN'T AS SIMPLE as he had thought, but then things with Tory seldom were. She insisted that there was another, shorter run of pipe leading to the body than the one she had initially walked. She further insisted that if Alvarez was going, she would go with him, because she might as well get in one last bit of inspection. Alvarez insisted on going first just to save face.

Scott watched them climb down through the opened manhole into the new inlet box Tory had selected. Then Tory started explaining about storm-sewer design and common causes of leaks as she and Alvarez headed toward the box with the body. Alvarez listened and even asked questions, patiently waiting while she stopped to point out examples of what she was talking about. He figured she wasn't too anxious to reach their destination, and anything that kept her mind off the contents of the inlet box ahead was fine with him.

When they got there, he suggested that she sit in the pipe opening and wait for him, and she didn't argue. He entered the concrete box and angled the beam from the torch onto the face of the corpse, muttering an involuntary curse under his breath as he did so.

"What is it?" asked Tory immediately.

"Nothing," he replied automatically.

"It didn't sound like nothing," she said. "You wouldn't even be down here if it wasn't for me. If you start playing the closemouthed detective, I'll head back and start replacing all the manhole covers.''

"Scott wouldn't let you," he said absently, as he ran the beam from the torch carefully over every visible inch of the body hanging suspended in front of him.

"I'll bet I could think of something plausible to tell him," Tory replied.

"I wouldn't be surprised. But I'd start yelling, Scott would hear me, and then he'd have to handcuff you and put you in the back seat of my car." Alvarez turned his attention from the corpse to the box itself, carefully examining every surface in a manner that would have done Tory proud if she'd done it herself.

"Your car doesn't have a back seat."

"I was just testing your powers of observation, and engaging in a harmless fantasy. I have the feeling you didn't spend nearly enough time in the back seat of a car when you were a teenager.''

"You're an expert on this subject?"

"Yeah, as a matter of fact, I am. Want me to go into detail?"

"Is this how you avoid answering questions?"

"It worked, didn't it?" Alvarez turned his attention back to Tory, sitting and waiting where the pipe opened into the inlet box. She didn't look happy. "I'm done," he said. "Let's head back.''

"You're really not going to tell me anything?"

"Patience, *cara*. Wait until I can tell Scott, then I only have to say it once. I will tell you one thing right now, though.''

"What's that?"

"I've decided to let you go first on the way back."

THAT DIDN'T TURN OUT to be such a bad idea, since it was easier climbing into an inlet box with an arm in a sling than it was climbing out of one.

"What did you find out?" Scott asked, after he and Tory helped hoist Alvarez up to the surface. Alvarez switched off the flashlight.

"I think she was killed first, then put into the manhole," said Alvarez.

"Shot to death?" asked Scott.

"Point blank. One bullet hole in the forehead, took out most of the back of her skull."

Tory winced at his words.

"Probably s-someone she knew," mused Scott, "in order to get that close to her."

"Or someone grabbed her forcibly, abducted her," contributed Tory.

"Yeah, that would work for a gang shooting," said Scott. "What do you think?" he asked Alvarez. "Did it look l-like an execution?"

"It might be an execution, all right, but I doubt it's gang-related. I recognized her, Scott. It's Pamela Case."

Scott looked at his partner and let out a low whistle. "Sure hope they can replace her by next Friday," he said.

"What do you mean?" asked Tory. "Who is Pamela Case?"

"She works for the city," said Alvarez, "one of those people who causes problems, gets bounced from department to department."

"What kind of problems?" asked Tory immediately.

Was it his imagination, or did she sound defensive? Alvarez wondered if the time Tory had spent alone with Pamela had been enough for female bonding. "She was a bigot," he said baldly.

"What?" asked Tory, shocked.

"What do you want me to say? That she didn't get along very well with certain groups of people?"

"Why do you say she was a bigot?" persisted Tory.

"When I first met her, she worked in Personnel," began Alvarez.

"Why would anyone put a bigot in Personnel?" Tory interrupted.

"You have to put them somewhere," Scott offered.

Tory looked at him a moment, then turned her attention back

to Alvarez. "How do you know she was a bigot?" she asked again.

"From how she acted. She got slapped with a discrimination suit," said Alvarez, "back when she worked in Personnel. I happened to be there when this guy went berserk in her office, and I helped get him out and calmed down. Instead of thanking me, good old Pamela looked like she wanted to spit in my face. Anyhow, the suit got bargained away and Pamela got moved to Purchasing. Then something happened there, but I don't know what it was."

"She g-g-got in trouble campaigning against affirmative action," said Scott.

"Why should that get her in trouble?" asked Tory. "People can campaign for whatever they want to, can't they?"

"Yeah, but she used city p-p-postage meters," replied Scott.

"How come you know this and I don't?" asked Alvarez, affronted.

"Because P-Purchasing threatened to have the EPPD investigate if she didn't agree to be transferred to another department," said Scott.

"Where was I when all this went down?" Alvarez asked.

"On one of your fact-finding missions," said Scott. "The one to Las Vegas," he added, sounding as close to surly as he ever got.

Alvarez grinned at his partner and turned his attention back to Tory. "Anyhow, about a year ago, Pamela got transferred to Payroll."

"That's why I hope they can replace her by Friday," explained Scott.

"So who would kill her?" asked Tory.

"Hell, Tory," said Alvarez. "I'm a great detective, but I don't have the answer to that question. It sure wasn't me."

"Why, you have an extensive weekend alibi?" asked Tory.

"Want to find out?" Alvarez countered. When she didn't answer, he continued, "It's probably a simple grudge killing. I doubt the EPPD Special Case Force will have anything to do with it."

"But why dump her body here?" Tory asked.

"Why not? It's isolated enough that you can see if there's anyone else around, and like you explained, the city was cooperative enough to remove the manhole covers. All someone had to do was drive up, roll the body out of the car, and drop it down the nearest hole. Pamela's body would have probably fallen all the way down into the box if it hadn't gotten caught up on some of that exposed steel stuff—what do you call it?"

"Rebar. She was caught up on exposed rebar. But why go to all the effort to put the body out here when it would just be discovered on Monday?"

"Because," said Alvarez patiently, "not everyone sees opened manholes and knows that means a test is coming up. Murderers are usually not your most intelligent people, which is why Scott and I excel as detectives. Right, Scott?" Scott just shrugged. Alvarez figured he was still bitter over the memory of Alvarez's all-expenses-paid jaunt to Las Vegas. "Anyway, hiding a body long enough to make a getaway usually fits the bill," he concluded.

"Then she was put out here sometime after the city pulled off the manhole covers," said Tory, thinking out loud. "I assume they pulled them late Friday, but I'm not absolutely sure. I can find out tomorrow."

"Oh, God," said Alvarez. "Don't tell me this means you're going to start helping us again. Finding the bodies is enough, Tory, you've done your civic duty. We're trained detectives. We can handle the rest."

Tory ignored him; she had thought of something else. "Is this going to delay the test?"

Alvarez sighed and looked at Scott. "Shit," he said, "she's getting ahead of us again. We need to make sure Engineering gets notified, so they don't have people out here tomorrow morning pouring water down on top of the CSU techs. Tends to make them grumpy."

"It's always a problem, letting the l-left hand know what the right hand is doing," Scott told Tory.

"I want to see how this test comes out," she said doggedly. "How long will the CSU take?" Alvarez shrugged.

"You know what this means, don't you?" inquired Scott suddenly.

"What? When it rains, it pours?" asked Alvarez, bracing himself for one of the classical quotations Scott was always tossing out at the most unlikely moments.

"This is going to be known as the C-Case c-case," said Scott slowly and distinctly. "Do you know how hard that is for s-someone who stutters?"

THEY WOULDN'T let her go home, of course. That was the problem with modern-day law enforcement, thought Tory. Every time you reported something like you were supposed to, the reward was having to wait around for someone to take your statement. Scott and Alvarez decided it would be better if one of them went with her to the station, as though she needed a chaperone. Then they decided it would be better if she went with Scott, since she and Alvarez together had something of a media presence that the EPPD would be just as happy to avoid, and since Alvarez was officially on restricted duty. So she couldn't leave until Scott did, and Scott couldn't leave until the ME and the CSU came, and God only knew how long that would take.

She needed to call home and tell them that she would be delayed, assuming that someone there would eventually notice her absence. Her mood was not improved when there was no answer at home, not even from the answering machine. All the technology in the world couldn't compensate for human interaction. Someone, probably that girl, had switched off the answering machine and forgotten to switch it on again. Thank God for her secretary, Sylvia Maestes, the Las Cruces alternative to mass communication systems. Tory was convinced that Sylvia slept with the phone next to her ear; she was also convinced that Sylvia was somehow related to at least 50% of the population of the Southwest.

"Hello?" Sylvia's vibrant voice, eager for whatever news

would be forthcoming from the other end, sang into Tory's ear before the second ring.

Tory told her as briefly and concisely as possible what was going on, and asked her to leave a note at Tory's house for Cody and her father. After listening to Tory's explanation, Sylvia went right to the heart of the matter.

"So after two weeks of making excuses, you called Dahveed?" she asked. Sylvia had decided that David Alvarez walked on water ever since he showed up to interview Tory as a suspect in one of his cases. Sylvia thought he had come to deal with the threats Tory had been receiving, and had embraced him with an exuberance that had never lessened. The fact that she was convinced Tory needed a steady man in her life didn't hurt Alvarez's standing in Sylvia's mind, either.

"That's all you have to say? Don't you care that there's a dead woman out here, shot in the head? Or is all you care about the fact that it gave me a reason to call David Alvarez?"

"Well," said Sylvia reasonably, "tell me who the woman is, and I'll give you an answer." Sylvia had never met a grudge she didn't like.

"Her name is Pamela Case," said Tory. "They say she works for the City of El Paso."

"Pamela Case?" asked Sylvia.

"Don't tell me you know her. Maybe the police should just install a direct line to your house."

Sylvia was immune to sarcasm. "No, I don't know her. But I recognize the name."

Tory couldn't believe it. Maybe she should have called Sylvia instead of Alvarez. "What?"

"I recognize the name from when you had me get all the records about Monte Vista Heights. Pamela Case was the Permitting official in charge. Her name was all over those documents."

"Are you sure?"

"Of course I'm sure. Do I make mistakes about things like that?"

She had a point there. Tory kept turning the information over in her head, trying to see the connection. First her company's report was rejected. She decided to do more research, then a body turned up on a project that had been condemned by the city fifteen years ago, with fatal results for the contractor. Now Sylvia was telling her that the body in the drain inlet a few hundred feet away was the woman in charge of permitting the project all those years ago. A project constructed by a successful Hispanic contractor, and a Permitting agent with a reputation as a bigot. "I need to tell David about this," she said.

"Tory," said Sylvia, "don't hang up. There's one more thing."

Oh no. "Don't say it," Tory interjected, but she was too late.

"I really don't think you need to keep finding dead bodies to keep Dah-veed interested," Sylvia told her earnestly.

Tory hung up.

Tory found Alvarez talking to one of the uniformed officers now on site. She pulled him aside and told him her news. He asked her to repeat some of the information she had told him earlier. She waited while he stood, thinking over what she had just told him. He nodded. "It's a date, then," he said.

"What?" she asked, wondering just what conversation he thought they were having. As long as she focused on the situation at hand, she figured she could successfully sidestep other issues raised earlier.

"Eight o'clock, tomorrow morning, City Hall." He grinned at her. "Isn't that where you plan on being?" And that was how David Alvarez managed to ask her out in a way she couldn't turn down.

FOUR

ADMINISTRATIVE SYSTEMS

DRIVING HOME to Las Cruces after giving her statement, Tory carefully limited her thoughts to Alvarez's comments about her relationship with her father. Maybe she needed to look at her current domestic situation in a new light. Yeah, right. Sometimes striving to be an adult really sucked.

There were lights on inside the house when she drove up, apparently indicating that everyone had returned home safe and sound from the afternoon's entertainment. Tory walked in the front door and encountered her father in the living room, seated in her favorite chair, a bowl of pretzels and a drink at hand, reading the newspaper.

She tried not to grit her teeth before she even said hello. She knew there would be opened packages of snack foods strewn all through her kitchen, and that the newspaper would be creased and folded into strange configurations before she ever got her hands on it. She told herself that surely she was too young to be so set in her ways that these things could drive her crazy. She also knew she lied.

Usually Tory would have tossed off a curt greeting and gone in search of her son, but on the drive home she had determined to try something different. She set her things down, sank into her least favorite chair and regarded her father. Although Tom Wheatley's hair had long since turned gray and there were lines in his face, he was still a handsome man, tall and spare with a carriage worthy of a patrician, which was what she supposed he was, after all.

"Hi," she said. "Sorry I missed dinner. Sylvia leave a note for you? Everything okay? Where's Cody?"

Her father slowly lowered the paper and regarded his only surviving child with one eyebrow raised. "You always were in more of a hurry than anyone I've ever met," he said. "How do you expect someone to keep track of three questions at once, much less pose intelligent answers?"

Tory took a deep breath instead of getting up and leaving the room. "Did Sylvia let you know I was detained?" she asked carefully.

"Miss Maestes was kind enough to convey that information," her father replied. "We went to a movie this afternoon, Cody, Kohli and I. In case you're interested."

Tory took another deep breath. "Of course I'm interested." What really interested her was whether Cody and Kohli had held hands in the darkened theater, but she wasn't quite desperate enough to ask. "I think it's great that Cody is getting to spend some time with you, which is one of the reasons I felt like I could go down to El Paso this afternoon. Have you had dinner?"

"Yes, no thanks to you."

"Cody is pretty handy in the kitchen," she said immediately. They both heard the unspoken *because he's had to be* that hung in the air between them.

"No need for that, at least not while I'm here. I took the young people to dinner, and Miss Maestes kindly agreed to join us."

Tory closed her eyes a moment. The thought of her father and Sylvia engaged in dinner conversation did not exactly top off her day. "So Sylvia explained what happened?"

"She said you'd gone off on your own to look at some project and discovered yet another body," her father replied. Tory wondered if discovering a lifetime total of two bodies really warranted that phrasing. "Maybe I'm old fashioned," continued her father, "but I think it would have been better if you'd stayed home and gone to the movie with us."

Better. Tory bit back a hasty retort. Was it possible that there was a hint of fatherly concern beneath what she had always interpreted as constant criticism? "You're probably right," she said, and her father's eyes widened in surprise. "Where is

Cody?'' she asked, continuing to work through her list of questions.

"Cody and his friend are in the den studying," her father said.

And when was the last time you looked in on Cody and his friend? "Studying?" she inquired casually.

"Diligently," her father answered.

"Should I check on them?"

"I imagine they're doing just fine on their own."

It was a stand-off. Tory took another deep breath. Talking to her father might qualify as Lamaze exercises. "The body I found, it was a woman," she said. "Someone killed her and put her in a storm drain we were supposed to inspect."

"You weren't supposed to inspect for bodies, were you?" her father asked, shocked.

"Of course not. We didn't find anything wrong with the drains, but supposedly they were constructed so badly that the whole project was condemned fifteen years ago. I went out there today to take one last look before they're tested again. It was a coincidence that I happened to find this woman's body, at least, I think it was. It bothers me, all the coincidences. I'd like to talk to you about it; some of it has to do with things I don't know much about."

Tory's father stared at her. "I can't remember the last time you thought I knew something you didn't," he said.

Was I really *that* awful as a teenager? she wanted to ask, but she didn't. She figured she was on a roll; her best strategy was to keep right on going. "This project was built by a Hispanic contractor fifteen years ago. I'm told that he got successful all of a sudden, about the same time affirmative action programs were in vogue with the city, so he got inspired to run for city commissioner."

She had said the magic words to pique the interest of a former Florida State Senator. "Fifteen years ago was about the right time for that," her father said. "The federal programs were in place, and local governments were trying to figure out how to implement them. There were two main approaches—ignore everything, or overreact so much that everyone white and God-fearing was up in arms about it."

"You mean everyone white, God-fearing, and male, don't you?"

"Good point," her father said. Tory was so shocked at the experience of having her father agree with her that it took her a moment to pick up the threads of her story again.

"So this contractor had a lot of people claiming his success was just because of the affirmative action programs."

"Makes sense," said her father, agreeing with her two times in the same night.

"Part of his campaign platform was to implement more minority set-asides," Tory continued. "But when his project got condemned, he went bankrupt, everything fell apart, and he killed himself. He drove out to the abandoned subdivision and shot himself."

"You know that for a fact?"

"Well, no," she said, momentarily sidetracked again.

"Could bear looking into," her father suggested. He took a sip of his drink.

"So now, fifteen years later," Tory continued, "we take a look at this subdivision, and we can't find much wrong with it."

"Sounds fishy to me," said her father. Tory couldn't believe it. She and her father were actually sitting in her living room and having a conversation, and he was agreeing with her.

"When I found the woman's body, I called a police detective I know."

"This would be the one Sylvia said you spent the night with, that night that Cody and I decided to drive back here, and we couldn't get hold of you." Tory's father didn't make it a question.

"He was injured," she said immediately. "Everyone was concerned that he might have a concussion."

"Sounds fishy to me," her father said again. Hot, angry words rose to Tory's lips, but then her father gave the faintest of smiles. "Go on with your story."

"This police detective recognized the woman."

"David Alvarez, you mean," interjected her father. "Miss Maestes told me that—"

"Please don't say it," Tory interrupted, to no avail.

"—that she didn't think you had to keep finding dead bodies to keep him interested in you."

Tory was at the end of her patience. "Do you know you're the third, no, the *fourth*, person to tell me that today? Don't you think I know it would be easier to take out an ad in the personals if it's a man I'm looking for?" She glared at her father.

"Calm down," he said, unperturbed, "and finish your story."

It took her another moment to remember where she was. "The dead woman's name was Pamela Case. She worked for the city, kind of a troublemaker who gets moved from place to place. Her last scrape was getting caught using city postage meters to campaign against affirmative action programs."

"She was probably drumming up support for one of the recent Civil Rights Propositions," said her father.

Tory looked at him in surprise. "Why on earth would a group against affirmative action support something called a Civil Rights Proposition?"

"Because it's all in the wording and the spin attached to it. Would you support a referendum to treat everyone fairly, regardless of sex, religion, or race?"

"Of course," said Tory automatically.

"Then you support affirmative action programs," said her father. "Would you support legislation requiring that positions be filled according to the experience and qualifications of the applicants?"

"Sure," said Tory.

"Then you just reversed your stance."

"That's confusing."

"You've just hit the nail on the head—that's about the only thing everyone agrees on." And Tory had hoped that talking to him might shed some light on the subject.

"How did we get off on this tangent?" she asked. "I didn't finish telling you everything. It turns out that this Pamela Case was the Permitting official for the Hispanic contractor's project, back fifteen years ago when it was condemned.''

Tory and her father sat in almost companionable silence while he thought that over. ''That does seem coincidental,'' he said finally. ''What does your detective say?''

Now her father was calling David Alvarez ''her'' detective. She was too tired to argue. ''He hasn't said. But he's planning to meet me at the El Paso Engineering Department first thing tomorrow morning.''

''I hope you're not getting in over your head,'' said her father, disapproval plain in his voice again.

Getting in over your head. That was good, after an afternoon in storm sewers. ''There are technical questions I need to answer,'' she said evenly. ''But it's the coincidences that bother me—two people found dead on the same piece of property, two people with opposing political philosophies. Is that enough to kill over?''

Her father contemplated his drink for a moment. ''Considering the fact that certain people have killed over things like whose daughter gets to be cheerleader, I think it's a possibility. Not probable, but possible.''

''What do you think about affirmative action programs?'' asked Tory impulsively.

''I think they can work for the same reason we need them,'' said her father. ''Which is one of those unfortunate paradoxes of modern society.''

''What do you mean?''

''People tend to hire people just like themselves, so minority-owned businesses tend to hire minorities. So, helping minority businesses helps minorities find jobs. Kind of like going full circle to get to the same place.''

''What's the problem with that?''

''The problem is that helping minority-owned businesses is complicated.''

''Why?''

''Because whenever you have regulators trying to address complex social situations, you end up with a nightmare of policies and procedures. The next thing you know, you have a whole department of people whose sole purpose in life is to run around trying to enforce rules that don't make sense.''

"Like what?"

"Well, start with the definition of minorities. What if someone is one-eighth American Indian? Does that meet the definition of 'minority,' and how do you go about documenting something like that? Then how do you define a minority-owned business? There are entire case files about whether a woman can be considered to have started her own business if she used any money held jointly with her husband.''

"What's she supposed to do? Get divorced, then start a business?"

"It's been done," said her father.

"That sounds like enough to drive someone to murder."

Her father laughed. "I don't know about murder, but a woman in Florida stood up in the middle of a hearing and slapped one of the state minority program officials."

Tory had entertained similar fantasies on occasion. "What happened?"

"A lot of factors led up to the final confrontation—the innate prejudices of the people running these programs, for one.''

"Prejudices in affirmative action programs?" Tory was aghast. This was as appalling as hearing Scott Faulkner explain that the city had to put a bigot somewhere. "I would think that people working in affirmative action programs would be the least prejudiced," she added.

"Then you're naive," replied her father. "The people running those programs are no less prejudiced than anyone else. There are always arguments over who deserves to be included in the definitions and who doesn't. There's a lot of resentment that in Florida, white women are eligible for minority classification.''

"How did that result in a woman slapping a state employee?"

"It didn't; it's just one factor. Florida certifies minority firms in small, strictly defined categories. A hardware store isn't considered to be a plumbing equipment supplier unless the business is certified in both categories, and the categories are defined by inventory."

"Inventory is expensive. What about JIT?"

"The people running these programs are mostly lifetime government employees with no experience in running a business. They wouldn't recognize the acronym for just-in-time inventory, much less the theory behind it, or why it saves money."

"The system you're describing sounds punitive, not helpful."

"That's exactly what Kiki Stearns said. She started a building supply company. Her philosophy was to win a contract first, then get certified in that category later. She was white, well-educated, and so successful that it drove the minority program people nuts. They kept telling her that she wasn't supposed to expand into new business areas until she got certified in that area. Kiki cut some corners mighty thin, but she never actually broke any rules, so they couldn't shut her down for non-compliance. But, one day Kiki started getting calls from government purchasing agents who couldn't find her in their computers anymore. Overnight, her firm had been purged from the state purchasing system. Of course, no one knew how it happened, but the upshot was that Kiki would have to start all over in getting her certifications, which would require inventory in all categories, and months to process."

"What'd she do?"

"Yelled bloody murder, kicked and screamed, and wrote letters to everyone from the governor on down." Tory's father chuckled. "I've been out of office for years, and even I got a few."

"A few?"

"I guess Kiki couldn't air all her grievances in one letter, so she wrote a series. They kind of became collector's items. Purchasing agents who hated the minority program people would get copies and pass them around. Then Kiki hired a lawyer and got a hearing date set, but it cost her thousands of dollars." Tory shuddered at the thought. "So Kiki was already pretty frosted by the time she got to the hearing. When the specific woman

Kiki had been feuding with for years got up and testified under oath that it was not the purpose of minority programs to help minority businesses be profitable, Kiki snapped. She stood up, leaned over the table, and slapped the woman.''

"Then what happened?" Tory would never have thought that minority programs could be such a riveting subject, or that any adult woman answering to the name Kiki could be such a potential role model.

"The hearing officer found in Kiki's favor, but he had to do something about her behavior. He remanded her to a minimum security prison for two weeks."

"That sounds harsh."

"Not really. Turns out the purchasing agent at the prison was a real fan. At the end of the two weeks, Kiki had the inside track on a major building supply contract for the facility. Heard she made a killing on that one."

Tory was thinking that over when her father set down his glass, got up, and stretched. "I'm going to bed," he said bluntly. "Don't you think you should look in on that son of yours?" And then, without lifting a finger to pick up either the empty bowl or glass he was leaving behind, he walked out of the room. Tory guessed that signaled the end of their father/daughter quality time. She remembered hearing her father once say that a politician, like a lover, should never leave his audience completely sated.

Resigned that some things would never change, including the behavior of a man who had always been waited on hand and foot, Tory picked up her father's dishes. She dropped them off in the kitchen, which looked even worse than she had imagined it would, and went off in search of her son. She found Cody stretched out on the couch, watching TV, alone except for the company of Tango the Transylvanian Hound, who was snoring on the floor beside the couch.

"Where is she?" asked Tory, figuring bluntness could run in the family.

Tango didn't move a muscle, but Cody came to his feet in one fluid movement. "Hi Mom," he said. He kissed his mother on the cheek, which immediately made her suspicious. "Glad to see you're okay," he added. "Sylvia told us what happened. Must have been a shock, finding a body like that."

"And I'm looking for another one, unaccounted for. Where is she?" asked Tory again. There wasn't any lipstick on Cody's face, but then, except for once, she couldn't remember seeing Kohli wear lipstick.

"Her name is Kohli, and I walked her home," Cody told his mother, and smiled charmingly while he said it.

Tory looked at him sternly, wondering if it would seriously impair the trust between them if she hightailed it down the hall to his room and looked under his bed. Protecting her teenage son's virtue was turning out to be a time-consuming, thankless effort. "You didn't tell me you were walking her home," she said accusingly.

"You and Gramps were actually talking," her son answered. "To each other. I didn't want to interfere." Tory couldn't think of an answer to that. "It's been a long day for you," Cody continued. "Why don't you take a shower and go to bed? I'll lock up."

Tory didn't know what it boded, this sudden solicitousness on the part of her son, but suddenly she didn't care. She grabbed his head between her hands and gave him a serious goodnight kiss on the top of his head. She might not be the only person to kiss him tonight, but she was damn well determined to be the last.

FIVE

PROJECT MANAGEMENT

TORY WAS CHAGRINED to find Alvarez already waiting outside Cal Cortez's office at 8:05 Monday morning, but she told herself that he had the shorter commute. The fresh white sling on his arm looked almost jaunty in contrast to his dark brown slacks and jacket. Tory felt underdressed in serviceable pants and a sweater that had seen better days, but then she had chosen her outfit optimistically—optimistic that the afternoon might find her out at Monte Vista Heights, watching the city run a water-tightness test.

Alvarez immediately put down his magazine and stood when he saw her. "Good morning, *querida*. Sleep well?"

As a matter of fact, she hadn't. "Are you always this cheerful in the morning?" she asked.

"Would you like to find out?" he countered.

Tory sat down and Alvarez followed suit. She decided to try another tack. "I know what I'm doing here," she told him, "but what about you?"

"Freelancing," he said. "We've got a city employee found dead on city property, the same property she worked on as a Permitting agent, according to the all-knowing Sylvia Maestes. It warrants asking some questions, not to mention the fact that I get to spend time with you. I just hope we can find something to do more enjoyable than crawling through sewers."

"We walked, we didn't crawl, and they were storm sewers," said Tory. "You make it sound like we were in a sanitary sewer. Believe me, there's a world of difference."

"You're the expert, I'll take your word for it."

"Besides, I thought you were on restricted duty."

"I am. I can pretty much do what I want as long as it's not overly physically demanding. Have something specific in mind I need to know about?"

Tory ignored his question. "I talked to my father last night," she said. "He knows quite a bit about minority business programs in Florida. He says there's a lot to get hot and bothered about, on both sides of the issue."

"Why don't you know about these things?" asked Alvarez. "Doesn't your firm qualify as a woman-owned business?"

"I'm sure it would," said Tory, "if we were willing to jump through all the hoops. Sometimes clients ask us to get certified to fulfill some kind of quota or something. Sylvia decided that filling out the forms would take about a month and kill off a small forest of trees, so we never pursued it."

"You think there's a connection between the two bodies found at Monte Vista Heights, having to do with the contractor's race and Pamela Case's bigotry?"

Alvarez had an uncanny way of summing up things before Tory had completely clarified them in her own mind. "Maybe there's a connection between the two deaths," she said carefully, "having to do with Craig Diaz's initial success and Pamela Case's politics."

"What, now it's not politically correct to call a bigot a bigot? You haven't answered my question. Are you trying to tell me that you have a theory?"

Tory felt like an amateur, but Alvarez wouldn't even know about Pamela Case's connection to the Monte Vista Heights subdivision if it weren't for her. Or, more accurately, if it weren't for Sylvia. "I think it's possible," she said.

Alvarez surprised her by saying, "You may be right. Stranger things have happened."

Before Tory could reply, Cal Cortez arrived, looking disheveled and harried. The usually mild-mannered city engineer fixed her with a baleful look and said, "You. You're the last person I want to talk to."

"I'm not here to hassle you," Tory said, "I'm just trying to get some answers.'' She was going to add "we're all on the same side," but she never got the chance.

"Answers?" interrupted Cal. "Answers are gonna be in short supply. Those prima donnas at the EPPD are looking for some needle in a haystack, so, being a mere mortal, I have to kowtow and grovel until they release my site back to me. And will they tell me anything in the meantime? Of course not. The only time I get answers from the EPPD is when they have an engineering problem, then they tell me just how fast they want me to fix it. I hope their damn cooling system goes down again this summer."

"Cal—" Tory interrupted, trying to introduce Alvarez before the city engineer could continue his rant.

"Don't 'Cal' me. I've got bigger problems than your rejected engineering report. Twenty-five years I've been with the city—why should I be the one to get the Project from Hell?" He looked accusingly at Tory, who didn't have an answer. "This is worse than trying to build a city facility next to some rich gringo subdivision."

"Surely racial slurs are unnecessary," said Alvarez.

"What racial slur?" asked Cal, blinking, noticing Alvarez for the first time.

"You said 'gringo' in front of the lady," replied Alvarez. "She might find it insulting."

"What lady?" Tory wanted to smack Cal when he glanced around the waiting area. He looked back at them, understanding dawning. "Not Tory. She's okay, she knows that zoning issues can be a bitch. Who are you? You with her?" He focused on Alvarez's arm. "You here about a worker's comp claim? That's all I need to top off my morning."

"Don't worry," said Alvarez helpfully, "this didn't happen on a city project. It was the result of a car bomb."

Tory used the pause to interject, "This is Detective David Alvarez with the EPPD, Cal. David, this is Cal Cortez. He's the project manager for renovating Monte Vista Heights." Seeing the horror on Cal's face, she took pity on him to add, "Alvarez is an okay guy, Cal."

"Yeah," said Alvarez pleasantly, "she calls me spic and I call her honky. Works for us."

Cal winced, then reluctantly shook Alvarez's hand. "Now I know who you are," he said with a visible lack of enthusiasm. "Should have figured it out, you being here with Tory. Kind of like the dynamic detecting duo, or something, aren't you?" He made an obvious effort to stop himself. "Sorry," he muttered, not trying to clarify exactly what he was apologizing for. "It's been a long day already. The City Manager wants me to participate in a press conference at eleven. That is not why I became an engineer, to participate in press conferences."

"I hear you," said Alvarez sympathetically, pumping Cal's hand. "This one here, she became an engineer because she couldn't make it as a secretary. Lacks people skills," he added confidentially.

Tory glared at Alvarez, Cal looked even more bemused, and the Engineering Department secretary had given up all pretense of doing something besides listening to their conversation. Cal cleared his throat. "Maybe we better talk in my office."

Alvarez said, "I thought you'd never ask."

TORY DECIDED the best approach was to give Alvarez as little chance to talk as possible. After all, this was the Engineering Department, her home ground. Also, it appeared that Alvarez's recent brush with death had changed his humor from sardonic to cheerful, and she couldn't decide which was worse. "What about the water-tightness test?" she asked as soon as they sat down in Cal's office, with the city engineer regarding her and Alvarez warily from behind his desk. "Do you know how long it will be delayed?"

"Don't ask me, ask your friend there," Cal replied. "I got a call last night telling me to keep our people off the site, or heads would roll. I understand they found a body out there, stuffed down into one of the inlet boxes."

"Actually," said Alvarez, "it was Tory who found the body."

Tory could have kicked him. Cal stared at Alvarez, then turned to look at Tory. "You found another body?"

Tory remembered her conversation with her father the previous evening. "Two in a lifetime doesn't exactly constitute significant double digits, Cal. It's not a new engineering specialty with me."

"Tory told me about Craig Diaz, the original contractor," interjected Alvarez. "So I understand some of the background with this piece of property, but why call it the Project from Hell?"

Cal Cortez looked relieved to find a subject he could warm to other than the EPPD. "It's been a pain in the butt from the beginning," he said flatly, "like sitting on a damn time bomb. The city commissioners thought we could resurrect this project and not relive its history. They're wrong."

"How so?" asked Alvarez.

"The Commissioners want to show how they're saving money and spending tax dollars wisely. But PR means reporters. So far, this time around, we've managed to keep Craig Diaz's suicide out of the story, but this will blow it wide open. Not that it wouldn't have made the papers eventually, anyway."

"Why is that?"

"Because there are other people around here besides me who remember what went down fifteen years ago."

"So?"

"Some of them have more than a passing interest in this project, dropping by to check on things two, three times a week. With all that interest, it's just a matter of time before the press catches on."

"What people?" Alvarez asked.

"Irma Lujan, Tommy Diaz, Pamela Case," Cal said without hesitating.

Tory found herself holding her breath, but Alvarez never broke his conversational stride. "I know who Pamela Case is," he said. "Should I assume that Tommy Diaz is Craig Diaz's son?"

"You got it," said Cal.

"Who is Irma Lujan?"

"She works in the Business Advocacy Department. It used to be the Minority Business Advocacy Department, but that got too controversial, so they changed it to the Small Business Advocacy Department. Then some big firm said it was reverse discrimination to have a Small Business Advocacy Department, so they changed it to the generic Business Advocacy Department."

"What does this department do?" asked Tory, fascinated in spite of herself.

"Damned if I know," said Cal, "but it's a great acronym."

"Why would these three individuals be so interested in the renovation of Monte Vista Heights?" persisted Alvarez.

"I guess Craig's son is still trying to understand what happened to his dad. Your report sure didn't help in that regard," Cal shot in Tory's direction.

"How about the other two?" Alvarez asked before Tory could reply that it wasn't her job to write a report to reassure the son of a dead contractor.

"Irma Lujan was a summer intern here when Craig decided to run for city commissioner. She was getting her political science degree, and she built Craig up as some kind of Hispanic role model. She took what happened real hard; she was young and idealistic back then."

Tory bet that working in something called BAD would cure anyone's idealism.

"And Pamela Case?" continued Alvarez. "I thought she worked in Payroll."

"She does," said Cal, blissfully unaware of the error in his choice of verb tense. "She used to work in Purchasing, too, but a long time ago, she worked in City Utilities."

"As a Permitting official, right?" asked Tory.

"Yeah, that was a long time ago, back when all the permitting was done department by department. Now it's been streamlined into One Step Permitting."

Tory remembered the office slang for it: One Stop Permitting.

"What was Pamela's interest in the project?" asked Alvarez.

"She'd been involved with the original development, thought

it was a shame the property stood abandoned all this time. She wanted to know how much work it was going to take to make the subdivision useable for the housing grant.''

"Wasn't that kind of an unusual interest for her to have after all these years?'' asked Alvarez.

"Pamela's kind of an unusual person,'' said Cal. "She has a reputation as a troublemaker. If she wants information, I give it to her, no questions asked. That way she doesn't stick around my office any longer than she has to.''

"Makes sense to me,'' said Alvarez, and Tory wondered if he thought it made sense because of Cal's last name. "What did you tell her about the amount of work required to renovate the project?''

"I told her there were conflicts that had to be resolved.''

Tory found herself sitting on the edge of her seat. "Did you tell her you were going to run another water-tightness test on the storm sewer?'' she asked.

Cal looked at her like she was clairvoyant. "How did you know she asked about that?''

"When did you tell Pamela Case about the test?'' asked Alvarez.

"Monday, a week ago, the same day I told Tory,'' Cal said.

"And did you tell Craig Diaz's son—what's his name—Tommy Diaz, about the conflicts, and the testing?'' asked Alvarez.

"Yes.''

"When?''

"Not on Monday. Some time later on that week.''

"Can you remember when?''

Cal took a moment to think. "It was Wednesday, late Wednesday. He came to see me without an appointment, and he had to wait because I was in a meeting. He teaches at Coronado High School, so he never comes until after school is out.'' Cal looked at Tory and Alvarez curiously. "Why? What's with all these questions? This doesn't have to do with the testing, does it?'' The blood started to drain from his face. "Don't tell me someone died from falling through an opened manhole. Man, oh man, I'm the one who requisitioned that work to be done on Friday afternoon.''

Tory watched Cal Cortez appear to age before her eyes. She knew what it was like to make a decision that seemed perfectly reasonable at the time, only to realize later that there were potentially devastating consequences involved. ''No, Cal,'' she said quickly. ''Don't put yourself through that. The woman didn't die from a fall, and she was dead before she was put in the inlet box.''

''Woman?'' Cal asked.

''I hate to add to your stress level,'' said Alvarez, ''but you'll probably find out when they brief you before the press conference, although I don't know if they're releasing the information yet. You can't disclose this until they've notified her next of kin, but the dead woman in the inlet box was Pamela Case.'' Cal looked at him in horror. ''Look on the bright side,'' added Alvarez. ''This will definitely limit the amount of time she spends in your office.''

SIX

PERSONNEL

ALVAREZ ESCORTED Tory out of Cal's office, leaving the city engineer looking more haggard now than harried. Tory barely waited until they were out of earshot before telling Alvarez, "I can't believe you said that."

He looked at her, perplexed. "Said what? That crack about you lacking people skills? I was just trying to get him loosened up, make him feel like we were on the same side."

"The part where you said Pamela Case wouldn't be spending any more time in his office."

Alvarez held up his good hand in the universal sign of surrender. "I thought the least I could do was say something to cheer him up. You sure are getting sensitive—must be all this discussion about affirmative action. Next thing I know, you'll start feeling like you're entitled."

"Entitled to what?"

"Entitled to go with me to my next interview."

Tory stared at him. "You're asking me to go with you to an interview? That's a switch. Are you sure it wasn't your head that got injured by the car bomb, not your arm?"

"Last time I checked, all the essential parts were in working order," said Alvarez, neatly turning Tory to the right to walk down a hallway she didn't recognize. "Of course, anytime you want to do some inspecting to satisfy yourself—"

"Where are we going?" she demanded. "Unlike you, I have a job to do."

"Smoking lounge. Best private place to meet people these days. No one wants to admit going there."

"Yuk."

"What do you mean, 'yuk'? Your good friend Lonnie Harper smokes."

"What does that—" Tory took a deep breath and cut herself off mid-sentence. It always brought her up short to remember that David Alvarez knew a lot more about her than she knew about him. She never, ever, wanted to become a subject in someone's investigation again. She also wanted to stop falling for diversionary tactics. She stopped walking. Alvarez went on a few steps without her, then turned back when it became clear she wasn't going any farther without some more answers. "Who are we going to see?"

"My own private Deep Throat," he told her. "I called her last night and she agreed to meet me," he looked at his watch, "in four minutes."

"You didn't schedule in much time to talk to Cal." Tory didn't know why that should make her feel surly, but it did. "What do you think about Pamela Case's interest in the renovation of Monte Vista Heights?"

Alvarez shrugged. "Too soon to tell. You in or not?"

"Who is this person you're going to see?" countered Tory. "Some sweet young thing you've conned into feeding you information?"

"Dottie Abbott is old enough to be my mother," said Alvarez, "and she's been working for the city since before Jonah."

"I didn't know Jonah worked for the city. Why is this Dottie Abbott person such a valuable source of information?"

"She's assistant secretary to the City Manager. City Managers come and go, along with their secretaries. But not Dottie. Dottie is an institution—she's been here over thirty years, and she's connected."

"Being an assistant secretary doesn't sound too connected to me."

"Her daughter is the head of Personnel," said Alvarez smugly.

Tory was aghast. "So her daughter feeds information to her mother and she passes it on to you?" If this Dottie Abbott ever vacated her position, maybe Sylvia could apply. She would feel right at home with the situation.

"Dottie loves gossip," said Alvarez easily, "and her daughter has access to basic information about city employees. I can't use anything they tell me unless I can get the same information independently, but talking to Dottie saves me time. She gives me hints—points me in the right direction."

Tory frowned. "I doubt it's as simple as that. And why should these two women do this hint dropping and direction pointing?"

"They're both big fans of mine."

"What does that mean, they're both fans of yours?"

"Has anyone ever told you that you ask a lot of questions?"

"Uh-huh. That's never stopped me," replied Tory, although it had occurred to her that she might not like the answer she sought. But a mother-daughter team aiding and abetting Alvarez? If she backed away from a question as enticing as this one, she could never look Sylvia in the eye again.

Alvarez sighed. "Dottie's granddaughter got involved with a punk in high school—a real winner. Knocked her around some, didn't want her to go off to college. Scott and I changed his mind."

"How?"

"Scott talked to him, stuttered at him 'til he agreed not to see her anymore."

"And what did you do?"

Alvarez took a moment to consider his answer. "I made sure he sat still and listened."

Tory digested this information. "What are we waiting for?" she asked.

"That mean you're in?"

"Was there ever any question?" she replied, taking off purposefully down the hall ahead of him.

"Just one problem," he called after her. She turned on a dime, ready to jump all over him if it turned out he was baiting her, this offer his idea of a joke. "It's the other direction," he said.

IF SMOKING HELPED with weight control, Tory hated to think what Dottie Abbott would look like if she stopped. The woman resembled a gnome, less than five feet tall and almost as wide. She wore no makeup and sported a limp gray hair cut in an outdated Dutch Boy that would have looked too juvenile on someone half her age, which Tory estimated to be over sixty. Dottie was sitting at a small round table in the deserted lounge, smoking. When she saw Alvarez, her lined face split into an impish grin that made her almost attractive.

"Hi, hon. Right on time, as usual. And you brought your friend. My, she's a big girl, nice and tall."

"Tory, this is Dottie," said Alvarez. "Dottie can squeeze three or four politically incorrect phrases into one sentence, but everyone ignores it because they think she's too old to know any better. Dottie, this is Tory Travers. She's not a big girl, she's a tall woman."

"I'll say, honey. When you're my size, five feet looks tall." Dottie Abbott directed her irresistible smile at Tory, offering her a cigarette from the pack in front of her. Tory declined, slipping into the chair between Dottie and Alvarez.

"How's Allison?" asked Alvarez.

Tory wouldn't have thought it possible, but Dottie's smile got wider. "Just fine, thanks for asking. Made the honor role at Rice last semester, she did."

"Good for her. Pamela Case, then," said Alvarez without further ado, pulling out a small notebook. For some reason, it galled Tory that Cal Cortez hadn't rated the notebook, while it appeared that Dottie Abbott did.

Dottie's smile disappeared. "Poor Pammy," she said, with genuine regret.

"You don't know she's dead," Alvarez reminded her.

Dottie gave him a ghost of her former smile. "Just like you don't know anything I'm going to tell you," she replied.

"You called her Pammy?" asked Tory. Somehow the diminutive nickname didn't correlate with the things she'd been told about Pamela Case.

"I call everyone by nicknames, dear. I knew Pamela from when she first started working for the city, that would be seventeen, eighteen years ago. She was a timid little thing back then, scared of her own shadow. I always called her Pammy, and if it bothered her, she never let on.''

Alvarez obviously wasn't interested in the subject of nicknames. ''What can you tell me about her? What made her tick?'' he asked.

''Her politics were extreme,'' said Dottie. ''I'd call her a little right of reactionary, myself. That's not really so unusual in itself, what's unusual is how outspoken she was about it.''

''What else?''

''She wasn't well liked by her coworkers.''

''Because of her politics?''

Dottie thought about the question, dragging deeply on her cigarette, then exhaling a thin wisp of smoke. ''That would be the easy conclusion, wouldn't it? It's more like asking which came first, Pammy's political leanings, or her off-putting personality? She didn't get along with people very well, although she was smart enough. Pammy was one of those people who always think they're owed more in life than they end up getting. Coming to El Paso was like a culture shock she never got over.''

''How so?'' asked Alvarez.

''Her husband was transferred here in the military. They were from up north somewhere, hadn't been around Mexicans before.'' It wasn't often anymore Tory heard someone say ''Mexicans'' instead of ''Hispanics'' or ''Latinos'' or ''Mexican-Americans,'' but Alvarez didn't even blink. ''When they got here, Pammy decided to go to work for the first time since she'd been married,'' continued Dottie. ''So there were lots of changes for the whole family, not easy changes. Pammy started out in what used to be the Utilities Permitting Department.''

''So where did the culture shock part come in?''

''They all had a terrible time adjusting. Her little sons, they must have been about eight or nine, kept getting beat up at school. Pammy said they got hassled just because they were white and had a northern accent, and she was probably right. But she handled it all wrong, never gave the kids a chance to get it sorted out for themselves. Then her husband got passed over for some big promotion. According to Pammy, they promoted a Negro instead just because he was black, and she took it really hard. That's when she started thinking other races were getting a better shake than members of her own family."

"What about her family?" asked Alvarez. "She got divorced, right?"

"Right. She and her husband broke up just before he got transferred out, which is why she ended up staying here."

"Never remarried?"

"No. There was talk that Pammy was carrying a torch for some married man, and that's what broke up her marriage. Her ex-husband was a hothead, I can tell you that. When she told him she wanted a divorce, he showed up here a few times like he was going to smell out the guy his wife was cheating with." Dottie thought for a moment. "I wonder if that's one of the reasons he came back."

"What do you mean, he came back?"

"He just recently retired and came back here, God only knows why. One of his sons still lives here, but neither Pammy or the boy had any use for the man after the divorce."

"How do you know he came back?"

"Because he was here, just a few weeks ago."

"He was here, as here, in the city offices?"

"Yeah, applying for a job. Pammy ran into him, and it was not a pretty sight, I hear. There was some shouting on her part. Said she'd rather have him dead than living in the same town with her."

"Did he threaten her back?"

Dottie tapped the growing snake of ash off the tip of her cigarette. "I know it would make things easier for you if I said yes, but no such luck. I heard he just kept on walking like she didn't exist."

"Any idea who she had an affair with?"

"Not a clue."

"What's the ex-husband's name?"

"Paul Case." Dottie pushed a piece of folded paper across

the table to Alvarez. "This is the address and phone number he put on his application."

"What about the son?"

"Sons. There were two of them, cute little boys, identical twins. It was kind of like they lined up and took sides in the divorce. Saul, he was on his mother's side. Stayed here, went to college, got a job teaching at a local high school."

"Do you know which one?" asked Tory.

"I'm not sure," said Dottie, "I think Coronado."

"Nice," Alvarez said, and Tory felt inordinately pleased with herself. "What about the other boy?" he asked.

"I can't even remember his name. He was trouble from the moment Pammy got divorced, always wanting to go live with his father, getting into all kinds of scrapes. As soon as he was old enough, he moved out and Pammy stopped talking about him. I have no idea what happened to him, or where he went."

"What about Pamela Case being a troublemaker, getting bounced from department to department?" asked Tory.

Dottie took a drag on her cigarette. "Well, that's a funny thing," she said.

"Funny-strange or funny-ha-ha?" asked Tory.

Alvarez raised one eyebrow. "Quite an interrogation technique, don't you think?" he asked Dottie.

"I couldn't have put it better myself," said Dottie, smiling her infectious smile. "Definitely funny-strange. All that most people remember these days is Pammy getting into trouble, first in Personnel, then in the Purchasing Department. But I've been here long enough to remember—that first transfer from Utilities Permitting was quite a feat—almost doubled her salary, and she didn't have any previous experience."

"What is that supposed to tell me?" asked Alvarez.

"That she had someone important looking out for her," said Tory immediately.

"You better watch your back," Dottie told Alvarez, "or she may be replacing you."

"No way," he replied. "She lacks my people skills, not to mention my vocabulary of Spanish profanity."

Dottie ignored him to nod at Tory. "I think you're right, dear. Pammy didn't get that promotion because of any kind of affirmative action program, that's for sure."

"Who was Pamela's benefactor?" asked Alvarez. Dottie shrugged. "What about her other problems?"

"There was that discrimination suit threat while she was in Personnel, but that was bargained away if she'd transfer to another department. You're out of luck if you want information about that; those records are sealed. The last thing I know about was her getting caught using city postage meters, and that got nasty. The head of Purchasing had your guys write up a report on that one, mainly to threaten her into agreeing to be transferred again."

"Do you know anything about Pamela Case being interested in the Monte Vista Heights subdivision project?" asked Tory.

Dottie looked at her blankly. "What's that?"

"Some abandoned property that's being renovated for a housing project," replied Alvarez.

"Sorry, but people are my area of expertise," said Dottie. "I collect information about people, not projects."

"Anything else I might find useful?" asked Alvarez.

Dottie thought a moment. "After the last episode in Purchasing, Pammy was pretty much on permanent probation. One more disciplinary problem, and she'd lose her job."

"Know anyone who might have wanted to kill her?" asked Alvarez.

Dottie took another drag on her cigarette. "Maybe her ex-husband? But it seems extreme to kill someone just to get them to shut up."

"Been done before," said Alvarez.

Dottie didn't look convinced. "And if he was going to kill her over having an affair and divorcing him, why wait all these years to do it?"

"How about other city employees?" asked Alvarez. "You said she had problems with her co-workers."

Dottie ground out her cigarette. "I can imagine Pammy wanting to kill someone, like the guy in Purchasing who sicced the police on her, but not the other way around." She smoked and gave Alvarez's question some more thought. "Lots of people didn't like Pammy much, but I can't think of anyone with a reason to kill her." She paused again. "Maybe Irma Lujan knows something. You should talk to her."

"Because Irma Lujan supports affirmative action, and Pamela Case was against it?" asked Alvarez.

"No, dear. Something else. Talk to Irma. Ask her about Pammy losing her job in Purchasing."

"Irma Lujan is in the Business Advocacy Department. Why should she know anything about what happened in Purchasing?"

Dottie shook her head and pocketed her cigarettes. "I don't mind telling you things that are common knowledge, dear, things that everyone talks about, or information you can get on your own, like Paul Case's address. But this is something I just have a feeling about, so you need to see what you can get out of Irma. She never got along with Pammy, so if you play your cards right, Irma may be willing to tell you things even I don't know."

Tory wondered if Alvarez would push Dottie on this, but he didn't.

"You can't make it sound much more challenging than that," he replied. "I appreciate the help you've already given me."

Dottie turned to Tory. "And you go along with him, dear. Irma likes men a little too much for her own good. You don't want our boy to face her alone in his injured state, do you?"

Tory ignored the reference to our boy; it wasn't as if she hadn't had previous practice. "We can start off by asking her about the Monte Vista Heights project," she said, already planning her questions. "I want to know why Irma Lujan is interested in that specific project after all these years, so much so that she's hounding Cal Cortez for updates."

Dottie showed no curiosity about the fact that Irma Lujan shared an interest in Monte Vista Heights with Pamela Case. "You've been talking to Cal Cortez?" she asked, grinning again. "Want to know something really interesting about him, something you'd never guess in a million years?"

Tory wasn't sure she wanted to know anything more about

the city engineer than she already did, but Alvarez didn't appear to share her scruples. "Sure," he told Dottie without hesitation.

Dottie's grin was back in full force. "He's been haunting the Personnel office, fighting with them over the group health insurance policy. He's trying to come up with a medical reason to have a hair transplant, so the insurance company will pay for it."

"Hey," Alvarez told Tory, "if Cortez continues to refuse to accept your engineering report, maybe you could threaten to leak his cosmetic plans."

Tory made an exasperated sound and tried to look morally superior. She didn't want to admit that the same idea had occurred to her the minute the words were out of Dottie's mouth.

SEVEN

ADVOCACY

ALVAREZ STOOD as Dottie left, then dropped back down in the chair next to Tory, and, to her surprise, started absently rubbing her shoulder with his good hand.

"Should you be doing this?" she asked.

"What, rubbing your shoulder? I thought maybe all this interrogation work was making you tense."

Tory decided to just skip the part where she asked if he rubbed Scott's shoulder after an interview. "What I mean is, should you be asking all these questions? It's not even your case."

"No one's asked if it's my case."

"Then why aren't we on our way to see Irma Lujan?"

"I'm trying to think of the best way to go about getting her to tell us whatever it is that Dottie won't talk about."

Tory tried to think about the problem at hand and not about how nice it felt to have her shoulder massaged. "Cal said she admired Craig Diaz. Why don't we say we're concerned that he wasn't treated fairly, and we're wondering if Pamela's death has any connection to discovering something that would clear his name."

Alvarez dropped his hand from her shoulder, tilted his chair back on two legs, and looked at her consideringly. "And you're not just another pretty face. But that's not too far off the mark, is it? You're describing what you really think happened."

"Well," said Tory slowly, thinking it through as she put it into words, "I don't know if there's really a connection between the two deaths. But yeah, I think that Diaz got the short end of the stick somewhere along the line."

"And that wouldn't be just because your firm put together an engineering report that differs with the city's opinion, would it?"

Tory tried to give the question fair consideration. "How can I answer that? Of course it affects my opinion; otherwise, I wouldn't have one. The fact is, we didn't find much wrong with the original construction, yet the city says it was so bad that they condemned the whole project."

"How could something like that happen?"

Tory took her time to phrase a reply. One of the things she'd learned about Alvarez was that when he asked a question, he wanted to know the complete answer, not just the quick sound-byte version. "Inspection is even less of an exact science than engineering," she told him. "On a construction site, things don't always happen according to a schedule. Work is progressive— if you miss the chance to inspect something, the next stage of construction may result in that work being covered up, never visible for inspection again. If a contractor gets off schedule, he may just forge on ahead, hoping he won't have to go back and tear out any work that missed being inspected."

"You realize that you're referring to this hypothetical contractor as a 'he'?" asked Alvarez. His question brought Tory up short; she didn't have a ready answer. "Interesting, isn't it," he continued, "the things we assume no matter how broad-minded we think we are. It's enough to make you wonder what comes first, the assumption or the stereotype."

"It's a matter of habit, and context," Tory said, trying not to sound defensive. "Would you have pointed out Cal using the word 'gringo' and Dottie using the word 'girl,' if we hadn't been talking about affirmative action beforehand?"

"Probably not," said Alvarez. "Would you?"

"No," said Tory. "Neither one bothered me. I don't think that's being hypocritical, I think that's where context comes in. On the other hand, if some asshole on a construction site calls me sweetie, it makes me want to pick up a two-by-four and deck him."

"I'll file that away for future reference," said Alvarez. "Gringo Girl is okay, but sweetie is definitely too much."

"It depends on the context," insisted Tory.

"Doesn't everything. But I didn't mean to get you side-tracked. Finish what you were telling me about construction inspection."

Tory tried to remember where she'd left off. "The main thing to realize is that any inspector has a lot of discretionary power. He—I mean, he or she—can let things slide, or make life miserable. A lot of it is arbitrary. A lot of it comes down to individual opinions and priorities, not to mention personalities."

"So we're sitting here on the sixth floor of the City Administration Building," said Alvarez, "and you're telling me that some inspector probably looked the other way on certain things when this building was constructed?" Tory nodded and started to elaborate.

"Never mind," said Alvarez quickly, and Tory wondered if he was thinking about the four floors above them.

"Anyhow, if the inspector on a project hates your guts," she said, "everything you do is wrong, and everything that goes wrong gets blamed on you."

"Could you tell if something like that happened to Diaz?"

"Maybe," said Tory. "And maybe not. All that's left now is the project documentation. A lot of it is reading between the lines. A lot of it, you would have had to be there to interpret what was really going on. That's why I want to see the city run the water-tightness test. If there's not a problem with the storm sewers, then I think you can take it as gospel that Craig Diaz was screwed."

"I love it when you get all intense and talk dirty at the same time," said Alvarez.

"Another thing," said Tory doggedly. "Are you certain Craig Diaz really committed suicide?"

"Why?"

"It just doesn't seem to fit. I mean in a way, developers almost have to be adrenalin junkies. They're used to setbacks, living life on the edge, schedule-and-money-wise. I've seen contractors in the parking lot outside a bid opening, tearing open their sealed bids and revising them three minutes before they're due, re-sealing the envelope with cellophane tape they keep in their trucks just for that purpose."

"Worth looking into. I plan to head out to Coronado High School this afternoon, talk to Craig Diaz's son and"—Alvarez consulted his notebook—"Saul Case. Convenient, them both working at the same school. Wonder how they feel about it." He shook himself out of his reverie and said, "Let's go talk to Irma Lujan."

"Should you call first, make an appointment?"

"That's for civilians. I like to see how people react when they don't expect me. Besides, we need to get going, because I'm taking you home with me and cooking you lunch."

Tory gave him a stern look, which was hard to do considering the fluttering feeling in the pit of her stomach. "I don't recall being asked, much less accepting. What makes you think I'd be free for lunch?"

Alvarez cocked his head, considered the question. "Because my dog misses you?"

Unbidden, numerous unrelated thoughts tumbled through Tory's mind. The look her son got on his face whenever Kohli was around. The look Sylvia got in her eye whenever she talked about Alvarez. Alvarez kissing her late one night after she'd tugged his shirt out of his pants trying to get to his gun to shoot someone. What underwear she had put on that morning, and whether it matched—Tory refused to think about that further. She bet Alvarez didn't try to remember what underwear he was wearing when he issued an invitation. Then again, maybe he planned ahead.

Alvarez appeared to be waiting patiently for an answer, hiding it well if he was thinking about his underwear. Since Tory's random thoughts hadn't melded into anything resembling an articulate reply, she went for brevity. "Well, okay," she said.

THE BUSINESS Advocacy Department was housed in a single small office, only slightly larger than a broom closet. When Alvarez knocked on the door and was told to enter, he and Tory walked into a room just large enough to hold a desk and two chairs. The woman behind the desk, who Tory assumed was Irma Lujan, wore a maroon satin blouse and a black mini-skirt, yet was not constrained from putting her feet up on the desk while she carried on her phone conversation. It made Tory's calves ache just to look at her stiletto heels.

Alvarez made a gesture of inquiry, but the woman motioned for them to sit down while she continued her rapid-fire conversation. "I don't give a shit what maintenance says about going to quarterly payments. Alfonso Hidalgo has provided janitorial services to the city for the last ten years, and he expects to be paid monthly, just like always."

The person on the other end was barely allowed thirty seconds to make a reply. "Listen, this man has done good work, and he doesn't deserve to be treated like a number. His wife is in the hospital, needs an operation for cancer. I want a check cut for him and available this afternoon. Or you can explain why maintenance has to go to all the hassle of putting those services out to bid again, and ending up paying twice as much for work that's half as good."

This time the pause was less than fifteen seconds. "Good. I'll believe it when I see it, and I mean this afternoon, not first thing tomorrow." She slammed down the receiver and looked at Alvarez with interest.

"David Alvarez, EPPD," said Alvarez, standing and proffering his identification. "This is Tory Travers." He made no effort to explain that Tory wasn't with the EPPD.

"Irma Lujan," said the woman behind the desk, standing up to take a good look at Alvarez's ID. She had sleek, shiny dark hair, and a figure that generously filled out the mini-skirt and satin blouse in all the right places. After Irma Lujan finished looking at Alvarez's ID, she took a good long look at him, flashing a smile as she sat back down. Instead of placing her feet up on the desk again, she leaned forward with earnest attentiveness, displaying a fair amount of cleavage. Tory was willing to bet that her underwear was a matching set fresh from

Victoria's Secret. "So, David Alvarez of the EPPD," Irma Lujan said, as though Tory didn't exist, "what can I do for you?"

"I'd like to ask you some questions," said Alvarez, sitting back down.

"I have some questions myself," said Ms. Lujan. "Are you married?"

"I beg your pardon?" said Tory.

"No ma'am, I'm not married," said Alvarez, smiling back, and Tory didn't think it was Irma Lujan's face he was looking at. "Is Alfonso Hidalgo's wife really in the hospital, waiting for an operation?" he asked. Tory was appalled to see Alvarez wink at Irma Lujan. This was not her idea of the way to conduct an interview.

Ms. Lujan gave Alvarez an even broader smile. "Nah, the old man doesn't even have a wife, not since his third one kicked the bucket a few years ago. But it sounded good, didn't it?"

"What exactly do you do here in the Business Advocacy Department, Ms. Lujan?" Tory asked.

Irma Lujan kept her gaze riveted on Alvarez. "Call me Irma. Can I call you David?" Alvarez nodded. Tory thought it would set a much better tone to insist on being called Detective Alvarez and Ms. Travers, but no one was asking her. "I do a little bit of everything," Alvarez's new friend Irma continued.

"Can you be more specific?" asked Alvarez. He pulled out his notebook again. Tory was beginning to wonder if this was a sexist thing. Did he think only women talked enough to warrant him writing something down? Or was it meaningful that it was a black notebook?

Irma put her elbows on her desk and her chin in her hands, leaning even farther forward toward Alvarez. "I'll be as specific as you want me to be, David," she said helpfully.

"I'd appreciate that, Irma," replied Alvarez.

Irma Lujan's eyes never left Alvarez's as she recited her job description. "I assist private businesses that work for the city. A year ago I would have said that I assist small businesses, but now that's called reverse discrimination. If a business has a problem getting city work, performing that work, or getting paid for it, they come to me. I try to cut through the red tape, help them out. I've developed a lot of skills helping out various people over the years, David. Various people, various skills." She flashed another smile at Alvarez.

He smiled back, then asked, "Didn't your office used to be called the Minority Business Advocacy Department?"

Irma raised an eyebrow and lifted her chin out of her hands. "That was a while ago," she told him. "Everyone knows we don't need affirmative action programs in El Paso, right, David?" Irma switched to rapid fire Spanish. "Everyone knows that no one here discriminates against anyone because your skin is brown and your last name is Alvarez, right? Just like it's coincidental that being brown-skinned overwhelmingly correlates with a lower socio-economic group in our bustling egalitarian metropolis," she added in the same language.

"You might be interested to know that Ms. Travers speaks fluent Spanish," said Alvarez in the same tone one would use to remark upon the weather.

Irma Lujan directed her attention at Tory for the first time, giving her an appraising look. "Do you now?" she asked.

"Por cierto," said Tory. "Although it took me a minute to translate the word for egalitarian. Do you remember Craig Diaz?"

"Why do you ask?" responded Irma. She sounded markedly less friendly than when she talked to Alvarez.

"We think there are discrepancies concerning the Monte Vista Heights subdivision renovation," Tory said, going for broke. "Cal Cortez told us you have a special interest in this project. Why is that?"

Irma Lujan looked at Tory for a moment. "I'm keeping track of what happens with Craig's project," she said finally. "He deserves no less than that from me."

"Why? What was Craig Diaz to you?" Tory asked before she even knew she had framed the question in her mind.

"He was a goddamned hero, that's what he was," said Irma Lujan, all flirtatiousness a thing of the past. "Someone who wasn't afraid to stand up for what he believed in. Someone who wasn't afraid to take chances, reach for the stars. Someone who tried to give back some of what he had been given. Someone who came from nothing to run for city commissioner, that's who Craig Diaz was.''

"And maybe something more, at least to you?" Tory suggested.

Irma glared at her. "There'd have to be a damn good reason for me to answer a question like that.''

"Fair enough," interjected Alvarez. "Speaking of Craig Diaz, it seems that some people feel like he got some breaks he shouldn't have. Know anything about that?''

Irma stared at him for a moment. "The things some people choose to remember.'' She sighed. "How much do you know about minority business programs?''

"Not much," said Alvarez. Tory didn't say anything.

Irma Lujan sighed again. "Back then everyone was trying to decide how to react to the federal affirmative action program. Some wild and crazy things went on, let me tell you.''

"What kind of wild and crazy things?" asked Alvarez.

"Random acts of liberalism," said Irma dryly, "enacted by the conservatives in power who were afraid that their past actions wouldn't stand up to public scrutiny.'' Tory couldn't begin to think of a question to phrase in response to that. Before Alvarez had to come up with one, Irma continued. "For example, take Craig's situation. He was a one-man contracting outfit, scraping out a living, hiring temporary workers on a job-by-job basis. Then someone came to the bright realization that all the sidewalk jobs in the city had gone to the same three firms for decades. So, the Commission, in their great wisdom, picked out a cushy job and went down the list of bidders until they came to a company owned by a brown person. They threw out three, four other firms with lower bids, and awarded the job to Craig.''

Tory was as aghast as Alvarez would be if the EPPD suddenly mandated all officers to carry guns loaded with blanks. "You've got to be kidding," she said. "They could never get away with that.''

Irma gave her a level look. "What you mean is, they couldn't get away with it today. Back then, nobody understood the new rules we were supposed to be playing by. All anybody could see was that there was a new movement afoot, and they were scrambling to get ahead of it. Sure, there were some disgruntled parties, but they realized that if they made an issue out of it, the past awards wouldn't stand up to a lot of scrutiny. This was long before anyone coined the term reverse discrimination. Anyhow, that's what happened, and that's what gave Craig his start. It was probably the only break he ever got, poor guy. And the reason he got crucified later on was because he wanted others to get the same kind of break he got."

"What do you mean, he got crucified?" asked Alvarez.

"Do you really think the people in power wanted to let him get away with it? Getting a break, getting successful, and then having the balls to run for city commissioner with a platform of more minority set-asides? Craig was practically a one-man lightning rod."

"And what was the lightning?" asked Alvarez.

"Permitting officials, inspectors, lending institutions," said Irma flatly. "They all stuck it to him."

"Can you prove that?"

Irma Lujan glared at Alvarez for a change, not a hint of cleavage in view. "Do you think if I could prove it, I would be sitting here talking to you now? Not that many people remember what happened to Craig back then, but I do. I'm waiting to see just what goddamn problems they find with Monte Vista Heights this time. If it turns out the way I think, then I'm going to the press."

"Might not be too good for job security," observed Alvarez mildly.

Irma Lujan gestured at her surroundings. "Don't you think I've worked hard to get where I am, one step down at a time? Someday the name on the door will read Bureaucracy Advocacy Department."

"So you think Craig Diaz got sandbagged because certain people didn't want him on the City Commission?" Alvarez asked. Irma Lujan nodded. "You remember who got elected to the seat he was running for?"

"Harry Montoya." Irma made the name sound like it had a bad taste to it.

"That's a Hispanic name," pointed out Tory.

Irma shot her a look of pure disdain. "Harry Montoya was about as Hispanic as you are, cookie."

"You must have misunderstood," said Alvarez immediately. "Her name is Tory, not Cookie. Refresh my memory, Irma. Wasn't Montoya an incumbent?"

"Incumbent enough to be in bed with every business interest in town."

"Including developers?" asked Tory.

"Especially developers," said Irma.

"Can you prove it?" asked Alvarez.

"How often can you prove things like that? Reverse discrimination is now considered a blatant political sin, but try proving something as nebulous as long-standing preferential treatment. It was a coincidence, they say, that Firm A got nine out of ten of the last airport expansion jobs, regardless of the bottom line. It all has to do with bid analysis, they say. Firm A had lots more experience than Firm B, or someone heard something really bad about Firm B, so why take a chance? Or, isn't it interesting that Firm A got a little extra clarification about the job, so they were able to bid it more exactly? Well, I say that Firm A has something more going for it, something called contacts. The kind of contacts Craig Diaz never had. I can tell you for a fact that none of Montoya's cohorts ever had inspectors come down on them the way they came down on Craig."

"Montoya's dead now, isn't he?" asked Alvarez.

"Yeah," said Irma bitterly. "It was the only way he'd ever give up his Commission seat. My mother always told me that the mills of God grind slowly. Well, they grind too damn slowly for me."

"Was one of the people who gave Craig Diaz a hard time named Pamela Case?" asked Tory.

"Why?" countered Irma, raw hostility in her voice. Maybe it was time for Alvarez to wink at her again.

"I'm going to tell you something not too many people know

yet," said Alvarez, "and I need you to keep it confidential until you hear it on the news, which will probably be later today. The body of a woman was found out at Monte Vista Heights yesterday. She'd been shot. It was Pamela Case."

If Irma Lujan wasn't shocked to hear Alvarez's pronouncement, she was a good actress, Tory thought. Irma looked at him, stunned, for several moments before she replied with the inane, "You're kidding."

"Police officers seldom kid about finding bodies," said Alvarez, "and never about the identity of those bodies."

Irma Lujan frowned at him. "So what's this all about? Why are you really asking these questions? Do I need an attorney?"

"Whoa," said Alvarez. "Not unless you did something I shouldn't know about."

"My handsome friend, that covers a wide range of topics," replied Irma, her friendly smiles a thing of the past.

"I was told you might know about people who didn't like Pamela Case," said Alvarez.

"Lots of people didn't like Pamela Case," said Irma flatly. "She was a bigot."

"My source said you might have information about someone who didn't like her, something having to do with her transfer from Purchasing," persisted Alvarez.

"Screw your source," said Irma Lujan. Alvarez sat quietly with a faint smile on his face and looked at her like he was willing to wait forever. "How deep are you prepared to dig on this?" Irma asked finally.

"As deep as I have to," replied Alvarez. "I don't want to overlook the possibility that Pamela Case's death might have some connection to what happened to Craig Diaz."

"You're telling me the truth about that?"

"I'm telling the truth about that," replied Alvarez.

"In that case," said Irma grudgingly, "you might as well hear it from me. Pamela Case is the reason that Jeff Harding got divorced."

"Jeff Harding being—"

"The head of Purchasing." That brought Alvarez up short; Tory knew it wasn't the answer he was expecting.

"I don't understand—" he began, but Irma held up a hand to silence him.

"Pamela Case got caught using city postage meters to campaign for one of her reactionary causes," said Irma. "Jeff caught her here red-handed, using the meters late at night, after everyone had gone home." She gave a humorless laugh. "Or, you could say that Pamela caught Jeff."

Alvarez was looking confused, so Tory came to his rescue. "What was Jeff doing here late at night?" she asked.

"He was here with me," said Irma. "He reported Pamela's unauthorized use of city resources, so she called his wife. Presto, Jeff Harding got divorced."

"And you and Jeff—" asked Alvarez, trying to catch up.

"You've got to be kidding," said Irma. "It was just a one-night stand. He's almost old enough to be my father, and besides, I've never found the guys from Purchasing to be particularly worth pursuing. There's something about them, must be related to always trying to economize. It's like they're still bean-counting while they're having sex, or something—" Irma failed to find the exact words she was searching for to describe the shortcomings of certain individuals in the Purchasing Department. "You know what I mean?" she asked Tory.

Tory couldn't help it; she was beginning to enjoy herself. "Maybe it's because they're always figuring the cost-benefit ratio," she suggested, thinking it sounded pretty good for the spur of the moment.

"You think?" said Irma thoughtfully.

"Jeff Harding hold a grudge against Pamela Case because of his divorce?" asked Alvarez, shooting a warning look in Tory's direction.

"I wouldn't think so. It's not like there were any kids or anything. Jeff is dating Sandra Simmons in the Computer Department now, and the last I heard, she was screwing his brains out. You know," Irma added, directing her remarks at Tory now, "some of those techno-nerds in the Computer Department are pretty hot stuff. Must be the result of everything they missed out on in high school.''

"I think you're right," said Tory. "People with technical backgrounds, they—'' she faltered for a moment. "They pay attention to the details," she said triumphantly. God, she could hardly wait to tell Sylvia about her contributions to this conversation.

Alvarez was not looking amused. Tory couldn't remember the last time he had written something down in his notebook. "How about Mrs. Harding?" asked Tory, figuring that someone needed to close the loop on this line of questioning.

"I wouldn't know," said Irma. "Last I heard, the old battle-ax had left town."

Tory felt like she was getting the hang of this interviewing stuff. "Ms. Lujan," she said in what she hoped was a businesslike manner. "One more question. How close was your friendship with Craig Diaz?"

"Will this go any further?"

"Of course not," said Tory. She avoided looking at Alvarez, who was now openly glaring at her.

"Well," said Irma, talking directly to Tory again, as though Alvarez was no longer in the room. "Let's just say that if Jeff Harding was a three on a scale of one to ten, Craig was a nine. But I was only nineteen then, and things seem different, you know, when you don't have so many other guys to compare someone to.''

Tory couldn't think of anything to say in reply to that, so she jostled Alvarez's arm to get him to come to his feet. She had just about got him to the door when she thought of something else. "Ms. Lujan, did you say your office helps businesses get paid by the city for the work they do?"

"Yes," said Irma hesitantly, apparently confused by the quick change in subject. It had the opposite effect on Alvarez, galvanizing him back into life.

"Thanks for your help. We'll be in touch if we need anything else," he told Irma Lujan, firmly grabbing Tory's arm and dragging her through the door.

EIGHT

LUNCH BREAK

"GOD, I'VE CREATED a monster," said Alvarez as soon he got Tory out of Irma Lujan's office.

"I thought it went pretty well," Tory replied.

"I was waiting for the two of you to start critiquing the sexual prowess of police officers."

"We could go back," Tory offered. "Irma might have some interesting observations about people you work with." She paused. "I'll never be able to look at Cal Cortez the same way again."

Alvarez took Tory's hand and started down the hall. "Time for lunch."

"It's only ten forty-five," she countered.

"I'm supposed to take long lunches as part of my rehabilitation," he replied.

"Am I going to regret this?" asked Tory. Alvarez could tell he was making the mistake of giving her too much time to think. They exited the City Administration Building, and not a moment too soon.

"Not if I can help it," he said fervently, but Tory didn't look convinced. "And besides," he added, "I'm going to call in, find out what's been going on. I'll recommend getting the crime scene cleared as soon as possible so Cortez can run that test on the storm sewers."

"But you'd do that whether I went to lunch with you or not," she protested.

"Yeah, but this way you'll get to hear the latest." He was betting this would be hard for Tory to resist. They reached his beloved bronze Corvette; he went around to the passenger's side and opened the door for her.

Tory looked at the opened car door as though trying to remember how she had arrived there, and why he was waiting for her to get into his car. "I have my own car," she said, "I can drive."

"No way," he replied. "I have absolutely no assurance that if I let you out of my sight, you'll put in an appearance."

She kept talking without looking at him. "I'm in a two-hour parking zone, and I'm over the limit already. I'll have a parking ticket when I come back."

Alvarez deftly guided her into the passenger seat. *"Querida,"* he said, "when you are with me, there are definitely some things you don't have to worry about."

CARUMBA COTTON CANDY, the white Puli that had come to live with Alvarez as a result of his last case, was overjoyed to see Tory. Or at least, she was overjoyed to sense Tory's presence. Since the dog's eyes always remained hidden from sight, Tory wasn't sure how much Cotton actually saw or didn't see.

Tory fussed over her while Alvarez pulled a casserole out of his refrigerator and put it in the oven. "Mexican rice and chicken," he told her. "I hope you like it hot."

Tory was surprised at this show of domesticity, but she didn't say anything. She started to feel faint stirrings of panic when Alvarez turned on the oven and set the timer for an hour. An hour seemed like an awful lot of time to kill before lunch was ready.

She accepted a glass of iced tea and sat at the kitchen table while he made his phone call. It appeared he had timed it right to get put through to Scott. Alvarez asked several short, cryptic questions, then gave Scott a summary of the information he and Tory had gleaned from their three morning interviews. True to his word, he finished by telling Scott that he thought it was important to turn the crime scene back over to City Engineering as soon as possible.

When Alvarez hung up, Tory noted that there were forty-seven minutes left on the oven timer.

"Damned if they didn't give it to him," said Alvarez.

"Give what to whom?" asked Tory. She wondered how long she could stretch out this conversation by talking very slowly.

"They gave Scott the case. At least for now, unless something more urgent comes along."

"Why are you surprised?"

"It means this isn't being treated as a routine homicide. Admittedly, Pamela was a city employee found dead on city property, but it's the connection to Diaz that's a concern. People at City Hall are afraid that the Case case has more than alliteration going for it; they think it has the potential to be sensationalized by the press."

"What does that have to do with Scott?"

"It's politically expedient to say that the investigation is being handled by Special Case."

"The Case case being handled by Special Case?" asked Tory, trying it out.

"Don't be a wise-ass. It's what our press liaison calls 'positive spin.' They don't even have to say any progress is being made, just that it's been turned over to us. Presto, everyone feels better. Hell, a year ago I suggested we change our name from the Special Case Task Force to the X Case Task Force, just so we could refer to our active investigations as the X Files. No one seemed to appreciate the idea."

"So are there any developments?"

"They didn't find Pamela's car at her house, so there's an APB out on it. They haven't been able to locate her son, Saul, yet. No one answers the phone at his house, and the school says he called in sick today."

"Isn't that kind of unusual?"

"Not if he's home with the flu and not answering the phone. We'll send someone out to his house later this afternoon. You'd be surprised at how long it takes to track people down sometimes, whether they're local or not. I remember when a small plane crashed into a house out toward Dell City, killing two senior citizens. Their son and his wife lived in Seattle, but no one could locate them. A week later, the Dell City Police get this hysterical call from the guy. He and his wife had come down to visit his parents, gone camping, been out of touch, and didn't know anything about what happened 'til they drove up to the house and found it flattened.''

That was a homecoming Tory didn't want to contemplate. ''Anything else?'' she asked. Three more minutes had elapsed on the oven timer.

''It's too soon for the autopsy results, but CSU thinks they've found where she was killed.''

''And where was that?'' asked Tory faintly.

''From what I understand, about fifty feet west from where you parked your car.''

Tory did what she was trying so hard not to do—she let a significant lull creep into their conversation. She wondered what evidence had been discovered, and whether she had walked over it unknowingly.

Alvarez removed his gun from his shoulder holster and laid it on the kitchen counter, then held out his hand. ''Stand up,'' he said.

''Why?''

''So we can move into the den. It's more comfortable—there's a couch in there.''

''It's perfectly comfortable in here,'' she replied, even as he took her hand and pulled her to her feet. She came to a standing position holding her iced tea glass in her other hand. ''Besides, this way we'll know when your casserole is done.''

Alvarez took the glass out of her hand and set it on the table. ''The oven turns itself off when the time is up,'' he told her. ''You of all people should recognize the benefits of modern technology.''

Then he moved his good hand to the back of her neck and pulled her toward him. He ducked his head and nudged her chin up until he could reach her lips. Then he started kissing her. After a while she found herself kissing him back.

This wasn't so bad, she decided. He stepped back and took

her hand again. He led her out of the kitchen into his den and pushed her down to sit on the couch. Before she could decide that there was a pause needing to be filled with conversation, he sat down next to her and brushed her hair off her neck. Then he started to feather light, breathy kisses between her ear lobe and where her neck met her shoulder.

"I've started to wonder," she said, "how you learn to do things like that. I mean, does someone tell you how, or do you just figure it out for yourself?"

Alvarez brought his head up to look at her with dark, intent eyes. "What are you talking about?"

"How do you learn to do this? How do you manage to get someone from your kitchen to your couch so smoothly? Is this something Cody will know instinctively, or do all the boys get together and give each other pointers?"

"Tory," said Alvarez, "has it ever occurred to you that there are some things you don't have to analyze?" His voice held a familiar tone of exasperation, but the timbre had changed. It was husky, breathy, and preoccupied. Tory started to panic at the same instant he started kissing her again, then she forgot what she had been concerned about.

When she came up for air the next time, she was beneath him on the couch, and he was looking into her eyes in that same intent way. She wondered if he could feel her heart pounding, and if his sexual experiences included reviving someone who hyperventilated and passed out from nervousness. She supposed she should be grateful that he was trained in first aid; if her quickened breath wasn't from nerves, she was in deep trouble.

"Do you know how much I've wanted you?" he asked.

"No," she said honestly. Did he really think that she was adept at making small talk in this kind of situation? Did he have any idea how out of practice she was at such things?

"I've wanted you since the first time I met you," he said in the same husky tone of voice, "when you thought I was a plant foreman and you went out of your way to put me in my place." He punctuated this declaration by kissing the tip of her nose.

"I didn't really go out of my way," Tory said. She looked

down her nose to where his hand rested at the base of her throat. Two buttons on her sweater were undone, and he was working on liberating the third. She didn't want to think where she would be right now if he had the use of both hands. The way things were going, she would soon solve the mystery of just what underwear she had put on that morning. "You know," she said desperately, "this probably works out for you just fine most the time, but you don't understand. I can't possibly do this."

"Do what?" he asked, watching his hand work its way down the next three buttons. Tory felt an amazing sense of relief as a pale peach satin bra came into view. That bra and the matching panties were both relatively new and reputable, if memory served her correctly.

"This," she answered succinctly. "I can't do this." Even to her own ears, her voice seemed to lack conviction. Maybe she could pretend she was wearing old, worn-out underwear. Surely someone wearing old, worn-out underwear wouldn't end up in a situation like this.

"You don't have to do anything," Alvarez told her in that comforting, reassuring tone she had heard him use on other occasions. "That's the beauty of it," he continued. "You just relax and go along for the ride." He eased her sweater off her shoulder and started kissing the top swell of her breast above the peach satin bra.

Tory knew she was in trouble when his simplistic answer seemed to make sense, and when his weight started to feel safe and comforting instead of confining. At this rate, she was going to lose her license to conduct smug maternal lectures about safe sex. "Aren't we supposed to have some kind of discussion?" she asked as she felt one bra strap smoothed off her shoulder.

This time Alvarez didn't lift his head to answer. "I plan to take very good care of you, *cara*," he told her, his breath warm against the top of her breasts. "You don't need to worry about anything. I'll take all the necessary precautions."

His hand was at the back fastening of her bra when the doorbell rang. Tory immediately stiffened and would have sat straight up except that Alvarez was stretched out on top of her. The doorbell didn't seem to faze him, but then he wasn't the one partially undressed. The good news was that his hand was back where she could see it—he laid a finger gently against her lips. "Shhhh," he told her reassuringly. "Don't worry about it. Whoever it is will go away."

The doorbell rang twice more while Alvarez went back to kissing her.

"What if it's important?"

"Are you kidding?" he replied. "What could be more important than this?" He shifted his weight slightly and she could feel his hand at the zipper to her pants.

"You don't understand," she said, keeping her eyes squeezed shut so she didn't have to look at him. "Sex hasn't been an issue in my life like…like forever. And if you say it's the same as getting back on a bicycle—"

"Tory," Alvarez said warningly.

"It might be better if we just stayed friends. In fact, I'm sure of it—"

"Christ."

Tory knew very well that he wasn't calling her name, but she answered anyway. "What?"

"Just close your mouth and be quiet. No, don't close your mouth, but be quiet. Can you do that?" Tory felt her pants being unzipped at the same time she heard tapping on the sliding glass door. The sliding glass door that was within her range of view if she opened her eyes and turned her head slightly. Cotton had wandered over to the door, and was standing wagging her tail at the person doing the tapping.

If Alvarez noticed the sound, he was doing a good job of hiding it. He seemed to be completely focused on kissing her stomach.

"David?" Tory said tentatively.

"What now?"

"What does Keaton look like?"

"Why?" he asked, barely pausing as he worked his way up from her navel. "Didn't we go over this already? You can hold your own with anyone, *cara*."

"Does she have long, red curly hair, and look like a star on a soap opera?"

"That's a pretty fair description," he admitted, his hand at the back of her bra again. "But why are we talking about Keaton at a time like this?"

"Because I think she's standing at your sliding glass door, tapping on it to get your attention."

NINE

PEER REVIEW

ALVAREZ WENT perfectly still. "Stay right here," he told the hollow between Tory's neck and shoulder. "Don't move. I'll shoot her; it will just take a minute."

"It will take more than a minute," Tory said, studying the ceiling, "because you left your gun in the kitchen."

Tory felt his weight shift and the zipper to her pants slide up into its original position, then her dangling bra strap was smoothed back into place. Alvarez sat up beside her while she quickly buttoned her sweater. "Just a goddamned minute," he called in the direction of the sliding glass door. He used his good hand for a perfunctory swipe at straightening Tory's hair. "Remember where we left off," he told her. Like that was something Tory was going to forget.

She sat up. It was dark in the den compared to the sunshine outside, and the couch was angled away from the sliding glass door. Tory wondered how much Keaton was able to see looking in, and what Irma Lujan would do in a situation like this.

Alvarez opened the sliding glass door and Keaton Crandell came inside along with a rush of cold air. "I knew you had to be here," she told Alvarez triumphantly. "I could see your car through the garage window." She gave him an enthusiastic kiss followed by a hug, affording Tory a chance to study the woman who had briefly been a suspect in Alvarez's last case.

Keaton Crandell was tall and slender, probably only a couple inches shorter than Tory. Her most outstanding feature, besides all that white creamy skin, was her tousled, red curly hair. Tory figured Keaton's deliciously rumpled hairdo was probably about as expensive as the cream-colored designer slacks and sweater she was wearing. Tory doubted that her own rumpled look, achieved by good old-fashioned means, was anywhere near as flattering. She gave a mental sigh. So Keaton was every bit as gorgeous as Scott had reported. Tory wondered if she was also as crazy.

Instead of concluding the hug and stepping back, Keaton kept her arms wrapped around Alvarez and spoke directly into his chest. Tory thought that was just as well, since the expression on his face was enough to turn someone to stone.

"It happened again, and no one believes me," Keaton told Alvarez's chest. "Ryan and Marshay think I'm crazy. Dale won't be back for two more weeks, and there's no way to reach him on that stupid Alaskan trout fishing expedition—it's one of those things where you pay more and get less, like no phones. Don't even suggest his parents—they hate me now. You're my last resort." Keaton lifted her head from Alvarez's chest to look up into his face. "What can I possibly do to convince you to stay over?"

Alvarez disengaged himself from Keaton. "Where's Hero?" he asked. Tory wanted to hear the answer to this: if Alvarez had some generic hero on call to help out women in distress, she wanted the details.

"Marshay is picking her up after school," Keaton told him. "Ever since Hero inherited most of my mother's money, Marshay has become a regular Super Aunt."

There seemed to be no better time to enter the conversation. "You named your daughter Hero?" Tory asked in amazement.

Keaton gracefully swiveled from Alvarez to look at Tory, staring fixedly at her with ghostly pale blue eyes. "My daughter's name is Hero Dominique," Keaton said, giving no indication of whether she had previously been aware of Tory's presence.

"This is Tory Travers," Alvarez interjected.

"Really," said Keaton, drawing it out into about four syllables as she looked Tory over.

"Tory is the engineer who helped us figure out what caused the collapse in your mother's house," added Alvarez, which was better than "this is the woman I've been trying to undress on my couch during my lunch hour.'' Tory squared her shoulders and tried to look prepared to answer any structural engineering questions that Keaton might send her way.

Keaton gave Tory a searching look. "But there's nothing to discuss anymore—that case is closed, right?"

Tory felt as though the memory of aiding and abetting a fugitive was written all over her face, but Alvarez didn't miss a beat. "It's probably about as closed as it's going to be," he said. "Tory is over here to discuss a new case."

"How nice," said Keaton. "How versatile. I remember now. David told me about you. You're the one who found a body in that cement column."

"Concrete," said Tory automatically. "It was a concrete column. Cement is what comes in bags."

"How does this work, exactly?" asked Keaton, but Tory didn't think she was interested in the difference between concrete and cement. "You do engineering as your day job, and moonlight as a detective? Maybe you can help me. No one else seems able to," she said, sending a look in Alvarez's direction.

"Tory and I were going to discuss the new case over lunch," said Alvarez pointedly.

"Perfect," replied Keaton. "Is there enough for three?"

"Looked like it to me," said Tory, ignoring Alvarez's reproachful look.

"Can I have a drink?" Keaton asked immediately.

"Iced tea," said Alvarez.

Keaton wrinkled her nose in distaste, then seemed to remember her short-term goal and looked pleadingly at Alvarez. "So, can I stay for lunch? I really, really need some help."

Alvarez didn't look happy, but he nodded. "You two can stay out here and get acquainted while I finish getting lunch ready," he said. Tory felt certain he was punishing her for telling the truth about the size of the casserole.

"What's to do?" she asked. "You explained that the oven turns itself off."

Alvarez shrugged. "I've decided that takes too long," he said. "I'm going to use the microwave. Stay, talk." He seemed to be warming to the idea of turning Keaton over to Tory. "You two have a lot in common," he added.

"Just what," Tory asked evenly, "do you think we have in common?"

This was as close as Tory had ever come to seeing Alvarez nonplussed. Well, with the exception of the time she'd held a gun on him. "You're both single parents," he threw out.

"I am not a single parent," Keaton said indignantly. "Dale may be on a fishing expedition to God knows where, but that does not make me a single parent. If anything," she continued, "I am part of a parenting triangle, and the problem is that there're too many parents."

"What I meant," said Alvarez, "is that both of you have one kid."

"I have a fifteen-year-old son," said Tory.

"And I have a seven-year-old daughter," chimed in Keaton. "I don't see a lot in common there."

Alvarez seemed to be thinking. "You both have trust funds," he said, and beat a hasty retreat into the kitchen.

Keaton shifted her pale gaze to Tory and cocked her head as though she were listening to some distant strains of music audible only to her. Tory hoped she wasn't going to be asked to sing along. "I think," said Keaton after a pause, "that you are the reason he won't sleep with me."

Being crazy didn't keep this woman from cutting right to the chase. "I think," said Tory, carefully, "that maybe he won't sleep with you because he doesn't think it's the right thing to do."

Keaton appeared to think that over. "You may be right," she said. After another pause, she added, "You aren't what I expected. I thought you would be younger."

"Well," said Tory. "I'm not." She couldn't think of anything to add, and the silence stretched between them.

"David says I need to make some friends," said Keaton suddenly. When Tory didn't reply, she added, "Besides him. I'm really afraid," she blurted, looking intently at Tory. "Really, really afraid, and I don't know what to do." Her pale eyes were striking, dramatically accentuated by deftly applied eyeliner, but it wasn't the makeup giving them a haunted look.

Shit, Tory thought, feeling that familiar urge to try to solve someone else's problems. "Do you want to tell me about it?" she asked, hoping she wasn't going to regret the question.

Keaton dropped into a chair across from the couch. "Maybe we can be friends," she said. "And, if I were your friend, I'd tell you something," she added.

Tory took a deep breath. "What would you tell me?"

"That your sweater is buttoned crooked." Tory looked down and saw that Keaton was right. She wondered how Irma Lujan would handle this. For herself, she couldn't think of anything more suave than re-buttoning her sweater as unobtrusively as possible.

Keaton watched Tory's every move. "A cigarette would be really good right now, but David won't let me smoke in his house."

"He sounds like quite the paragon of virtue," said Tory through clenched teeth as she struggled with the last button. "Well," she said, as much to distract herself as Keaton, "are you going to tell me what's frightening you, or not?"

Keaton looked at her a moment, as though making up her mind. "No one believes me because they all think I'm crazy," she said obliquely. "Maybe you'll believe me because you don't know me."

"Why do people think you're crazy?"

Keaton thought it over. "Well, because I am, sometimes, I guess. Sometimes I get depressed, sometimes I get manic, and sometimes I have eating disorders. So I take a lot of pills, and sometimes I drink more than I should. But I'm not so crazy that I don't know when someone has been in my house at night, going through my things."

That didn't sound like a common garden variety delusion to Tory. "How do you know someone has been in your house?"

"Things get moved around."

"If you drink and take pills, maybe you just imagined it," said Tory carefully.

"No," replied Keaton, shaking her head so hard that her curls fell into even more disarray. "Hero has to have everything just so. Sunday morning she showed me where someone had moved things around on her desk."

"Maybe Hero imagined it," suggested Tory gently. "She's only, what did you say, seven?"

"Hero doesn't imagine things. She's not that kind of kid. She kind of takes care of me." Keaton paused. "How do I explain this? My mother was a bitch." Tory didn't think this was a competition, so she didn't say anything. "I fell in love when I was fifteen," Keaton said. "In love, forever, the one and only, the whole nine yards." Cody was fifteen. Tory didn't think she wanted to hear this, but Keaton wasn't giving her a choice. "His name was Gary Cabrioni, but he was half-Jamaican. My mother wanted me to marry the son of my father's business partner. She threatened to ruin Gary's family if I didn't do what she wanted. I was young, I'd just discovered I was pregnant, and I was afraid that if my mother found out, she would kill me. Or kill him. Do you understand?"

Of course Tory didn't understand. How could she? "I understand," she told Keaton.

"So I married Dale and said Hero was premature. Then everyone was happy, mostly, except for me. Gary never knew he was Hero's father, and neither did anyone else. Then my damned mother got herself killed and left half her money to Hero, in a trust to be administered by her biological father. Even from the grave, she wanted to make sure I would stick it out with Dale. The damned lawyers required a blood test to prove paternity. They'd hated my family forever, and they thought they were really sticking it to us. They ended up sticking it to a seven-year-old girl instead."

"That's horrible," said Tory.

"My brother is an asshole," continued Keaton, as though Tory hadn't said anything, "his wife hates me, my husband has gone into the wilderness to find himself, and Gary—Gary is the worst. He won't even talk to me. He's going to sue for sole custody of Hero, on the basis that I'm an unfit mother. He can afford to do that now, and his money will hold out longer than mine if he can get a judge to let him use Hero's trust to pay for the custody suit. If my mother knew that Gary Cabrioni was spending her money, it would send her straight to her grave. But that doesn't do me any good, you see, because she's already dead.''

"Surely he can't take your child away, just like that," Tory said. "Maybe he's just threatening a custody suit because he's hurt and angry.''

"He can be hurt and angry all he wants, as long as he doesn't fuck with my daughter," said Keaton. "He might win the custody suit. It's still okay to discriminate against crazy people, which sucks." She looked at Tory. "There are more of us crazy people than you know. Think of your three closest friends. Are any of them crazy?''

Lonnie, Sylvia and Jazz had various vexing eccentricities, but Tory wouldn't call them crazy. "I don't think so," she said cautiously.

"Well," Keaton replied, "then you're lucky, because medical studies have shown that twenty-five percent of the population is mentally ill." She paused, considering. "If those statistics are right, and your three best friends aren't crazy, what do you think that says about you?''

Tory couldn't think of a ready answer. "It sounds like you're under a lot of stress," she said instead. "Hero must be, too. One instance of a child thinking things are out of place isn't really a reason to conclude that someone is walking around in your house at night.''

"I know," said Keaton. "But it happened again last night. Someone went through my desk.''

"How do you know?''

"Because of Hero's TBR pile.''

"What's a TBR pile?" asked Tory. She had never met an acronym she particularly liked.

"A 'To Be Read' Pile. Hero stacks her nighttime stories on my desk, because I read to her in my room right before I put her to bed, and she's really particular about the way the books are stacked. We're reading a series, and Hero is the kind of child who has to hear them in order. This morning, the books were arranged differently."

Tory had to ask. "Could Hero be playing a prank?"

Keaton looked at her wanly. "Do you think a child in Hero's situation would be playing pranks?"

No, thought Tory. She would bet Hero was working hard on being very, very good, hoping that would somehow make the adults resolve all their problems and live happily ever after. "Are you sure your husband has really gone out of town?"

"He said he wanted to get as far away as possible," Keaton said dismally. "And why would he sneak back into his own house?"

She had a point. "Maybe someone is trying to set you up?" asked Tory. "This Gary person, could he be trying to make you nuts so he has more leverage in the custody battle?"

"Believe me, he already has plenty of evidence that I'm nuts," said Keaton wearily.

Tory tried to help Keaton go through the possibilities of people with a key to her house, but she steadfastly maintained that except for herself and her husband, only the weekly cleaning service had a key. Since Keaton lived in an older home on prestigious Rim Road, it had never been wired with an alarm system. Tory could only come up with a few trite suggestions and empty reassurances before Alvarez declared that lunch was served.

The food was surprisingly good, as was the conversation. Alvarez gave Keaton a general summary of events since Sunday, which seemed to take her mind off her troubles for a while. In turn, Keaton told them that she vaguely remembered Harry Montoya. He had been a friend of her father and her father-in-law, the founders of Pinnacle Development. But Keaton's father had succumbed to an unexpected heart attack when Keaton was thirteen, and she had had little contact with the business world until her husband and brother took over Pinnacle. She didn't really know any specifics about Montoya, and she had no memories of the political climate in El Paso fifteen years ago.

The only uncomfortable lull in the conversation came when

Keaton offered to drive Tory back downtown on her way home. Alvarez sighed, then shrugged. "It's okay with me if it's okay with Tory," he said.

"And what about tonight?" asked Keaton. She picked at the food remaining on her plate.

"For heaven's sake," said Tory. "It's not necessary to be scared to sleep in your own house. What you need is a plan. If you and Hero have more problems, call me. I have a hound, a big friendly hound, who loves kids but barks like the dickens if he hears anything at night." Tory hoped Alvarez wouldn't say anything about how this particular dog slept the sleep of the dead. "I'll bring Tango down and lend him to you for a few days if you need me to," she added.

She couldn't believe she said that. From the way Alvarez was looking at her, it was obvious he couldn't believe she had, either. This meant that she had to give Keaton her phone number, but maybe that was a good thing. Maybe Keaton would constitute the required 25% quota of crazy personal acquaintances.

"Won't your son miss the dog?" asked Keaton.

"No," said Tory, "he's a little distracted by other things these days."

"That's an excellent idea," said Alvarez, just a couple of beats late. "I'd lend you Cotton, but she can't see anything anyway, so I doubt she'd be much help."

"This way," continued Tory, "everyone can sleep soundly. In their own beds." She did not look at Alvarez.

"I'll do my part, too," he added. Tory stared at him. If he offered to keep Tango company, she was leaving. "When I get a minute," he told Keaton, "I'll call Cabrioni. If he'll talk to me, I'll tell him I think he's being an asshole." Keaton's face lit up with gratitude.

Alvarez walked the two women out to Keaton's car and kissed Tory goodbye in spite of her efforts to avoid it. "I'll be in touch," he told her. "We have some unfinished business." Before she could pretend he was talking about Pamela Case, he added, "And I'll let you know the minute I hear that Monte Vista Heights is cleared for the water-tightness test." He squatted down by the passenger car door and said quietly, "Thanks for being so nice to Keaton. I know she's a flake, but she's going though a rough time."

"She's a drop-dead gorgeous, richer-than-God flake," Tory reminded him.

He continued as though she hadn't said anything. "I don't know if she's stressed out or just trying to get attention, but maybe talking to you about her imaginary midnight visitors will help her get it out of her system."

Tory looked at him. "I need to tell you something," she said, matching his quiet tone.

"This thing you're going to tell me, does it have to do with finding another body?" Alvarez asked. "You need to remember that I'm on restricted duty."

"Yeah," said Tory, looking out Keaton's windshield. "I could tell." She turned back to look at him. "Do you remember when I kept telling you we needed to figure out what was going on with the stadium column, and you thought I was crazy?"

"Yeah."

"Well, I have this gut feeling that Keaton isn't imagining things."

Alvarez studied her for a minute. "This was fun," he said. "We'll have to do it again sometime."

Keaton drove away from Alvarez's house like a bat out of hell.

TEN

RELATIVE LOCATION

ALVAREZ WATCHED Keaton drive off, grimacing at both her driving and the outcome of his lunch date with Tory. He hadn't put such high-pressure moves on a woman in years, preferring his sexual partners ready and willing, requiring only reciprocal participation on his part. Regressing backward into high school behavior patterns was not exactly high on his list of personal goals.

He happened to know that Tory's impressive record of police arrests, all accumulated before she was eighteen, successfully disguised a sexual neophyte. But even under duress, when questioned as a suspect in one of his cases, she had admitted to only one sexual encounter since her husband's death. So he couldn't claim he hadn't been forewarned; all the signs pointed to someone who took sex seriously, as some kind of commitment. Alvarez shook his head, not wanting to face the dilemma this raised. Ultimately, commitments always yielded hostages to fate, something he had avoided to date.

Alvarez went inside and called Coronado High School. He verified that teachers were on duty in their classrooms from three to four PM after school was dismissed. The person on the other end of the line informed him that Thomas Diaz and Saul Case were instructors in chemistry and math, respectively. Alvarez wondered how often their paths crossed, and whether they were aware of a connection to each other through their parents' histories.

Then he cleaned up the lunch dishes and went to throw a tennis ball for Cotton in the backyard, which should please his physical therapist, since, in addition to the repetitive movements

of tossing the ball, accuracy was required to throw only into the
cleared portion of the yard. Past experience had taught Alvarez
that having Cotton retrieve a ball close to trees or bushes in-
variably resulted in her running head-on into something, and he
didn't figure she had so many doggie brain cells that she could
afford to lose some in high speed collisions with inanimate ob-
jects.

Cotton, though initially ecstatic, flatly refused to fetch the tennis ball on the sixteenth throw. He tried to exhort her into going
for twenty, but had no luck, leaving him no choice but to go
inside and look at the address for Pamela Case's ex-husband. It
was either that or think about when Tory would get back to her
office, and it wasn't cool to call someone when you had no idea
what you were going to say.

Conveniently, the address for Paul Case indicated an older
apartment building some fifteen minutes from Alvarez's house.
Plenty of time to drop by, check out who might be home, and
then drive out to Coronado High School.

CASE LIVED IN A two-story apartment building built in a U-shape
around a swimming pool which yawned gray and empty, drained
for the winter. In spite of the cool weather, the door to apartment
247 was standing wide open, which could either mean Case was
home or a burglary was going down.

Alvarez was relieved to discover that the jeans-clad man inside the apartment appeared to be taking things out of crates
instead of putting them in. When Alvarez knocked on the open
door, the man inside immediately straightened from the box he
was standing over. He was tall and rawboned, with an athletic
build that belied his gray hair, the color barely discernible because of the shortness of his military buzz cut.

"Paul Case?" asked Alvarez.

"Who wants to know?"

Alvarez flashed his badge. "David Alvarez, Detective, El
Paso Police Department. If you're Paul Case, I'd like to ask you
some questions."

The man crossed to the doorway and took his time looking

at Alvarez's badge, something people seldom did. Then he looked at Alvarez and said, "I'm Paul Case, all right, but I don't know about answering questions. My ex-wife put you up to this?"

"No," said Alvarez. "But it involves her. I'm afraid I have some bad news for you."

Brown eyes as dark as Alvarez's own continued to look steadily at him. "A policeman comes to the door, says something like that, it usually means someone is dead." Alvarez didn't say anything; he didn't want to have this conversation standing out on a second-floor landing. After a long moment Case said, "You better come inside then." He shut the door behind Alvarez, making no move to invite him to sit on the couch which was the sole piece of furniture in the room. Case jutted his chin in the direction of Alvarez's sling. "What's with the arm?"

"Injured in the line of duty."

"Couldn't move out of the way fast enough?" Case leaned back against one of the two crates keeping the couch company in the living room.

"I was running toward the problem at the time."

Case thought this over, then nodded as though satisfied with the answer. "Guess you better say whatever it is you've come to tell me."

"Your ex-wife was found dead yesterday afternoon, out on an abandoned piece of property."

Case nodded again, not showing any emotion. "I thought maybe something like that, soon as you told me who you were."

"This is confidential, until notification of next of kin," continued Alvarez. "As of noon, the police hadn't located your son yet."

"You must mean Saul."

Alvarez nodded. "He didn't go to work today; hasn't been answering the phone. Any idea where he might be?" Case shook his head. "Well, it's been less than twenty-four hours, sometimes people are out of touch, go out of town for a few days."

Case's gaze never faltered; he didn't seem inclined to discuss his son's potential whereabouts. "How'd she die?"

"Shot."

Case didn't flinch. "Die quick?"

"Appears so."

Case nodded again. "That's good, then. She was the mother of my sons. Wouldn't want to think she suffered."

"About your other son. You in touch with him?"

Case looked surprised. "Of course. He's my son, isn't he?"

"Could you make sure he's notified?"

Case looked at Alvarez curiously for a moment before answering. "If you want to handle it like that, yes."

"For now, that would be helpful. If it turns out we need to involve him, talk to him for any reason, we'll get back to you."

Paul Case Senior shrugged. "Sure."

"With all respect, you don't seem too broken up."

"What was between me and Pam was over and done with a long time ago. At least on my end."

"Why move back to El Paso, then?"

"I don't have other family, and my son's not in good health. This seemed like as good a place as any to try out my retirement." Case shrugged for a second time. "If it doesn't work out, I can always move on."

"Sorry to hear about your son's health. Any particular reason why you applied for a job with the city?"

"Any particular reason why I shouldn't? It's not the only place I've applied."

"I hear your ex-wife wasn't happy about it."

Case gave a short, humorless laugh. "Like there're so few city jobs, there wouldn't be room for both of us. Did you also hear that she told me to get the hell out of Dodge? And that when I didn't agree, she started yelling that she wished I was dead? Guess that doesn't help too much with your investigation, does it?"

"Not unless it was a reason to retaliate," Alvarez replied.

Case stared at him. After a moment, he said, "If I was going to kill my ex-wife, doesn't it seem a little strange that I'd wait all this time? We've been divorced for over a decade.''

"Doesn't it seem a little strange that shortly after you come back to town, she ends up dead?''

"You have a point there,'' Case conceded, but he didn't seem concerned, or even insulted by the observation. Either the man had ice water in his veins, or he felt secure in his innocence.

Alvarez considered asking Case to account for his whereabouts during the weekend, but decided not to risk antagonizing the man. He didn't have a time window for the death yet, and there was other information he wanted. "Know anyone who might have wanted to harm your ex-wife?'' Alvarez asked.

"Sorry. I've only been back a few weeks. I'm not going to be any help there.''

"Weren't you in contact with her?''

"Not really.'' Alvarez let the silence hang between them, willing the man to expand on his answer. "When we split up,'' added Case finally, "I tried to make a clean break, move on, but Pam was never the kind of person to let go of a grudge. If something went wrong with the boys, or the house, or anything she could blame me for, she phoned, until I wised up and stopped taking her calls. Then she started writing me letters whenever she wanted to vent. Those letters were stuff nobody should have to read, so I stopped reading them. If something came up, or I needed an update, I called her. As the boys got older, there wasn't so much of that. That little encounter at City Hall was the first conversation I'd had with Pam in over a year.''

"Must have been hard,'' said Alvarez, "with children involved.''

"Nothing's easy with kids involved. Especially in the military.''

When Alvarez's long-gone father joined the Army, he didn't deign to take his family with him. "Thought it was kind of like having a support system already in place, wherever you moved.''

Case gave a mirthless grin. "Whoever told you that, told you wrong. For kids, it's like being an outsider, wherever you go. Hell, I move back here, first thing I see is a picture on the front page of the paper, police breaking up gang fights at Austin High School.''

"There have always been gangs at Austin." Alvarez spoke from experience.

"Yeah, but they used to beat up the white kids. Now there aren't any white kids left, guess who gets beat up?" Case didn't give Alvarez time to supply an answer. "Kids the same color as the others, all right, but with parents in uniform, living on base.''

"It's the universal adolescent pastime, defining who belongs and who doesn't," replied Alvarez. He didn't want to get into a discussion about how this pastime sometimes had fatal results. "So, the divorce wasn't exactly amiable?''

"No, but don't get me wrong," Case said. "Pam wasn't all bad. She tried to be a good mother, and she worked hard for things she believed in. But it was like she just turned bitter at some point, couldn't ever get past it.''

"When do you think it was, this point at which she turned bitter?''

Case never dropped his eyes, never hesitated. If there was something he was trying to hide, Alvarez sure couldn't figure out what it was. "Pam never admitted it, and I never caught her at it, but she was having an affair. My guess is that he was married; she must have thought if she divorced me, he would leave his wife. Obviously that never happened. Guess something like that would go a long way toward making someone bitter.''

"You never remarried?''

"Never wanted to go through all that again.''

"Sometimes you don't have to catch someone to know what's going on. Are you telling me that you have no idea who she was involved with?''

Case's eyes narrowed for the first time in the conversation. "You're asking me to go places I don't want to go," he said.

"I'm conducting a homicide investigation," replied Alvarez. "No matter what was between the two of you, or what kind of woman your ex-wife was, she didn't deserve to be shot to death.''

There was a long moment when it could go either way, but then Case nodded again. "Guess not," he said. "You really think this might have something to do with her death?"

"I didn't, I wouldn't be asking."

There was another pause, not quite so long this time. "You know how it is sometimes, when you know something, but you don't really want to know it?" Case asked.

"Sure," said Alvarez, not wanting to think too closely about his own answer.

"One night, when things were already bad between us, and the boys were visiting her mother, we had a fight. I got drunk, passed out. I came to, hearing her go out. She stopped in the hall, where we had a mirror, and damned if she didn't brush her hair. Who rushes out to get some air after a fight and brushes her hair?" he asked Alvarez. Alvarez didn't have an answer. "So I got up, stinking drunk, and I got my service revolver. I got in my car and I followed her. I saw her pull up at a fancy house and go inside. I parked on the street and thought about going in and shooting someone. I decided to do something else instead I went home and packed, moved out." Alvarez didn't say anything. "Sometimes, I still wonder," said Case. "If I'd followed her into that house, showed her that I cared enough to go after her, if maybe things would have turned out differently."

Alvarez wasn't about to voice an opinion about that. "Where is this house, the one you followed her to?"

"Why? You think I sat there and wrote down the address?"

"No," said Alvarez, "but I'm damn sure you remember where it is."

Case looked at a place between Alvarez's head and the ceiling for a while. "Got your car outside?" he finally asked.

"That's how I got here."

"You feel like taking a drive?"

"Works for me."

"Don't lose me. I'm not planning to do this twice."

Alvarez didn't lose him. Fifteen minutes later, he pulled up behind Paul Case's car at the curb of a residential street. As soon as Alvarez brought his car to a halt, Case gunned his motor and sped off. Alvarez didn't notice which street he turned down. He was too busy studying the outside of Keaton Crandell's house.

ELEVEN

TEACHER CONFERENCE

ALVAREZ DIDN'T QUITE dismiss his first hypothesis out of hand; he mentally filed it under highly unlikely, but not absolutely impossible. As crazy and conniving as Keaton might be, it didn't seem plausible that she had listened to him relate the facts regarding Pamela Case's murder at lunch, dropped Tory off downtown, hightailed it over to Paul Case's apartment, and bribed him to lead Alvarez to her house.

Alvarez sat in his car and remembered a conversation in which Scott's father had recited the long list of women Keaton's husband had supposedly slept with. If Pamela Case's name had been on that list, he would have remembered it.

He considered Tory saying that she thought Keaton was telling the truth about her nighttime visitor. What if this latest problem wasn't another ploy for attention? Worrying about a real nocturnal intruder in Keaton's house wasn't something he wanted to add to his job description right now. Alvarez sighed, got out of the car, and walked up the long winding sidewalk to knock at the imposing front door of Keaton's Rim Road residence.

She answered the door with a drink in hand, looking every bit as good as she had when she'd showed up at his house. Her surprise at seeing him immediately changed to delight. "David, hello, come in. Would you like to have some lunch?"

Alvarez shook his head. "We already had lunch. Remember?"

Keaton was not a bit embarrassed. "Right. Come in and have a drink, then."

"*Creo que no.* I'm working."

"Well, come in and I'll have a drink."

"I'm on my way somewhere. I just want to ask you something."

"Ask away. Anything." Her smile was as bright as the afternoon sun.

"These problems you say you're having at night. Can you think of anything in your house that someone might want to get their hands on?"

Keaton's smile turned into a frown, but it was still a pleasant sight. "That's what's so scary. I'm always leaving jewelry out, and the artwork on the walls is worth a small fortune. But nothing is missing."

"How about something less obvious? Records, deeds, insurance policies?"

Keaton shook her head. "We have a wall safe in the upstairs bedroom. Dale keeps everything important in there, or in a safe deposit box at the bank. Why?"

"Just a thought. Don't worry about it."

"I do worry about it."

"Try not to. There's probably some simple explanation."

"Right," said Keaton flatly. "So simple no one has thought of it yet, other than the fact I might be crazy." Alvarez was reminded that whatever her problems, Keaton wasn't stupid.

"If you get too rattled, call Tory and have her bring her dog to spend the night." He couldn't believe he was echoing Tory's suggestion, but after all, the dog was some rare breed—a Transylvanian Hound. Therefore, Tango the Hound should feel right at home on Rim Road, although he couldn't quite picture it himself.

"You think she was serious about that?"

"Yeah, I think she was serious about that. Tory can be a good friend."

"Is that what she is to you?"

Alvarez looked up at the afternoon sun for a moment, considering possible replies. "When I get a chance, I'll give Gary Cabrioni a call. Maybe he's just pissed, maybe he'll settle down once he gets used to the idea of having a daughter. You need to decide what you'd like to do, who you'd like to be with if things work out. It'd be easier to figure if you'd lay off the pills and booze.''

Keaton looked forlorn. "It would be a lot easier to lay off the pills and booze if I knew what I wanted.''

"It's hard for anyone to know what they want," he told her.

"Yeah," she said, "but everyone else has had a whole lot more practice than I have.''

"Come here," he said. He enfolded Keaton in his arms. His ideas about what she needed to do were hard and unyielding; she was not, and she smelled delicious. He took the drink out of her hand and emptied it into the potted plant beside the door, then kissed the top of her head and returned the glass to her hand as he disengaged himself from the embrace. "You have a nice afternoon," he told her, and walked back to his car. Keaton stood in the doorway, swirling her glass as though it still contained a drink, and watched until he drove away.

ALVAREZ ARRIVED at Coronado High School at 3:10 p.m. A giggling female student was willing to be distracted from loitering in the hall long enough to direct him to Mr. Diaz's chemistry class. There, Alvarez found a short, husky Hispanic man bent over papers spread on a lab bench, earnestly talking to a gangly, pimply-faced teenaged boy. The boy looked up when Alvarez entered the room and obviously saw his appearance as a form of deliverance. The student began fervently repeating, "I understand now, Mr. Diaz. I got it. No problem," like he was reciting a religious chant. In less than five minutes, the boy had gathered his belongings and disappeared.

Tommy Diaz looked at Alvarez and sighed. "When will kids ever realize that staying after school for individual help isn't a form of cruel and unusual punishment?''

"Probably about the time they realize they don't already know everything worth knowing," said Alvarez mildly. "Which never happens for some people, kids and grown-ups alike.''

"Can I help you?" asked Diaz. "I'm sorry, I don't recognize you. Which student are you here to discuss?"

Alvarez flashed his badge. "I'm not here to talk about a student," he said. "I have some questions about your father and Monte Vista Heights."

"What's this about?" asked Diaz, no longer quite so friendly.

"A murder was committed out at the site over the weekend."

Diaz stared at him. "Who was killed?"

"I can't tell you that, not until the next of kin are notified."

Diaz continued to stare. "Out at Monte Vista Heights? Are you sure? That's just abandoned property."

"I know," said Alvarez. "Abandoned property that's currently being developed by the city, something you took a healthy interest in, according to Cal Cortez."

Diaz flushed. "I have a reason to be interested. That project was the death of my father, and I mean that literally."

"I know some of the background," said Alvarez. "I know that the project had problems, your father got in over his head financially, and he committed suicide, but I don't know the details. It's the details I'm interested in."

Diaz had regained some of his composure. "Why should I answer your questions?"

"So I can make sure the project history doesn't have anything to do with finding a body stuffed into the storm sewers out there," said Alvarez bluntly.

Diaz winced. "Those damn storm sewers. Sometimes I think they'll haunt me 'til the day I die."

"You worked on the storm sewers?"

"I worked on the whole damned project, but yeah, the storm sewers were my responsibility."

"So how come they failed inspection?"

"Damned if I know," said Diaz, sufficiently distracted from seeking the reason for Alvarez's questions. "After all these years, I still don't know the answer to that question. We were under so much heat, inspectors on our case over every single little thing, but I wasn't sweating the water-tightness test. I knew those sewers had been constructed right. You could have knocked me over with a feather when we got the first set of results. I told my dad something was screwed, there was no way we were leaking that much water. But when we failed the second test, that was it. That was the end.''

"Why? I thought developers were used to weathering setbacks like that.''

Diaz looked down at his hands. "We'd already weathered setback after setback. The storm sewers failing the watertightness test was the last blow.'' He shook his head at whatever memories he was reliving. "Working on that project was like being in combat. Everything that could go wrong, did. Every single little thing that could be held against us was.''

"Think your father was set up?''

Diaz looked up. "I'd bet my life on it. If I'd had more time, maybe I could have done something about it. But I was just eighteen then, fresh out of high school, and my father was too far out on a limb. After he died, what did it matter? No one was going to listen to a kid like me, and besides, I was too busy trying to help my family deal with the fallout.''

"What do you mean, your father was too far out on a limb?''

"You know anything about how developments are financed?'' Alvarez shook his head. "Haven't you wondered how the city came to own that property?''

"Tell me,'' Alvarez suggested before Diaz could ask another question.

"Usually, developers get a loan, buy a piece of property. They develop it, get their permits, then start selling lots. After you pay back the loan, the rest is profit, usually rolled back into another project. When my father took on Monte Vista Heights, he was already committed to run for city commissioner. He needed cash for his campaign. Not a good situation when all your money is tied up in property.''

"So what did he do?''

"He bonded the development to the city in return for the right to sell lots before it was complete. Before it had all the necessary permits and approvals.''

"Kind of like a second mortgage?'' asked Alvarez.

"More like robbing Peter to pay Paul," said Diaz. "I don't really blame him, not anymore. My dad was a zealot; he had a cause. He was an optimist, he thought big, or he would never have gotten as far as he did. But when the development got shut down for faulty construction, he didn't have money to pay the bank or reimburse the initial lot sales, and the property was bonded to the city."

"Sounds like a bad position to be in," Alvarez said when Diaz fell silent. The chemistry teacher was studying his hands again.

"Maybe someone who knew what they were doing could have gotten him some breathing room, I don't know," Diaz said. "Like I told you, I was eighteen at the time, not exactly a financial or legal wizard. I'd made a little money on the side, and I offered it to him, but he told me it wasn't enough to do him any good."

Certain phrases always caught Alvarez's interest. "What do you mean, you'd made some money on the side?"

"Doing odd jobs, this and that," said Diaz vaguely.

"So what happened after your father turned down your offer of financial support?"

"The bank and the city worked out a deal where the city took possession of the property, reimbursed the bank for some discounted amount on the loan, and refunded the purchase price on the pre-sold lots. That left my father owning nothing but the debts, with no way to repay them. He must have figured his life insurance was the only solution to the problem."

Diaz was now looking intently at some spot in a distant corner of the room. Alvarez waited a moment to let him get a grip on his emotions, then asked, "You think there were people at City Hall who didn't want your father to succeed?"

Diaz looked directly at Alvarez. "Do you think my father spoke with a heavy Mexican accent?" he asked by way of an answer.

"Cal Cortez said that you were one of three people showing a marked interest in the resurrection of this project. Why?"

"Isn't it obvious? I want to see what problems they find this time around. I'm not eighteen any more. Maybe this time I can get some things rectified, like my father's good name."

"Irma Lujan and Pamela Case—they're interested in the Monte Vista project, too. Know either of them?"

"Yeah," said Diaz. "I know both of them. Irma Lujan used to administer affirmative action programs for the city, back before those went out of vogue. Now she does business advocacy, whatever the hell that's supposed to be. Irma knew my dad; she has the same interest I have."

"What about Pamela Case?"

"Pamela Case does something else for the city now, but fifteen years ago she was the pissy Permitting officer who did everything she could to bring my father to his knees. She's probably wondering how things will go down if some of the problems she found fifteen years ago aren't there anymore."

Alvarez decided to leave the subject of Pamela Case for now. He'd already told several people about her death before notification of next of kin, and Diaz had less reason than any of the others to keep it confidential. "What happened to your family after your father's death?"

"Not anything good," said Diaz. "My mother died within a year of my dad. I don't care what it said on the death certificate, she died of a broken heart. I had two older sisters. One died in a drunk driving accident two months after our mom passed, the other one got married and moved to Minneapolis—probably increased their Hispanic population by a full percentage point. I'm the only one left around here. The only link to Craig Diaz and all he tried to accomplish. And you wonder why I'm interested in the renovation of Monte Vista Heights?"

"Married?" asked Alvarez.

"Never. Aren't we getting a little far afield with the questions here?"

"Just got a few more," said Alvarez quickly. "Any reason to doubt that your father committed suicide?"

Diaz stared at him. "I hope you have a good reason for these questions, man, because I can tell you, I'm not having much fun answering them. My father shot himself, that's for sure. He didn't leave just one suicide note, he left four.'' Alvarez raised his eyebrows in inquiry. ''One for each of us,'' Diaz said shortly. ''He was a caring kind of guy.''

Since Alvarez had gotten most of the information he'd sought, he decided to go ahead and throw out the next question, the one most people balked at, and see where it got him. ''Can you account for your whereabouts this weekend?''

Instead of taking offense, Diaz grinned. ''This sounds like one of those TV shows. What are you going to tell me next, that I'm a suspect, and you won't even tell me who I'm supposed to have killed? I turn to murder to do what? Revenge my father's death? Embarrass the city? Save yourself some effort. I can account for my whereabouts. I spent the weekend with my girl-friend—Irma Lujan.''

Alvarez hoped his surprise didn't show on his face. ''You didn't mention she was your girlfriend.''

''You didn't ask. It's a recent thing—I met her when I was hanging around City Engineering, trying to get updates on what was going on. We started talking, realized we had a lot in com-mon, and there you are. It happened kind of fast, I'd be the first to admit it, but that's how things go sometimes.''

Alvarez definitely did not want to ask Diaz to elaborate on the things he had in common with Irma Lujan. He would have to think about the possible implications of this relationship later. Right now the ice was getting much too thin for a moonlighting detective on restricted duty.

''I understand Pamela Case's son teaches here,'' he said as casually as possible. ''Given that you don't think too highly of Ms. Case, is that awkward for you?''

Diaz shook his head. ''I'm not going to tell you that I didn't think about it at first, but no, it's not a problem. Saul's a pretty decent guy. And you know how they say what goes around comes around. Well, he's dating an English teacher here.''

If that was the punch line, Alvarez didn't get it. ''So?''

A full-fledged smile lit Diaz's face. ''She's black, man. Don't you suppose that just makes good old Mrs. Case want to shit bricks?''

Now there was an engineering metaphor he would have to point out to Tory, thought Alvarez. He moved to conclude the interview.

"I wanted to stop by, tell Saul hello," he said, hoping he sounded as though he knew the man. Diaz hadn't really pushed for the reason behind all his questions, and Alvarez didn't want that to change. "I understand he wasn't at work today. Maybe if you told me where his room is, I could leave a note."

"It'll be a while before he comes in to pick up any notes, would be my guess," said Diaz. "Don't you city employee types talk to each other?"

"What do you mean?"

"It made the news this morning, but they weren't releasing names, so I didn't put it together 'til I came to school, heard about it here."

"Heard about what?"

"Saul and his new lady friend went out to a movie last night, came back and found his house burned to the ground."

TWELVE

TELEPHONE FACTS

"WHAT THE HELL do you mean, they can't give us the address?" asked Alvarez, incensed. "We're supposed to be the good guys, remember? Or has something changed, and no one bothered to tell me?"

"I d-didn't say they couldn't give it to us," said Scott calmly. "We have to g-go through channels. It's a new policy; now the location of arson victims is treated as c-confidential for forty-eight hours after the incident."

"Great," grumbled Alvarez. "If there's some big vendetta against the Case family, I'll bet the hitman gets the information before we do."

Scott refused to argue the point. "What's bugging you?" he asked instead.

"I keep running into surprises—things I never anticipated. It's getting on my nerves, making me wonder if I'm losing my touch." Scott tilted his chair back and regarded Alvarez expectantly. "And, on top of everything else, I'm sexually frustrated."

Scott nodded. "No wonder you think you're losing your touch."

"What really pisses me off," said Alvarez pleasantly, "is how you can throw out certain comments without stuttering once."

"It is interesting," agreed Scott. He took a deep breath. "Donna has me taking a class," he said carefully, "to reduce stuttering through breathing techniques."

That was the Donna Faulkner Alvarez knew and loved, always at work on improving the people around her. That she hadn't found someone for Alvarez to marry was a source of continuing frustration for her and endless blind dates for him. "Is it working?" he asked.

"Are we talking about Tory Travers, or my stuttering?" Scott asked slowly and deliberately. There wasn't much chance of acting like you'd misunderstood the question when someone put so much effort into enunciating every word.

"Hell if I know," said Alvarez. "This feels kind of like coming down with a stomach flu. You know, where you can only think of one thing you want to eat, and nothing else interests you."

"I wouldn't d-describe it like that t-t-to Tory." The very thought seemed to be enough to bring back Scott's stutter in full force.

"Enough about me," said Alvarez. "What about Pamela's ex leading me straight to Keaton's house? Remember when your dad told us about all the women Dale Crandell has supposedly slept with?"

"Dale Crandell *Junior*."

"What?"

"Fifteen years ago Keaton's husband lived in that house with his p-parents. They gave it to him when he got married."

Alvarez was pissed that he hadn't thought of that himself, since it was something he vaguely knew. "What do we know about Dale Crandell Senior? Is infidelity like child abuse, a trait that can be inherited?"

"I don't know," said Scott, "but it's worth checking out."

"Keaton says she's been having uninvited nighttime visitors."

"I know."

"What do you mean, you know?"

"She c-called me, asked me to come over and check it out."

"Did you?"

"No."

"Did you consider it?"

"I'm married, not dead," said Scott.

"That isn't what I meant." Alvarez thought a moment. "What did Donna say?"

Scott grinned. "To call you."

"And?"

"I told her Keaton would take care of that."

"You think it means something?"

"That Keaton called me first?"

"No, *pendejo*. I like you better when you stutter. Do you think there's a connection between Pamela Case's death, her ex-husband leading me to Keaton's house, and Keaton thinking someone's wandering around her home at night?"

Scott shook his head. "Keaton's crazy," he said simply.

"Tory talked to her," Alvarez threw out. "She thinks there's something going on."

This definitely got Scott's attention. "Tory talked to Keaton?"

"Yeah. I took Tory home for lunch and Keaton showed up, so they ended up talking to each other." Scott let the silence between them lengthen, but Alvarez wasn't in the mood to go into more detail. "Anyhow, like I said, Tory thinks there's something going on."

Scott considered this. "Tory doesn't have as much experience with crazy as we d-do," he said finally.

Alvarez couldn't argue with that. "So far, I've been doing all the work. What do you have?"

Scott opened a file on his desk. "Cause of d-death, one .38 bullet to the head."

"Maybe I'm not losing my touch after all. When I noticed the hole in her forehead and the fact that most of the back of her skull was missing, I ruled out suffocation right away. How about you?"

Scott continued unperturbed. "No d-defense wounds, no sign of a struggle. Looks like she was transported t-to the site by car, shot, then put in the storm sewer."

"I'd pretty much ruled out hang-gliding and helicopters as the means of transportation. Too obvious, and how many murderers have access to hang-gliders, anyhow? An automobile was going to be my first guess."

"Time of d-death estimated between three and seven p.m., Saturday," continued Scott. "The ME thinks she was put in the inlet box soon after death, or rigor mortis would have m-m-made it difficult to stuff the body down the manhole.''

"I'm three for three,'' said Alvarez. ''Tell me something I don't know.''

"Where they found her car.''

Alvarez named the first thing in the vicinity of Monte Vista Heights that came into his head. ''Ascarate Park.''

Scott looked up in surprise. ''That's good. You sure you have an alibi for Saturday afternoon?''

"That's not good news,'' Alvarez said. ''The weather was great Saturday afternoon—Ascarate must have been swamped with people. Not likely anyone will remember seeing her coming or going. Unless she was tearing her clothes off and screaming at the top of her lungs, my guess is that no one remembers seeing Pamela Case at all.''

"So far, you're batting a thousand,'' said Scott glumly.

"Feel free to stutter if it cheers you up,'' Alvarez told him. ''So Pamela Case meets someone at Ascarate Park Saturday afternoon, gets in the car with whoever it is, and they drive out to Monte Vista Heights for some unknown reason. Pamela steps out of the car, gets shot in the head, then stuffed into the sewer. What else do we have?''

"The son's house burns to the ground Sunday evening.''

"And what does that tell us?''

Scott considered the question. ''He failed the wrong student?''

"A possibility, but it doesn't help us out. Give me something else.''

"Someone is methodically attacking m-members of the C-Case family.''

"Why?''

"Revenge.''

"For what? If it's related to Monte Vista Heights, the timing's off. Why wait fifteen years? Saul Case was just a kid back then. You'd have to be really bent to include him in some revenge scheme.''

"Still.''

"Yeah, still. I guess we can assume that Saul Case is safe

and sound for tonight, courtesy of the Fire Department. When we talk to him, maybe he can tell us where his twin brother is. If the brother just had a fatal accident, the vendetta theory gets my vote."

"How about blackmail?" asked Scott suddenly.

Alvarez perked up. "I like it," he said. "Pamela Case is just the kind of person I could see holding something dirty over someone else's head. Her type, she'd think she was justified. Maybe she sent something to the son for safekeeping. She gets killed by the person she's blackmailing, then the murderer burns down the son's house to destroy the evidence. The problem is, what did Pamela Case know that would be worth blackmailing someone over?"

"Tory thinks there are d-d-discrepancies in the permitting of Monte Vista Heights," Scott said after a pause.

"Ah yes, discrepancies. Our girl Tory does seem to have a special talent for turning up discrepancies."

"And she likes to see them resolved," added Scott.

"She's wasting her talents inspecting storm sewers," Alvarez said thoughtfully. "Wonder if we could convince her to go into a new specialty, maybe call it homicide engineering."

"Insurance would cost too much."

"Trust you to take the economic perspective. I kind of like the sound of it—homicide engineering."

Scott shook his head. "Too much p-potential for misuse. We'd get s-serial killers calling themselves homicide engineers."

Alvarez considered Scott's statement. "Then the guys who came up with the idea would probably be liable or something."

"You might get sued."

"No way. I'm half spic—it'd violate affirmative action to haul me up on liability charges."

Scott winced. "One day you'll say that in front of the wrong p-people, and we'll get sent to sensitivity training."

"Not me, I'm already a sensitive guy. You're just worried you'll get stuck with the liability now. After all, you were in on the conversation. That makes you an accessory."

Scott shook his head. "ADA protection," he said cryptically.

"What's ADA? American Dance Academy? Has Donna got you in some self-improvement class you haven't got the *cojones* to tell me about?"

Scott shook his head again. "Americans with Disabilities Act. I deserve protection because I stutter."

"Yeah, but if this class works, and you stop stuttering, where will that leave you?"

Scott was mulling that over when the phone rang. Alvarez pounced on it. It was Tory, calling him by his first name and sounding breathless on top of it. Maybe she'd decided she wanted warmed-up casserole for dinner. "I've found a discrepancy," she told him.

Alvarez sighed. "Yeah, we were just talking about you and discrepancies."

"What?"

"Have you heard the term homicide engineering?"

"What are you talking about?"

"We just wanted you to know, if you come across the term, that Emmett Delgado originated it." Scott gave Alvarez a thumbs up sign, obviously relieved that his partner had found a solution to their current dilemma. Emmett Delgado was a structural engineer who had become a complication in two murder investigations, and Alvarez couldn't think of a better guy to stick with liability.

"Do you want to hear what I have to tell you, or not?"

"Always, *cara.*"

Tory skipped the part where she told him not to call her *cara*.

"When Sylvia first requested all the documents on Monte Vista Heights, we got the Permitting report for both watertightness tests, but the second test didn't have the actual results attached."

"That unusual?"

"Not as much as you'd like to think. Records get lost on a daily basis, and the city has had over fifteen years to lose these. The unusual part is that we've got Sylvia Maestes on our side. Most secretaries would have figured that the test results got detached, got thrown away, got misfiled, something, end of story. Most secretaries would have given up right there.''

"But Sylvia isn't most secretaries."

"Right. These days the city has One Step Permitting for development projects. But back then, utilities, traffic, building, they all had separate Permitting programs. Sylvia checked with all the other departments she could think of, and presto, the Building Department went digging in their files and came up with a copy of the Permitting reports, and both their copies had test results attached."

"Why would the Building Department care about storm sewers?"

"Because they had to make sure all the t's were crossed and the i's dotted before they issued any building permits."

Alvarez didn't want to come right out and admit that he had no earthly idea where all this was leading. "And there's a point to you telling me all this, right? You're not looking for an excuse to call me up—because if you are, it's kind of like finding dead bodies, you don't have to keep—"

"Don't go there. Listen to me—the first water-tightness test was a whole system test—that means they plugged the outfall and filled all the storm-sewer pipes with water. The water loss significantly exceeded allowable standards."

"Sounds exciting," Alvarez said to keep up his end of the conversation.

"Keep in mind, that was the first test. Then they went back, divided the storm-sewer system into five parts, and ran the test on each part separately. That's really how they should have done it to begin with. Anyhow, each segment yielded virtually identical percentages of water loss."

Alvarez couldn't understand why Tory sounded so excited, unless she was planning a nocturnal visit and hadn't seen fit to tell him yet. As far as he was concerned, Tory Travers could wander around his house at night any time. "I must be missing the punch line, or something."

"Don't you see? There's virtually no way that five different parts of the same system would yield the same results. If anything, you'd expect three or four to pass with flying colors, with just one, maybe two segments showing significant water loss, which would help pinpoint where the problems were. You wouldn't expect a sewer to leak water at an overall constant rate throughout the entire system."

Actually, Alvarez hadn't expected anything much at all regarding sewer systems prior to this particular case. "So you think someone doctored the results?" he ventured.

"Without a doubt. And it's Pamela's signature on the second test," Tory said triumphantly.

"How about the first one?" asked Alvarez automatically.

There was a pause on the other end, which wasn't a good sign. Alvarez could hear Tory flipping pages. "Well," she said reluctantly, "that's a problem. The first test was signed off on by someone named Michael Mendoza."

"Who's he?"

"How should I know?" Tory sounded irritated that he couldn't immediately resolve all the loose ends in her new-found hypothesis. "You're the detective," she told him. "I'm the engineer."

"Okay. Let's do some detective-like thinking. How likely is it that two Permitting officials would be in on falsifying results?"

"Not very likely, I wouldn't think," Tory admitted. "The more people you have in on something, the more likely it is to be discovered. And it sounds like this Pamela Case didn't have too many friends on the job."

"And I don't think there were too many Mendozas on her list of good pals. So how else could the test have been doctored?"

"Well, if you wanted a real hands-on approach," said Tory slowly, "you could just drive out to the site in the middle of the night, pick an opened manhole with a water level within reach of a bucket, and start bailing."

That was so simple it was shocking. "No kidding. How come there's not more security when these tests are run?"

Tory made an exasperated sound. "Get a grip. Rigging a

storm sewer water-tightness test doesn't just occur to most people. Cyanide in Tylenol bottles has a much more direct, satisfying result.''

She had a point. ''If someone bailed water on the first test,'' he said, thinking it out as he went along, ''they might be worried that the contractor would have someone stick around for the second test.''

''Or,'' Tory was back to being excited again, ''if you didn't understand what was going on too well, you might be afraid that you couldn't access the right parts of the system to bail.''

''So if someone bailed water during the first test, they might resort to falsifying the data for the second test,'' said Alvarez.

''And after the first set of dismal results,'' continued Tory, ''no one would look too closely at the second set, especially not on a project with chronic Permitting problems.''

''But would this be enough to blackmail someone?'' The words were out of Alvarez's mouth before he remembered who he was talking to.

''Blackmail? Blackmail who? If Pamela Case was involved, she's already dead.'' One of these days, Alvarez would learn not to think out loud where Tory was involved. He could almost hear the gears turning at high speed in her head. ''You think someone else was involved, don't you? And that Pamela was blackmailing that person, and so that person killed her. What have you found out?''

Alvarez figured he'd lose his leverage if he told Tory that at this point, the blackmail scenario was only a brain-storming hypothesis, nothing more. ''Want to drive down to my house tonight and collaborate on this case?'' he asked instead. Scott handed Alvarez a piece of paper with a message scrawled on it.

''No, I don't want to drive down to your house to collaborate on this case. This is what telephones were invented for. What have you found out?''

''Scott just wrote me a note. The site was released back to the Engineering Department this afternoon, and they're planning to run the third water-tightness test first thing tomorrow. Will you be there?''

"I wouldn't miss it for the world."

"Look me up tomorrow when you're down here, and we'll compare notes."

"Why are you being so difficult?"

"I'm not feeling well."

The immediate tone of concern in her voice almost made him feel guilty. "What's wrong? Is your arm bothering you?"

One of the fine arts of interviewing technique was knowing just when to lay all your cards on the table. Alvarez took a deep breath, decided that made him sound like Scott trying to control his stuttering, and exhaled his reply in one run-on sentence. "I've been thinking it over and I've decided I'm either coming down with intestinal flu or I'm in love."

"I can't believe you said that."

Alvarez's detective instincts told him that Tory wasn't thrilled by his declaration. "So what do you think?" Alvarez heard himself ask, sounding amazingly lame. If Scott related this conversation to Donna, it was really going to tarnish his image.

There was a long pause on the other end of the line. "I think," said Tory finally, "that either alternative presents a problem." Then she laughed. "But look me up tomorrow, and we'll compare notes." She obviously got a big kick out of feeding his words back to him. The next thing Alvarez heard was the dial tone. He looked at Scott, shrugged, and hung up the phone.

"Man," said Scott sincerely. "You are definitely losing your touch." But Alvarez wasn't listening. He was trying to analyze just how much promise he could read into a laugh.

THIRTEEN

RELATIVE BENEFITS

"WHAT A PLAN," said Alvarez as he and Scott walked up to the condominium where Saul Case was staying. "It's nothing less than inspired. Case is staying with his girlfriend. I'm so glad the Fire Department decided to keep that information confidential while they investigate their arson case. If I was trying to locate the guy, it would never occur to me to check the girlfriend's house."

"Diana Hooper," said Scott helpfully.

"Diana Hooper," repeated Alvarez. "Now there's an ethnic-sounding name if I ever heard one. I'll bet Pamela Case could tell she wouldn't like this woman the moment she heard the name. Kinda reminds you of Diana Ross big hair, sequined dresses—"

The door opened abruptly before Scott could reach for the doorbell. The slightly-built black woman standing in the doorway had hair shorter than most of the uniformed officers Alvarez knew, peppered through with undisguised gray. Her attractive features were marred by a severe frown. She had obviously heard them coming.

"You must be the EPPD detectives," she said in a tone far from welcoming. "I'd ask for ID, but I know who you are from your stupid remarks coming up the walk. Before you see Saul, I want to make it clear that in the last forty-eight hours, he has lost his mother, house, and most of his possessions. I don't care about your opinions of me or Pamela Case, I don't want him subjected to any more stress. Have I made myself clear?"

Alvarez and Scott nodded obediently. If Diana Hooper had

assigned three essays due by Friday, Alvarez wondered if he and his partner would have had the nerve to argue.

"And if you forget what I've told you, your visit will be very short," Ms. Hooper added before leading them into a sitting room occupied by a young man wearing jeans and a denim shirt. Saul Case resembled his father in height and body build, with tawny blond hair and healthful good looks that made him look more like a surfer than a high school teacher. Alvarez would bet that there were more high school girls with crushes on Mr. Case than on Mr. Diaz. But it appeared that Tommy Diaz had Irma Lujan for a girlfriend, so maybe everything evened out.

Alvarez and Scott made short work of introductions and their condolences under the watchful eyes of Ms. Hooper, who sat next to Saul Case on the couch, holding his hand. The bureaucratic channels of notification procedures had caught up with Saul about the time that Alvarez had been talking to Tommy Diaz, so the young man had had some time to adjust to the news of his mother's death.

"I can't think of anything I can tell you that would be helpful," Saul said before they asked their first question.

"When was the last time you talked with your mother?" asked Alvarez.

"About a month ago."

"I thought the two of you were close."

"We were." Alvarez let the pause lengthen. "My mother wasn't happy about Diana and me," Saul added finally. "It caused a temporary estrangement, but in time she would have come around."

"You feel the same way?" Alvarez asked Diana Hooper.

"Why?" she snapped, surprising him with her vehemence. "Do I need an alibi? You figure I've got a white boyfriend with a mother who doesn't approve, so I do the mom?"

"Whoa," said Alvarez. He didn't have a chance to say anything else before Diana Hooper started in again.

"I'm from inner-city LA. I know how it works. When something goes down, the first thing you boys in blue look for is a black person to hang it on."

"We're a ways from inner-city LA," said Alvarez evenly. He looked down at his own maroon shirt and charcoal slacks. "I'm not dressed in blue, and I'm too old to qualify as a boy, so why don't you drop the hostility and help us find out who murdered Pamela Case?"

"Sounds great," shot back Diana Hooper. "If I hadn't heard you coming up the walk making snide remarks about my involvement with a white man ten years younger than me, I might even fall for it."

Alvarez held up his good hand in surrender. "I apologize for any offense—there was none intended. Investigating Pamela Case, we keep coming across race issues. We'd already assumed that she didn't approve of your relationship with her son. The fact that you're ten years older than him is something I had no way of knowing, and frankly, would never have guessed." He gave her his most winning grin.

"You think you can sweet talk your way out of everything, homeboy?"

"It's worth a try."

Diana Hooper grudgingly allowed the frown to leave her face. "All right," she said shortly. "I'll try letting bygones be bygones. But be forewarned, you're on thin ice with me."

"Noted," said Alvarez, turning back to Saul. "You know anyone who might have wanted to harm your mother?"

Case sighed. "If you've done any investigating at all, you already know that my mother didn't get along with some people. But I don't think anyone disliked her enough to murder her."

"Unfortunately," said Alvarez quietly, "you're wrong about that."

Saul Case winced at the truth in Alvarez's words. "Listen, my mother had her faults, she had opinions I don't necessarily agree with. But she wasn't a monster. She was a good mother, she was loyal to the things she believed in. She didn't get along with some people, and she had some political beliefs that aren't very popular. But that's not a crime."

"We're not here to judge her," said Alvarez. "Our job is to find out who murdered her."

"Was there anything unusual g-g-going on in your mother's life in the last few months or so?" asked Scott.

"Yeah," said Saul slowly, "now that you mention it, there was. The last time I talked to her, she said she'd had some things happen at the house. One morning she woke up to find it papered, another time someone threw a stink bomb."

"Sounds pretty juvenile," observed Alvarez.

"That's what I thought."

"Did your mother associate with any groups of teenagers?"

"You mean like the Boy Scouts, or something like that? No, her outside interests were with political issues. She was always involved in some campaign or other. I hardly ever saw my mother that she didn't have some petition for me to sign."

"And did you sign them?"

"Well, mostly—" Saul Case looked uncomfortable.

"Getting to know me made Saul take another look at some things he'd always taken for granted," interjected Diana Hooper.

"Yeah," said Saul glumly. "It's hard to support an end to affirmative action when you meet up with somebody it really helped."

"That would be you?" Alvarez asked Diana Hooper.

"You see any other darkies in the room?"

"I don't know if you've noticed," said Alvarez evenly, "but white Anglo-Saxon Protestant blood doesn't run pure in my veins."

"You could probably pass for Sicilian," replied Ms. Hooper.

"But who would want to?" Alvarez wondered how they had wandered off on this topic. "The phrase 'pot calling the kettle black' comes to mind." Alvarez saw Scott, who was sitting across from him, wince.

There was a moment it could have gone either way, then Diana Hooper laughed. When she laughed, she didn't look or sound so much like a disapproving teacher. "Well," she said, "this kettle ended up attending an Ivy League school, precisely because she was black, and not Sicilian."

"D-Did it bother you, being given preference because of the c-c-color of your skin?" asked Scott curiously.

''Not one single bit,'' said Diana Hooper emphatically. ''It will bother me the day all applicants are judged equally, and not before. These institutions already have preference programs in place and functioning, they just don't want to admit it.''

''Isn't that kind of an old argument?'' asked Alvarez. ''That the system is already biased simply because it was instituted by members of a certain class and race?''

''No, homeboy, I'm not talking about inherent system bias. I'm talking about out and out preferential treatment. You know what legacies are?''

''A windfall from someone rich?'' asked Scott automatically.

''Not in college admittance offices,'' said Ms. Hooper. ''Legacies are admission slots and scholarships set aside for applicants who don't meet the admission standards.''

''What kind of applicants?'' asked Alvarez.

''Relatives of certain people, like big donors and potential faculty members. John Doe gave three million dollars last year and has a son with a one-point-two average who wants to go to Yale? No problem, he just got admitted as a legacy. Dr. Jane Doe has an outstanding reputation in her field, but her daughter just got out of drug rehab for the third time. No problem, if Jane joins the faculty at Harvard, her daughter certainly deserves a chance to attend school there.''

''I never knew that,'' said Alvarez.

''Most people don't. Most people don't understand the first thing about affirmative action. They just like the buzzwords.''

''Ever discuss this with Pamela Case?''

''Once,'' Diana Hooper admitted, no longer quite so talkative.

''What happened?''

''My mom asked us to leave the house,'' said Saul.

They all sat and thought this over for a while. Then Diana Hooper broke the silence by asking, ''Is this the point where you ask for an alibi?''

''If you're so eager about it, go ahead,'' said Alvarez.

''Saul and I were together all weekend.''

''Somehow I thought you'd say that,'' replied Alvarez, and Diana Hooper went back to frowning at him. ''I talked to your father yesterday,'' Alvarez said to Saul. "He said that one of the reasons he'd moved back here was because of your health problems. You don't look sick to me.''

Saul shook his head impatiently. "Can't you guys get anything right? My dad doesn't give a damn about me. He moved back here because of my brother—he has Crohn's disease.''

Alvarez blinked. "I thought your brother moved away.''

"He did. He moved back about two years ago.''

"What's Crohn's disease?''

"A chronic bowel inflammation,'' said Scott. Everyone turned to look at him. "Serious, but seldom fatal,'' he added.

"Have you stuttered from birth?'' asked Ms. Hooper in a concerned school teacher voice. "It's interesting how you don't stutter when you're communicating pieces of information that you're sure of.''

"There are other times he doesn't stutter, too,'' said Alvarez, then moved on before she could start counseling his partner about his stutter. "Are you in touch with your brother?'' he asked Saul.

"Some. We're not close, but we're not exactly enemies, either.''

"Talked to him since your mother's death?''

"No. According to the Fire Department, I'm not supposed to be talking much to anyone 'til they complete their investigation. Which, hopefully, will be this afternoon. Then maybe I can start getting my life back to normal.''

"Your brother have much contact with your mother since he moved back to town?''

"No. They didn't get along. We kind of took sides when my parents got divorced, me with my mom, Paul with my dad.''

"Your brother has the same name as your dad?''

"Yeah, he's eight minutes older than me, so he's Paul Case Junior. Kind of fitting, don't you think, Paul sides with Paul.''

"Where does your brother live?''

"He manages the apartment complex where my dad is living.''

Alvarez could have kicked himself for relying on Dottie's

recollection that one of Pamela Case's sons had moved away. No wonder the father had looked at him strangely when he'd asked him to notify the other son. Alvarez felt like he was being told something important, but for the life of him, he couldn't figure out what it was.

"You said you weren't in c-contact with your m-mother lately," interjected Scott. "But did she give you anything to k-k-keep for her, maybe send you a letter recently?"

"No," said Saul, obviously puzzled. "If she wanted to talk to me, she called. Why would she send me a letter?"

"Was there anyone else, maybe a friend or a lover, who she would have confided in?" asked Alvarez.

"Not that I know of," replied Saul.

"Did your m-mother ever d-d-discuss her financial affairs with you?" asked Scott.

"Not since I moved out of the house," replied Saul, looking puzzled again. The trick was to maintain the pattern of quick, short questions, keeping the person being interviewed from having time to think about their meaning.

"Who will inherit?" asked Alvarez immediately.

If Saul had considered the question before, he didn't show it. "I imagine she left everything to Paul and me, I don't know," he said slowly, like he was thinking it through. "Look, if you think my mother was worth murdering for her money, you're barking up the wrong tree. The main reason she stayed with the city all those years was so she'd end up with a decent retirement income."

"Know why your parents got divorced?" asked Alvarez.

"They didn't get along. What does that have to do with anything?"

"Know who might have torched your house?"

The young man shrugged. "I'm a teacher," he said prosaically, and Alvarez's cell phone rang.

In true governmental fashion, the City of El Paso had resisted outfitting its police officers with cellular phones for a shameful period of time, then jumped on the technology bandwagon by purchasing equipment with all available bells and whistles. The display on Alvarez's phone flashed a caller priority code that he had given to only three people—Scott; the administrator at Horizon House where his sister Anna lived; and Tory Travers. "I have to take this," he said, and stepped out of the room into the hall.

When he returned to the living room, Scott was concluding the interview with the obligatory speech about getting in touch if anything occurred to anyone, and handing out his business card.

"We need to go," said Alvarez.

"What's up?" asked Scott as soon as they were out of the house.

"That was Tory."

"Hot date?"

"I wish. She's at Providence Hospital. Keaton is there in hysterics. She couldn't wake Hero up this morning—the little girl is in a coma. The doctors think it's some kind of drug overdose."

"Shit," said Scott.

"It gets worse. They ran into Gary Cabrioni when Hero was being admitted, now Cabrioni is demanding that Keaton be arrested."

"For what? Keaton's no criminal, she's just crazy."

"At best, gross negligence. At worst, wanting to kill her own child to prevent losing custody."

Scott shook his head in disgust. Whether it was at Gary Cabrioni in specific or the human race in general, Alvarez didn't know. "Where does Tory come into this?" Scott asked.

Alvarez sighed. "I guess Keaton's been trying to call everyone she can think of. There'll be a stack of messages for both of us down at headquarters. Anyhow, Keaton called Tory's home phone, talked to her father, and he tracked Tory down at Monte Vista Heights."

"Aren't families wonderful?" asked Scott rhetorically as he backed out of Diana Hooper's driveway.

Alvarez fastened his seat belt, no small feat with one hand, and tried not to think of a bright-eyed little girl with brown frizzy hair.

FOURTEEN

MEDICAL BENEFITS

ALVAREZ COULD THINK OF combat situations less intimidating than the Pediatric ICU waiting room at Providence Hospital. He didn't know if there was a dearth of other patients, or if the contentious group in the small room had managed to clear out everyone unrelated, because all ten occupants of the waiting room seemed involved in one single loud, on-going conversation.

Keaton, predictably, was in the middle of the commotion, dressed in gray sweats, her pale face streaked with tears and mascara. Tory stood next to her in jeans and a black-and-white plaid flannel shirt, looking like someone fresh off a construction site. On Keaton's other side, a tall, gray-haired man in a tailored black suit appeared to have a death grip on Keaton's arm. Next to him stood an immaculately coifed petite matron wearing a green jersey dress with matching heels.

Alvarez had met Keaton's husband, and the man gripping Keaton's arm was similar in both physical appearance and mannerisms. Alvarez mentally pegged the couple as Mr. and Mrs. Dale Crandell Senior, Keaton's in-laws. He was surprised to see them at the hospital, since the revelations about Hero's paternity were bound to have had an impact on Keaton's in-laws. One part of Alvarez's mind wondered how they managed to turn up for an early morning medical emergency so impeccably attired. Were they on their way to a formal meeting, or did they go to bed fully dressed in order to meet any upcoming contingency in appropriate style?

The dark-haired man in green scrubs confronting Keaton was Dr. Gary Cabrioni. There were two other individuals in scrubs standing uneasily at the edge of the group, a man and a woman. The group was completed by a short brawny black man in a white uniform labeled SECURITY, his shaved head glistening with a sheen of sweat in the overheated room, and two uniformed officers, one of whom Alvarez had worked with in the course of another investigation.

"You asshole," Keaton was shouting at Gary Cabrioni. "How dare you accuse me of hurting my own child? You don't know shit. Your stupid one-time sperm contribution doesn't make you a father—it doesn't make you anything."

"You crazy bitch," Cabrioni yelled back. "I'll see you rot in jail for what you did to that child. There's no one-time about it—screwing is the only thing you were ever good at. I wish I'd had a vasectomy before I ever had a part in making you a mother—"

"Find me a fork and I'll help you out," Keaton screamed at him. "I don't need a medical degree to do the job."

Tory caught Alvarez's eye as he and Scott entered the room, and Alvarez had a moment to reflect that whatever he did, he certainly wasn't going to be guilty of bringing the conversation to a lower level. He walked straight to Cabrioni, took the man's hand, and began shaking it enthusiastically. "Detective David Alvarez," he said. "We've met previously." Simultaneously, Scott displaced the man holding onto Keaton, murmuring sympathetic phrases while he did so.

"Thank God," said Cabrioni. "A homicide detective—we're finally getting somewhere. I can't get these two other idiots to do jack-shit."

"You mean Officers Kurita and"—Alvarez had to squint to make out the name of the second uniformed officer, who was shifting uneasily from foot to foot at the edge of the group— "Owens. They're two highly trained professionals, very good at doing jack-shit. They're just not sure what particular jack-shit they should be doing right now. Who's committed a homicide?"

"It's not a homicide yet—"

Alvarez cut Cabrioni off as soon as the words were out of his mouth. "Then let's not throw the term around incorrectly."

"This man should be removed from this room immediately," the older man in the black suit said imperiously, grabbing Alvarez's arm. Alvarez figured he must be in dire need of something to hold onto. "That's no way for him to talk to my son's wife," he added in a voice that sounded like he was used to be listened to and obeyed.

"Please, sir," said Alvarez, managing to shake off the man's hold without being too obvious about it. "I need you to be quiet while I sort this out. Who's the doctor here? And I don't mean you, Cabrioni."

"I am," said the woman in scrubs, and Alvarez mentally deducted two points from his feminism quotient for assuming she was a nurse. She had dishwater blond hair tied back in a limp ponytail, and a pleasant freckled face devoid of makeup. "I'm Dr. Taylor-Franklins."

"What's Hero's condition?"

"She's conscious but drowsy, which is understandable. Chances are she'll make a full recovery. She's really lucky; a drug overdose in a child her age is a serious thing."

"Sure about it being a drug overdose?"

"We can't be certain until we get the lab results, but she was unconscious when she came in. The mother had tried to rouse her with no success. All the symptoms point to an overdose."

"Tell him what kind of overdose," Cabrioni demanded.

The young doctor never faltered. "Again, it's too early to tell for sure, but I think the little girl was suffering from an overdose of anti-anxiety drugs."

"What she's saying is that Hero was full of tranquilizers," interjected Cabrioni. "Her mother's tranquilizers."

"Are you Hero's doctor?" Alvarez snapped.

"No, but—"

"Then be quiet and let Dr. Franklins-Taylor answer," he told Cabrioni.

"Taylor-Franklins," the young woman corrected him. "Hero's symptoms are compatible with an overdose of valium.

We've interviewed the mother to determine what drugs were in the home environment—"

"That must have taken quite a while," snarled Cabrioni.

"You want to see just what kind of jack-shit these officers can do?" asked Alvarez evenly. Cabrioni didn't say anything else, but he was breathing like he had just finished running a marathon. "I want you to be quiet until you're spoken to," Alvarez admonished him. He turned back to the woman in scrubs. "You were saying, Doctor—" For the life of him, he couldn't remember which of her names came first.

"Mrs. Crandell—the mother—confirmed that there was valium in the house," Doctor-hyphenated-name answered.

"Where?" Alvarez asked Keaton.

"In my medicine cabinet, my nightstand, my dresser, my purse, I don't know. It doesn't matter—Hero would never take any of my medicine. She knows better than that."

"Mrs. Crandell told us that the child was put to bed around nine o'clock last night, with no variation in the usual routine," said the doctor. "The last thing she remembers her daughter ingesting was a glass of apple juice around eight-thirty."

"And I made her brush her teeth afterward," Keaton added.

"Any chance Hero got up during the night, got something to eat or drink?" Alvarez asked her.

"No, she doesn't like to get up after I turn her lights out. We don't do the glass of water routine, either. She and I have matching crystal water decanters with a glass that fits over the top—you know, Barbara, you gave them to us for Christmas two years ago." The woman that Alvarez had pegged as Keaton's mother-in-law nodded wordlessly. "So Hero knows that after lights out, the only thing she's allowed to drink is water."

"Did she drink out of her decanter last night?" Alvarez asked.

"How would I know?" asked Keaton desperately. "I went in to get her up for school, and I couldn't get her to wake up. The last thing I worried about was—" Keaton went absolutely still and her pale eyes went opaque; Alvarez knew she was no longer seeing any of the people surrounding her. "Oh my God," she whispered. "Oh my God."

Tory put her arm around Keaton. "The worst is over, no matter what happens," she told her. "Hero is going to be okay. Tell us what you remember, Keaton."

"The water. The water in my decanter," said Keaton slowly. "It tasted funny. I had some right before I went to sleep, and I thought it was stale or something, so I poured it down the sink in my bathroom and got fresh water out of the tap."

"Like hell you did," exploded Cabrioni. "Someone like you doesn't drink water when they go to bed. Vodka on the rocks would be more like it—"

"No," wailed Keaton. "It wasn't like that. Dale isn't home, I'm responsible for getting Hero up in the morning, and we've been having weird things happen at night. I don't dare take a drink after I put her to bed."

"The only weird things happening at your house are in your sick, demented, drugged-out head—"

Alvarez clapped his good hand on Cabrioni's shoulder. Out of the corner of his eye he saw the burly man in the security uniform rock onto his toes. "I told you to be quiet," Alvarez told Cabrioni. He waited until he was sure Cabrioni was going to shut up before he removed his hand. "Here's what we're going to do," he said, looking at Keaton. "We're going to get to the bottom of this, so we can deal with facts instead of suppositions. Kurita—"

"Sir," said Kurita smartly.

"I want Mrs. Crandell's house treated as a crime scene."

"Noooooo," wailed Keaton. "You can't do that to me. You're supposed to be on my side."

Alvarez leaned forward to look directly into Keaton's eyes. "This is the best thing for you and Hero," he said firmly. "We need to get some answers so you don't have to live with these allegations."

She looked at him like a drowning woman focusing on a life jacket tossed in her direction. "Do you think I drugged Hero?" she asked.

"No," he told her. "I don't think you drugged Hero," he

added for emphasis, and hoped like hell he wouldn't be proved wrong.

"Is that your definition of police impartiality?" Cabrioni was back to shouting again. "What's in it for you? Are you sleeping with her?"

"S-S-Sir," said Scott. "You're under a great d-deal of emotional strain. But m-my understanding is that a p-p-patient in ICU is allowed one visitor every two hours or so."

"Every hour, in peds," clarified the young doctor immediately. "With children, it's really important to have someone with them as frequently as possible."

"If you c-can c-control yourself," continued Scott, "I'm sure the doctor here will be willing to work out s-something so you and Mrs. Crandell can rotate visits."

Cabrioni stared wordlessly at Scott, his Adam's apple working up and down furiously as though there were words in his throat he was trying to keep from uttering. As sometimes happened in a confrontation, a different voice, coupled with a different face, was able to halt the escalation of emotions spiraling out of control. "Okay," Cabrioni croaked, keeping his eyes on Scott, clenching his fists with the effort of limiting himself to a one-word response.

"Good," said Alvarez smoothly, "then that's settled. Keaton will need someplace to stay while she's not at the hospital, some place where we can get in touch with her—"

Once more Dale Crandell grabbed Alvarez's arm. "We'll take her home with us. We'll keep a good eye on her." He looked at Kurita. "You can be sure we won't let her go anywhere." Next the old man would be offering to keep Keaton under house arrest; Alvarez figured the details could be worked out later.

"Let's put a rush on this," he said. "We want Mrs. Crandell and her daughter to be able to go home as soon as possible."

Kurita nodded and he and Officer Owens left the room. The hospital security guard, knowing a good opportunity when he saw it, joined them. Now there were only seven people in the small room.

"Doctor," said Alvarez, "could you and your assistant step

outside with Dr. Cabrioni and arrange a visitation schedule? It would be a good idea to try to prevent any more misunderstandings.''

"No shit," muttered the unknown man in scrubs.

"Certainly." The young doctor looked at her watch. "Meanwhile, Mrs. Crandell, you can see Hero now."

The three individuals in hospital garb left the room together, while Keaton made a beeline for the door right behind them. Alvarez caught her arm. "Keaton, what are your in-laws doing here?" he asked quietly.

Keaton looked up at him and tears started rolling down her cheeks again. "When we got here it was touch and go. We didn't know if Hero was going to make it. Dale hasn't called, but I thought maybe his parents knew how to contact him in case—" Her voice broke. Alvarez pulled her toward him, gave her a hug, then pushed her toward the door.

"Well," said Tory quickly. "I think I'll wait out in the hall."

"Don't leave before I've had a chance to talk to you," Alvarez told her. She nodded and ducked out of the room, leaving only Scott, Alvarez, and Mr. and Mrs. Crandell Senior in a room that no longer seemed so small and overcrowded.

Scott gestured for the older couple to have a seat, then joined them. "I'm Scott Faulkner. My family lived d-d-down the street from you, when you still lived on Rim Road."

"I remember," replied Dale Crandell in frosty tones. Now that Alvarez and Scott had served their purpose in sorting out the waiting room commotion, it didn't appear that the senior Crandell was eager for chit-chat.

But it took a lot more than frosty tones to discourage the dynamic detecting duo. "Well, we'd l-like to ask you a few questions," Scott said.

FIFTEEN

IN-LAW INPUT

"WHY OF COURSE we remember you, Scottie," replied Mrs. Crandell, exhibiting a marked Southern drawl as she spoke for the first time. "The minute you opened your mouth, we knew who you were. Would it be a good idea to have your partner ask the questions, honey? It might take a lot less time."

Alvarez spun a chair around, straddled it, put his good arm on top of the chair back, his chin on top of the arm, and regarded Mrs. Crandell thoughtfully. "I'm not as polished as Scott," he said, "but if that's what you want. Does the name Pamela Case ring a bell, Mrs. Crandell?"

"I can't say as it does," she replied with just the right combination of politeness and puzzlement.

Alvarez turned to her husband. "How about you, Mr. Crandell. Were you acquainted with Pamela Case?"

"Why do you want to know?"

Alvarez skipped explaining that he was the one asking the questions. "Pamela Case worked for the City of El Paso in several positions over quite a few years. She was a Permitting agent for a while, and since you were a developer, I was wondering if you knew her."

"That still doesn't explain why you're asking the question," said Crandell in the tone of a reasonable man making a reasonable statement.

"She was found murdered two days ago. It didn't make the newspapers today because her next of kin wasn't notified until late yesterday. Anyhow, I talked to her ex-husband. When their marriage broke up, about fifteen years ago, he followed her one night. He says she drove to your house."

Crandell raised one eyebrow in an eloquent expression of polite interest. "I've met with many people over the years, often at night. Nothing sinister about that. Now that you mention it, I think I knew this Pamela Case, but I'm not sure. It would help to see a picture of her."

"That can be arranged," said Scott, making a great show of pulling out a notebook and jotting down a note to himself.

"Well, if that's all—" Mrs. Crandell made some brisk motions like she was brushing crumbs off her lap prior to standing up.

"No, that's not all," said Alvarez. He turned his attention back to Crandell. "You remember when Craig Diaz ran against Harry Montoya for city commissioner, about fifteen years ago?"

"No," said Crandell, "I can't say as I do."

"Diaz was a big proponent of affirmative action programs, set-asides, things like that."

"How interesting." Dale Crandell sounded as though they were discussing the weather and he had just become bored with the topic. "You can understand if we don't want to sit and chat; we have a granddaughter to check on."

"But not a granddaughter by blood," Alvarez said pleasantly. He watched the faint smile on Mrs. Crandell's face disappear as her lips compressed into a thin line. "Anyhow," Alvarez continued, "a construction project of Diaz's went belly-up, he went bankrupt and committed suicide. This was late in the day, so to speak, so Montoya ran unopposed and retained his Commission seat." Alvarez decided to take a stab in the dark. "You were a big Montoya supporter."

"And why not," said Mrs. Crandell, surprising Alvarez by answering for her husband. "We're staunch Republicans, and we've supported numerous political candidates over the years. My husband has a right to oppose affirmative action programs and set-asides for people who don't deserve them. Dale worked hard for what we have while I stayed home and raised my children. If that's not the very definition of affirmative action, then what is?"

Alvarez concentrated on what he remembered about Pinnacle

Development, the company Dale Crandell Senior founded in partnership with Keaton's father. Scott had unearthed a significant amount of information about Pinnacle during a previous investigation. "That's right," he mused, continuing to look at Mr. Crandell. "Pinnacle Development did quite well while Montoya was in office. It doesn't seem to be doing quite so well, now that it's been handed down to the second generation. Why do you suppose that is, sir?"

"I think," said Crandell, "that this conversation is at an end."

Alvarez considered Crandell's statement and decided he was right. "Thanks for talking to us. We appreciate your time."

"I'll be sure to tell my parents hello for you," Scott added.

THEY STEPPED OUT OF the waiting room and Scott arranged to meet Alvarez in the lobby after he checked on Keaton and Hero. He gave Tory, who was pacing in the now-deserted hallway, a thumbs-up sign as he walked by.

"Hey," said Alvarez, grabbing Tory's arm and pulling her to him. "That was nice of you to come here and be with Keaton."

"It was the least I could do," she told his chest in a muffled voice. "It was awful. For a while it could have gone either way." Alvarez patted her back with his good hand, wishing his injured arm didn't have to come between them.

"Looks like Hero's going to be okay."

"Yeah," Tory sniffed, "but I don't want to leave her alone with that maniac Cabrioni and her dragon in-laws. I'll stay 'til my dad gets here."

"Until what?" asked Alvarez, wondering if he'd heard right.

"Until my dad gets here. He's on his way. He's adopted Keaton as one of his causes."

Alvarez pushed Tory far enough away to look into her eyes. "That must be hard to swallow."

Tory shrugged. "It's not such a big deal, and it's right in character. It will give him something to do and maybe help Keaton out at the same time, although I doubt there'll be a photo opportunity at the end of it all. You know how they say it's easier to help strangers—" She made an obvious effort to change conversational direction. "Besides, I need to get back out to Monte Vista Heights. The test isn't turning out as expected."

"Aha," said Alvarez. It was about time that a piece of the puzzle fell into place. "That sewer is holding water tighter than a bathtub, right?"

Tory shook her head. "No," she said. "It's not. They can't get the system to fill past a certain level."

Alvarez stared at her. "You're kidding, right?"

"When have you ever asked me that question and the answer was yes?"

While unpredictability admittedly had a certain allure, the unexpected was not a welcome diversion in a murder investigation. "What does this mean?" Alvarez demanded.

Tory frowned at him. "I don't know."

"What do you mean, you don't know?" Surely it was his imagination that he was beginning to sound like Gary Cabrioni.

"I mean I don't know. Do you know all the answers in your job?"

Alvarez made an effort to sound calm and patient. "How do you plan to go about getting some answers?" Then he threw calm and patience to the wind. "Damn it Tory, you've had us all along thinking that Diaz was screwed somehow, that the permitting was rigged."

"I'm not saying it wasn't. I just need to figure some things out."

"How?"

Tory narrowed her eyes in concentration. "Craig Diaz's son was in charge of constructing the sewer system, right?"

"Right, and I already talked to him. He didn't tell me anything useful."

"Maybe you didn't ask him the right questions."

Alvarez sighed. "Your humility, that's what I've always loved about you," he told her.

"I thought it was intestinal flu," she shot back.

"You thought wrong." He pulled her to him and kissed her. His timing was off; he heard the door to the waiting room open, and from the corner of his eye he could see Mrs. Crandell peering out at the two of them. Tory pushed him away and tried not to look like the kind of person who would be caught dead kissing a homicide detective in a hospital hall.

"I'll give you a call later if I find out anything," she said in a business-like manner that would have come off better if she weren't furtively rubbing her mouth with the back of her hand.

Alvarez had a thought. "If you think you can ask the right questions," he told her, "see if you can get Tommy Diaz to tell you who his current girlfriend is." He laid a cautioning finger on Tory's lips before she could ask. "That would be telling," he admonished her. She turned and walked down the hall without a backward glance.

"I just now realized who she is," said Mrs. Crandell in her slow, honeyed tones. She had managed to find her smile again. "She's that engineer who helped you solve two of your cases. Isn't that sweet."

"Did you want to talk to me?" asked Alvarez politely.

Mrs. Crandell looked up and down the hall as though she would be relating top secret information. "There's a couple things you should know," she drawled.

"And you're going to tell me?" he prompted.

She focused back on him again. "Keaton's a sweet girl and all, but she's had problems for years. I don't want to go into it, but believe me, there's a whole history. I'm sure she didn't mean to harm Hero, but we all know it takes a diligent person to be a good parent, to—"

"To accomplish the affirmative action of parenting," he finished for her.

"Why yes." Her smile broadened. "So you were listening to me."

"I've made a career out of listening to people," he told her. "You said I need to know a couple of things. What else did you want to tell me?"

Barbara Crandell was back to not looking at him again, her gaze focused somewhere beyond his left shoulder. "Sometimes, to be a good mother and a good wife, you have to make certain sacrifices," she said obliquely.

Alvarez closed one eye as he considered what she had just said. It didn't help. "I'm afraid I don't understand."

"Well, you know, detective." She smiled coyly. "Men and women are different, have different needs. Dale is probably embarrassed to tell you, because he thinks I don't know."

Alvarez waited for her to complete her explanation, but she obviously thought she had. "He thinks you don't know what?" he asked.

Mrs. Crandell allowed herself an unladylike snort of exasperation. "About his other women," she said shortly.

"Oh," said Alvarez, because he couldn't immediately come up with a more original response.

"So, if you find out that Dale knew this Pamela Case, it really doesn't mean anything at all."

Obviously there was "knew," and then there was "knew," and Alvarez was savvy enough that he thought he could tell the difference. "I'll keep that in mind," he told her.

"You do that." She looked at him consideringly. "You know, I saw the newscast when you and that attractive engineer lady were on television together. You put your arm around her, shielded her from the cameras. I thought that was really sweet." She smiled up at him for a moment, then turned and disappeared back into the waiting room.

Alvarez stood in the deserted hall for a moment, wondering if he'd just been threatened, and if so, with what, and why. Or maybe he just didn't comprehend genteel Southern talk, and needed to ask Scott for a translation.

SIXTEEN

PROJECT DOCUMENTATION

PAUL CASE, MANAGER was posted plainly on the door of the first ground-floor apartment at the complex where Alvarez had interviewed Pamela Case's ex-husband. Alvarez looked at the name in disgust as they waited for someone to open the door; Scott considerately didn't say anything.

They waited so long for a response that Alvarez began to think no one was home, but then some minutes after the second round of knocking, the door swung slowly open and a thin young man peered curiously out at them, blinking his eyes as though the sunlight was an unaccustomed phenomenon. "Yes?" he asked querulously in an old man's voice.

"Detectives from the EPPD," said Alvarez. "Like to talk to you about your mother's death."

The door swung farther open, revealing a pale, shadow version of the young man they had interviewed earlier. Paul Case Junior was the same height and coloring as his twin brother, but there the resemblance stopped. Everything about him was gaunt and washed out. If Saul Case hadn't told them that his twin brother suffered from Crohn's Disease, Alvarez would have pegged him as an AIDS patient.

Case showed them into a sparsely furnished living room and perched on the edge of a chair as though he were prepared to leave the room at any minute. "Your dad tell you about my visit?" asked Alvarez.

"Yeah."

"We're sorry for your loss, and that you weren't given formal notification. I'm responsible for that; I was under the impression you lived out of town. You have any questions about your mother's death?"

Something akin to interest flickered in Case's eyes for the first time since he'd opened the door. "Yeah, I have some questions. Probably the same ones you do. Who killed her, and why?"

"That's what we're hoping to find out," said Alvarez.

"By talking to me?"

"You may know something that will help with our investigation, without even knowing it's important—" Alvarez had just barely transitioned into his interview spiel before Case interrupted him.

"There's something you need to know up front."

"We already know you were estranged from your mother," replied Alvarez, "but still—"

Case waved a thin hand at Alvarez, dismissing what he was saying. "What do you know about Crohn's disease?" he asked.

"Not much," admitted Alvarez.

"A little," said Scott.

"Except for the clothes and the setting, I look like some kind of wino derelict or drug addict, don't I?" Neither Alvarez nor Scott answered, but Case didn't seem to expect a reply. "You'd never guess I have a degree in computer science, and used to work for a big firm out in California. Well, Crohn's Disease changes your life, that's for sure. Other than generally feeling like shit, you've got cramps and the runs all the time. So if I suddenly leave the room while you're talking to me, you'll know what's going on."

"Noted," said Alvarez.

Case gestured vaguely at their surroundings. "This is the only damn job I can hold right now. At least working on apartments, I'm always close to the can."

"Isn't there any t-treatment?" asked Scott.

"Sure," said Case. "Drugs and shit, with side effects worse than the damned disease. That stuff works for some people; not for me. Last resort is to go in and cut out the diseased part of the intestine—I'm scheduled for that in a few weeks. Sometimes it works, sometimes it doesn't.'' Case shrugged as though it made no difference to him.

"Got health insurance?'' asked Alvarez.

"Looking for a motive?'' Case shot back, appearing animated for the first time. "Estranged son kills mother for money to have gut removed?''

Alvarez strove for a tone that was totally neutral. "We can do this easy, or we can do it hard.''

"You know anyone who would have wanted t-t-to harm your mother?'' asked Scott.

Case shook his head. "She was petty and hard to get along with, but there's no way anyone would want to kill her.''

Alvarez didn't bother to point out the flawed logic in the young man's statement. "What about her political activities?'' he asked instead.

"Ah, yes, mom's political causes,'' mused Case. "Her alternative to arts and crafts, or raising goldfish. She was always involved in the conservative cause of the month. What was the name of the latest one? The only reason I know about it is because it had Saul's lady friend all up in arms. I think it was the Committee for Equal Opportunity, or something like that. Great name, don't you think? Kind of like calling the NRA the National Safety Association.''

"It had Diana Hooper up in arms?''

"Yeah. Saul-The-Golden-Boy was close to Mom, always wanted her approval. He wheedled and wheedled 'til he got her to invite him and Diana over for dinner, which I could have told him was a mistake. Diana insisted on discussing politics, and dinner degenerated into a shouting contest. Diana told Saul that one of the advantages in being involved with an older woman was that both her parents were already dead.'' Case appeared to think over what he had just said. "Ooooops.''

"You think membership in one of these political groups might have made your mother a target?''

Case cocked his head. "You read about any other members of the Committee for Equal Opportunity getting shot in the head lately?''

Alvarez decided to move right along. "How often were you in contact with your mother?"

His question coincided with a knock at the door. The gaunt young man excused himself and returned with Paul Case Senior in tow. "I understand you've already met Dad. He saw you drive up, wants to sit in on the conversation," the son told Alvarez.

Alvarez made quick work of introductions. "How often were you in contact with your mother?" he asked the son again.

"I talked to her on the phone, maybe two, three times a year," said Case Junior.

"She by any chance send you a letter, or maybe a package in the last month or so?" asked Alvarez.

Case Junior gave a humorless smile. "Are you trying to check up on whether my mother sent me presents for birthdays and Christmas?"

"Just answer the question, please."

"What's the point?" inquired Case Senior abruptly. "Why keep badgering him?" That was the problem with letting people sit in on interviews, Alvarez reflected. They always intended to be quiet, but then they never were.

"We're not badgering him," said Alvarez evenly. "We just want to know if he received a letter or package from his mother recently."

Case Senior was getting inexplicably hot and bothered. "Why do you have to keep rubbing it in? Pam made him pay for his relationship with me. How do you think it feels to be ignored by your own mother? Hell, I had more communications from her than he did."

"Are you saying you received something from Pamela recently?" Alvarez asked the older man.

"Yeah," said Case Senior. "I got a letter from her last week, maybe the week before." He glared at Alvarez. "I already told you about this, remember? She used to phone me 'til I stopped taking her calls. Then she switched to writing, but I just pitch the letters."

"I thought this was in the past," said Alvarez. "You said

there was no need for communication now that the boys were grown."

"Did you p-pitch this particular letter?" asked Scott, leaning forward as though that would affect the answer.

"Think I did. Wasn't like there was anything Pam had to say to me that I wanted to read."

"When is the garbage p-picked up here?" asked Scott immediately.

"Friday," said the son, and Scott looked crestfallen.

"When I talked to you yesterday," Alvarez said, "you were unpacking. There a chance that maybe you haven't thrown away the letter yet, that maybe it's with the packing material?"

Case considered the question. "Guess there's a chance," he admitted.

"Then I suggest we head up to your apartment," said Alvarez. "Immediately."

GO LOOKING for stuff against all odds long enough, sometimes it pans out. This was one of those times. The discarded letter was in the bottom of a cardboard box, along with some packing material and other pieces of junk mail. Whatever Pamela Case had sent through the mail was contained in a standard white business envelope, addressed to Paul Case's apartment on the first floor. It had been delivered to the second-floor occupant with the same name by mistake, who never looked any closer at the envelope after determining who it was from.

The four men sat around Case's kitchen table, Scott and Alvarez intent on the task in front of them, Case Senior looking on curiously, Case Junior appearing bored by the proceedings. Handling the envelope only along the edges, for whatever good that was worth after its sojourn to the bottom of a packing case, Scott slit the top with his pocketknife and carefully extracted a sheet of notepaper and another sealed envelope. Using only the tips of his fingers, he put the handwritten note in front of Alvarez and opened the second envelope.

"'Dear Paul,'" Alvarez read out loud, "'I know you will be surprised to hear from me, but I need someone to keep the enclosed envelope safe. I'm asking you to do this instead of your brother, because everyone knows we don't get along, so no one would think of you if they went looking for this. A long time ago I did a favor for someone and the envelope contains my leverage for getting the favor returned, so please keep it safe for me. Thank you, Mom. PS. I know we haven't always gotten along, but that doesn't mean I haven't always loved you just as much as your brother.' "

Paul Case Junior's eyes went wide with surprise. Meanwhile, Scott removed two more sheets of paper from the second envelope, one full of typed text, the other containing a tabulation of some sort.

"Let's hear the rest of it," said the senior Case gruffly.

Alvarez centered the first sheet in front of him and began to read. " 'When I was a Permitting agent for the Utilities Department of the City of El Paso, a contractor named Mr. Craig Diaz was awarded numerous jobs and was given preferential treatment just because he was Mexican, although his work was substandard and did not meet codes. Because of his easy success, Mr. Diaz decided to run for city commissioner so he could create more minority set-asides and preferential treatment based on race, and because of this, he had a lot of support from the poor, uneducated Mexicans in El Paso.' "

"Jesus Christ, Mom," muttered Pamela Case's son. "It's a goddamn blackmail note, and you're calling him mister."

Alvarez waited to make sure the young man didn't have anything more to say before he continued. " 'Mr. Dale Crandell, the owner of Pinnacle Development Corporation, was a supporter of Mr. Harry Montoya, who was running against Mr. Diaz for city commissioner. Mr. Crandell and I had numerous conversations about how Mr. Diaz's politics would be bad for the residents of El Paso, and how his work was so substandard that it was unsafe. Mr. Crandell and I agreed that preventing Mr. Diaz from winning a seat on the City Commission would be to everyone's benefit, since very few people had the advantage of the knowledge we had.' "

"That's Pam for you," interjected the senior Case. "Always a higher justification for everything."

"'The project Mr. Diaz was working on, Monte Vista Heights, was on the verge of being shut down for failing to meet permitting standards,'" Alvarez continued reading. "'Mr. Crandell asked me to alter the results of one single test, and I did. This action, although not something I am proud of, only hastened what would have happened eventually anyhow. After the results were submitted, Monte Vista Heights was condemned by the city. Mr. Diaz went bankrupt and committed suicide. I am very sorry this happened but it was not my fault. If Mr. Diaz had worked honestly to accomplish what he had been given, none of this would have happened.'"

Alvarez paused again, but no one seemed to need to make a comment. "'Later,'" he read, "'I learned that Mr. Crandell paid someone to remove water from the storm sewer during the first test, which I didn't know when he asked me to alter the results of the second test. I also learned that Mr. Crandell had a lot to gain from Mr. Montoya being a city commissioner, things other than the political goals we had discussed. I learned that Mr. Crandell's company made payments to Mr. Montoya during his term in office, and that Mr. Crandell was given numerous city projects and political favors in return. When I learned this, Mr. Crandell and I ended our friendship.

"'Now the Monte Vista Heights project is being renovated, and I am afraid that some of the tests will be re-run. I am afraid that if my name is connected with Permitting irregularities, I will lose my job. This is not fair, since I never received any payment for what I did (and wouldn't have taken it if it was offered), but Mr. Crandell received significant financial reward for my efforts. Therefore, I am going to demand that he pay me an amount equal to my retirement benefits at the city. I have decided that this is a fair price for my help.'"

Alvarez had reached the end of the page. He turned the sheet of paper over; there was nothing on the back.

"She never said she slept with him," said Pamela's ex-husband, studying the table as though it held additional answers for him.

"No, she didn't," said Alvarez. The least he could do was agree with the man on this one factual point.

"The other page, it's the results of the s-s-second test, the data Tory couldn't find in the p-project file," Scott said into the silence. He didn't add that Sylvia Maestes had found the same data after she went looking for it.

Case Senior suddenly hit the table with his fist so hard that the typewritten sheet of paper fell to the floor. "Goddamn it, she screwed up everything she touched," he said, genuine pain in his voice.

His son reached out as though to comfort him. "She thought she was doing the right thing," he said. "She always thought she was doing the right thing," he repeated, as though explaining something to himself as well as his father. "She didn't think anything bad would come of it. She didn't say to release the information in case of her death, or anything like that. She just thought she'd ask for what she'd decided was fair, and that would be that." He shook his head in sorry amazement at it all.

The father ignored his son and looked straight at Alvarez, who had been left to handle this latest outburst alone while Scott dove under the table to retrieve the missing document.

"It won't hold, will it?" Case demanded.

"I don't know," said Alvarez simply.

"What do you mean, it won't hold?" asked the son.

"Can't you see what's in front of your eyes?" Case Senior asked roughly. "The only thing this proves is what your mother did."

"What about the payments to this Harry Montoya?" asked the son.

"Where's the proof?" countered the father. "Not here." He shook his head in disgust. "She didn't even sign and date the damn thing. God, Pam, what a cheap sale of your own life." He buried his head in his hands.

"Is he right?" asked Paul Case Junior.

"He's right about the lack of evidence," said Alvarez carefully. "It would have been better if your mother had signed this document, but the courts may uphold it, since it was in the same envelope as the note in her handwriting. But if we're lucky it won't get to that."

"What do you mean?"

"This document may not be hard evidence, but it certainly points to a prime suspect for your mother's murder. If we play it right, and we're lucky, that may be all we need."

"I still don't understand."

"This gives us enough justification to sweat Dale Crandell, ask him for an alibi, and start digging into the accusations of graft and bribery. Sometimes that's all you need."

"What happens now?"

"I don't know," said Alvarez honestly.

"I mean, to the letter."

"It'll be entered as evidence, held while there's an on-going investigation."

"And then?"

"Depends on whether there's a trial. Why?"

Paul Case Junior looked off meditatively into the distance. "Because," he said finally, "when you're through with that letter from my mother, the first one, I'd like to have it back."

SEVENTEEN

INVESTIGATIVE DESIGNS

ALVAREZ AND SCOTT had few rules governing their methods of
investigation, but avoiding making decisions on an empty stomach was at the top of the list. Even so, as they waited for their
lunch order at a small Thai restaurant, Scott drummed his fingers
on the table and Alvarez knew his partner was itching to start
searching for financial evidence to corroborate the allegations in
Pamela Case's letter.

"What do you think?" asked Alvarez.

"In gutter English, or g-gutter Spanish?" asked the ever-
accommodating Scott.

"English. After all, we're hobnobbing with the Rim Road set
again."

"We may be screwed."

"That's nice and concise."

"I think Montoya's last t-t-term in office was over ten years
ago."

"So?"

"Unlikely b-banks will have records going back that far. Possible, but unlikely." Scott paused while the waitress deposited
a heaping plate of chicken fried rice in front of him. "Now they
use laser discs, but t-ten, fifteen years ago, they used microfiche.
Fiche requires storage space, storage space c-costs money, banks
are philosophically opposed to things that c-c-cost money, so
obsolete records g-got dumped as soon as possible." After nav-
igating all the treacherous consonants in this explanation, Scott
turned his attention to the plate in front of him while Alvarez
contemplated his own stir-fried shrimp and vegetables. There

were few places where he didn't have to add extra hot sauce to the food, but this was one of them.

"But you'll meet the challenge and rise above it, right?"

Scott put down his fork for a moment, and Alvarez felt a quote coming on. "'Pray remember that I leave you all my theory complete, lacking only certain data for your adding, as is meet,'" said Scott.

Alvarez had long since quit accusing Scott of making these quotes up out of thin air. "What the hell is that from?"

"'The Old Astronomer To His Pupil.' A poem by Sarah Williams."

Alvarez chewed in silence, thinking. "I get it," he said. "You're telling me not to pin all my hopes on your talent for digging up obscure obsolete financial information against all odds, *que sí*? Well, I think you're just suffering from low self-esteem. So what's the plan?"

Scott plowed through half his plate of fried rice before phrasing an answer. "Dig into everything I can," he said finally, "having to do with the Crandells' finances."

"They're just going to love having a search warrant served on them. You plan to hit Pinnacle with a warrant at the same time?"

Scott chewed, swallowed. "Might as well, tick everyone off at one time, but I doubt it will get us anything. We're chasing a cold trail. P-P-Pinnacle changed hands about nine, ten years ago. What I'm looking for is probably prior t-to that."

"But maybe not," said Alvarez thoughtfully.

Scott had to swallow before he answered. "Maybe not," he agreed. "It's depressing to think bribery p-practices might be passed down from one generation to another."

"Especially if the new guard can't do it as well as the old," said Alvarez. He was starting to get depressed himself, trying not to think about the mess Keaton was in, and coming down from the high of obtaining the information contained in Pamela's letter. He had to admit that much of what Paul Case Senior had said was true; unsubstantiated, the letter gave them probable cause to investigate Dale Crandell Senior and his past business practices, but little more. That was a long way from nailing him for murder. And besides, Alvarez thought, considering the implications of a detailed financial investigation, they had too many people running around with the same, or similar names.

"Mrs. Crandell's version of affirmative action is maintaining the nuclear family structure while your husband makes money hand over fist," Alvarez told Scott. "She mentioned raising children. Plural. I thought Keaton's husband was their only child."

Scott had to think about it. "There was an older brother," he said slowly. "I'd forgotten about that."

"If there was an older brother, then why the hell is Keaton's husband named Dale Crandell Junior? Don't tell me that there's a new practice in affluent families, where they name all the male offspring after dear old dad. Is there really a Dale Crandell Junior One and a Dale Crandell Junior Two? We're going to have to start handing out name tags in this investigation."

Scott suspended the forkload of fried rice that was on its way into his mouth in midair. "I'm trying to remember. His n-name was Jonnie—Jonathan. He was quite a bit older."

"So why wasn't he named Dale Crandell Junior? Unless it's that class thing again, and he got his mother's maiden name instead. Except I've never known anyone with the last name of Jonathan."

"Davis," said Scott, as though he had just fished that name out of thin air.

"Which was it, Jonathan or Davis? Make up your mind, because I'm confused enough the way it is."

"It's coming back to me—he was from her f-first marriage. His name was Jonathan Davis, then Crandell adopted him and he changed his last n-n-name to Crandell."

"I think people should be issued one name at birth, like a social security number," grumbled Alvarez. "So whatever happened to this Jonathan Davis-Crandell? Why isn't he around to claim his portion of the Pinnacle Development dynasty?"

"I don't know," Scott said thoughtfully. "He d-d-disappeared from the scene right after high school. Maybe went off to college or a job somewhere, maybe went to l-live with his dad."

"I'm disappointed in you. And here I thought you knew everything about everybody on Rim Road."

"Sorry," said Scott, not sounding the least apologetic. "I can always ask my mom."

"That's what I call real courage under fire."

"So, how's your love life?" asked Scott, and Alvarez choked on one of those green peppers that sneak up on you after you bite into them. He drank half his glass of water glaring at his partner.

"I must not have heard you right."

Scott was chasing the last grains of fried rice around his plate. He took a deep breath and spoke slowly and deliberately. "Last I saw of Tory, it was just you and her standing alone in a hospital hall."

"So?"

"I hear those hospital linen closets are pretty hot."

Alvarez stared at Scott. He wondered if the classes in stuttering reduction were affecting his partner's brain. "Where did you get that piece of information?"

"Donna. She watches this soap opera, and they get it on in the hospital linen closets all the t-t-time." Scott sighed, obviously falling short of his own goals. "All the time," he repeated slowly, stutter-free.

"Donna needs to get a life."

Scott looked up just short of licking his plate clean and grinned at Alvarez. "That's what she says about you."

Alvarez sighed. "Instead of hanging out in a hospital linen closet, waiting for exciting things to happen, Tory is off chasing the technical mysteries involving water-tightness tests. Which is fine with me. I don't think she can get herself into too much trouble trying to figure out why a storm sewer does or doesn't leak water, and I don't think anyone is going to shoot her for asking questions about it." He stopped, remembering some assumptions he'd made about Tory's activities in the past. "At least, I hope not," he amended.

"It's an interesting question," said Scott. Alvarez had told him how the Monte Vista Heights storm sewer reportedly wouldn't hold water past a certain level.

"But not one that affects our investigation any more," said Alvarez, dismissing Tory and her hydraulic quandary. "It does present another problem, though."

"What problem?"

"If the sewer stuff doesn't affect our investigation, how am I going to come up with another reason to need her consulting engineering services in this case?"

"I think now *you're* suffering from low self-esteem," Scott replied. "You'll think of something."

"Your confidence in me is touching," said Alvarez, "and probably well-placed. Want to go play good cop, bad cop with the Crandells?"

"I want to get the search warrants."

"Yeah, but then I'll have to arm wrestle you to get you out of the office once you get started, and me with only one good arm to do it. You're just itching to get those search warrants in hand, access account records and start rifling through pages and pages of computer print-outs, which you seem to think rival centerfolds. So be it. Tell me how long you need, and I'll time the talk with the Crandells to be done before they get hit with the search-and-find team."

"Homicide with p-p-possible blackmail and bribery implications," said Scott, thinking out loud. "Give me an hour, tops. You sure you don't mind t-talking to them alone?"

"When have I ever had a problem playing bad cop all by myself?" asked Alvarez. "No, don't bother to answer that. Just send me on my way with an appropriate quote to lay on the old man."

Scott didn't hesitate. " 'Though my soul may set in darkness, it will rise in perfect light. I have loved the stars too fondly to be fearful of the night.' "

"What's that from?"

"Same as before."

"Convenient. What's it supposed to mean?"

"An appeal to Crandell's better nature."

Alvarez wasn't buying it. "Thanks, but I think I'll just rely on my natural wiles and craftiness instead. How's this for a story—I march up to Crandell's front door, tell him about Pamela's letter, he's overcome with guilt and remorse, confesses immediately, and then you don't have to worry about banks dumping microfiche records because it costs too damn much to store them. *Que sí?*"

"I think we've got two problems."

"Shoot."

"The operative word that describes Dale Crandell is ruthless."

"You were just telling me to appeal to his better nature."

"That was b-because it fit the quote."

Alvarez frowned. "You're supposed to come up with quotes to fit the situation, not the other way around. What's the second problem?"

"Remember the size of Lenora Hinson's estate?"

Alvarez certainly did. Keaton's mother, the widow of Dale Crandell Senior's business partner, had died an extremely wealthy woman. Alvarez was a minor beneficiary of her accumulated wealth, having serendipitously become the recipient of a trust fund left for the care and maintenance of her dog, the fluffy white Carumba Cotton Candy. Alvarez had never envisioned himself as a dog owner, much less the owner of a dog that looked like a stuffed animal fit for some teenaged girl's room. Life was full of surprises. "Lenora was an extremely wealthy woman," Alvarez replied, wondering where Scott was going with this.

"We both work for the city," said Scott, "s-so we already know we're not going to retire wealthy."

"That's why you married Donna," Alvarez reminded his partner.

Scott ignored him. "For someone with Crandell's kind of m-money," he continued, "what Pamela Case was asking for would be a p-pittance." Alvarez looked at his partner, knowing what was coming next. "So why kill her?" asked Scott.

Alvarez didn't have an answer to that. The waitress chose that moment to bring a small tray with the check and two fortune cookies. Chinese fortune cookies, now there was a genuine Thai touch. Alvarez pushed the tray over to Scott, who ignored the check and brought his hand to hover over first one cookie, then the other.

"Pick one," said Alvarez. "It's a damn fortune cookie, not a religion."

Scott picked up a cookie, broke it in half, and smoothed the fortune out on the table between them. "Much is revealed to those who seek," it said. Alvarez broke open the remaining cookie, spread the fortune next to Scott's and read, "'Not everything comes to those who wait.'" He picked up the bill, shoved it at Scott.

"Why do I get the bill?" protested Scott.

"Because you took my damned cookie."

EIGHTEEN

RELATIVE CONNECTIONS

SCHOOLS MADE Tory nervous, bringing back memories of an edgy time in her life, when balancing academics with various acts of juvenile delinquency had been a full-time occupation. As a high school student, Tory had existed in the nebulous shadow land between various peer groups. A single day could consist of such paradoxical behavior as skipping school with the shoplifting popular girls, smoking dope with the angst-filled radicals, playing pick-up basketball with the jocks, then meeting her physics teacher to go over her entry in the science fair. Sandwiched in between these activities would be a date with some interchangeable, hormone-driven young man who was convinced she was putting out for everyone but him. As an adult, Tory sometimes wondered where she had found the physical reserves to survive her adolescence.

The actual memories of her high school years, although fraught with anxiety, were blessedly vague. She remembered reading a quote about growing up in a dysfunctional family which claimed that the time-honored teenaged concepts of proms, best friends, and first kisses just didn't mean the same things to someone living in a combat zone. Tory couldn't have put it better herself.

Nervous to begin with, Tory had forgone the ruse of posing as a parent of one of Tommy Diaz's students; instead, she simply called and asked if he would meet with her after school to discuss the Monte Vista Heights project. Diaz agreed, although his reluctance was plain over the phone. What she hadn't anticipated was that when they came face to face, the chemistry teacher would begin pacing nervously back and forth in his classroom, cracking his knuckles incessantly and giving her sidelong furtive glances. She was tempted to tell him to sit down at one of the desks and stop fidgeting.

"I knew you'd come," he said, barely giving her a chance to identify herself by name. "I knew it, and I've been dreading it all day."

"I just want to try to clear up some things—"

"The first detective told me a body was discovered out at Monte Vista Heights. He didn't tell me who it was, but I found out last night. Shit, the minute I heard it was Pamela Case, I knew you guys would be all over me."

Tory realized that the chemistry teacher thought she was from the EPPD. It wasn't often that she got to be identified as one of the guys. Tory decided to sit back for the moment and enjoy the ride.

"Irma and I have decided to cooperate, come clean," said Diaz in a rush, as though he had been storing up the words all day. "I'm not proud of what I did, but I'm not going to say that there isn't some kind of ironic justice in what happened to Pamela Case. You have to believe me, though, we didn't have anything to do with it."

Tory was glad she had been resting her chin in her hand during his diatribe, or her mouth might be hanging open. "Slow down," she said, trying to think what Alvarez would say, and reflecting how handy it must be to go around equipped with a set of handcuffs, just in case the need should arise. "Let's take things one at a time," she told Diaz, whose face was glistening with a fine sheen of sweat although the room was January-cool. "Who is Irma?"

"I already told that other guy, what's his name, Alonzo or something—"

"David Alvarez."

"Yeah, whatever. Irma Lujan is my girlfriend. She's the one who called me last night, told me about Mrs. Case."

"I see," said Tory. She could hear Cody in her mind, saying, "Well, duh." Irma Lujan and Tommy Diaz, who would have ever thought? "What have you and Ms. Lujan decided to come clean about?'' Tory thought that was a good question until she started to imagine some possible answers. This was a high school chemistry teacher, for heaven's sake. Surely he didn't carry a gun, although the way the high schools were these days, maybe he'd taken one off a student recently. She sat up straighter and watched his every move.

''Like I told Alonzo—''

''Alvarez.''

''Yeah, Alvarez. Irma and I hooked up when we discovered we both had an interest in the Monte Vista Heights project. She knew my dad, you know.''

''Mmm,'' said Tory, thinking it was a pretty good response under the circumstances.

''Then we got started talking about other things, politics, philosophies, stuff like that. It's no secret that the Case woman gave my father hell while he was alive, and she was a problem for Irma, too, always trying to make trouble over the things Irma was trying to accomplish.'' Tory wondered if the Head of Purchasing was on the list of things Irma was trying to accomplish.

''What happened then?'' she asked.

''Then we got carried away, and we did some things that were, well, kind of inappropriate.'' Tommy Diaz actually hung his head, pretty amazing behavior for an adult high school teacher. ''We papered her house,'' he muttered.

''You papered her house?''

Diaz winced when she repeated his words in a normal tone. ''With toilet paper,'' he quickly clarified, as though determined to be accurate in his confession. ''Then I showed Irma how you make a stink bomb, and we drove by Mrs. Case's house one night and lobbed a couple into her front yard,'' he added in an even lower voice. Then he raised his head and looked at Tory. ''But we didn't kill her, Detective Travers. I work every day with her son and his girlfriend. How could I kill the mother of one of my co-workers?''

Tory didn't have an answer for his question. She was starting to wonder about the penalties for impersonating a police officer—it seemed so much safer when good old Alonzo was around. She thought over her options, then said the most merciful thing she could come up with. "Mr. Diaz, I appreciate you being willing to tell me these things, but that's not why I'm here."

Tommy Diaz frowned. "It's not? Then why are you here? And who are you?"

"I'm an engineer working on the Monte Vista Heights renovation. I'm trying to figure out some things about the storm-sewer system."

Diaz's relief made him surly. "Well why the hell didn't you say so in the first place? Why—"

"You see," said Tory quickly, "the sewer construction looks good. I couldn't understand why there were problems with leaks in the first place."

"No?" asked Diaz, momentarily distracted from his anger over thinking she was a police detective.

"No," Tory said firmly. "I thought the storm-sewer construction looked fine. That's what bothered me. So, when the city decided to run another water-tightness test, I thought it would prove that the permitting problems were bogus."

"Yeah, so where were you fifteen years ago?"

"But it's not that simple, is it?" continued Tory. "They've been pouring water into those pipes all day, and it stays at the same level. Your father may have been given a raw deal back then, but there's something else going on, isn't there?"

Diaz looked at her, his eyes narrowing, considering. "Even if there is," he said finally, "why should I tell you? Why should I tell anyone? What's in it for me?"

There it was, the age-old question that everyone ends up asking sooner or later. Tory figured it was important to come up with an acceptable answer, or Diaz might refuse to tell her another thing. Then what could she do? Execute a citizen's arrest for withholding storm-sewer details? "Because," she said carefully, "you were in charge, and whatever else is going on, it would be nice to prove that those storm sewers were constructed properly. And beyond that, wouldn't it be the right thing, to have that property finally used for something your father would approve of?"

Tory virtually held her breath in the silence. When Diaz didn't say anything, she added, "I can probably figure it out, or someone else will. But it will take a lot of time and effort. Why make it hard? I'm not a politician, I'm not a detective, I'm not a Permitting agent. I'm just an engineer trying to make a piece of property useable for low-income housing, so some people can have decent homes, people who wouldn't have them otherwise." Tory made herself stop. Much more, and she'd be humming the theme song to *Rocky*.

"Okay," said Diaz, so quietly she wasn't sure she had heard right. "Okay. But you didn't get it from me, lady, and I'm not repeating this to anyone else. Got it?"

"Got it."

"You're so hot to know the answer, what do you think it is?"

"An upgradient connection," she said immediately.

"Right. Where?"

"I don't know, or I wouldn't be here."

"Desert Ridge."

"Desert Ridge? But that's an established neighborhood."

"You mean it's an Eldon Carver development, don't you?" asked Diaz, naming one of El Paso's most reputable developers, now retired. "You mean Eldon Carver wouldn't go around making an illegal connection to someone else's storm sewer, right? Well, I'm here to tell you he did, and fifteen years ago I pocketed the money to prove it."

"What happened?"

"That posh neighborhood called Desert Ridge was way under-designed for drainage. Every time there was a big storm, it flooded and there was water standing in the streets, all the things you don't associate with an Eldon Carver project. Thing was, by the time he realized the size of the problem, the storm water regs had changed, and good old Eldon was going to be caught in a permitting nightmare. The fix was going to require a retrofit to reach the new discharge point, thousands of dollars in fines, and a building moratorium. Not things you associate with a name like Carver, right? Diaz maybe, but not Carver.'' Tory didn't say anything. "Well, guess what project was under construction, right over the hill, about the time that good old Eldon realized what he was up against?"

"Monte Vista Heights."

"Eldon started taking me around some that summer, showing me things, introducing me to some of his buddies. At eighteen, it was enough to turn a kid's head. Hell, I was such a stupid *cholo* I thought he wanted to be my mentor, seeing as he didn't have any sons. By the time Eldon told me what he wanted me to do, I would have been happy to do it, even without the bribe. Now there's irony for you."

Tory was busy thinking it out. "What about the water-tightness tests?"

"Eldon and I had it covered. He built his discharge line right up to an intake line in our system, but he didn't connect. That was our agreement, that he wouldn't connect 'til the permitting on my dad's project was complete. I wasn't supposed to know the details; all I had was his word. Eldon Carver's word. Shit, I used to go over and over it in my mind, wondering if he'd jumped the gun and that was what screwed the test results, if that was what caused—'' Diaz broke off, his thoughts obviously elsewhere.

"It wasn't," said Tory immediately. "Carver must have gone in and made the connection after Monte Vista Heights was condemned, figuring what would be the harm, someone might as well benefit from the storm sewer you'd constructed." Tory tried to visualize the area topography. "Do you know where he tied in?"

"No," said Diaz, sounding tired. "That was part of the deal. I didn't want to know. I still don't."

Tory stood up, wanting to leave, but not wanting to seem ungrateful. "Thank you," she said. "It really means a lot to me to know what's going on. For whatever it's worth, I'm sorry about what happened to your father, and to his project. I think it was a shame."

"You think someone will bring Carver up on charges over

this?" asked Diaz. "I can't say anything without implicating myself." Tory couldn't tell if he really cared about the answer to his question or not.

"No," she said honestly. "What Carver did was wrong, it was fraudulent. But unless you come forward, how could anyone prove what went down? And after all these years, who would care? Storm sewers aren't real high on the list of your average citizen's priorities."

"Ain't that the truth. Too bad my dad and Pamela Case aren't around to hear you say that." Tory couldn't begin to think of an appropriate reply, so she took that as her cue to leave.

She started to shake off Diaz's desolation as soon as she walked out of the school building into the sunny afternoon, already reaching for her cellular phone. Alvarez kept telling her that she didn't have to keep finding dead bodies to keep him interested. She wondered how he felt about secret subterranean drainage pipes, not to mention the recreational activities of Craig Diaz's former lover and his only son.

NINETEEN

HISTORICAL TIE-IN

ALVAREZ PONDERED HIS approach to the upcoming interview on the walk from his car to the Crandells' front door. When Scott headed downtown to get the search warrants, Alvarez picked up his beloved 1968 bronze Corvette. It had been lovingly restored in stages over the last decade as his finances permitted, and Alvarez felt it looked particularly nice parked in front of the Crandells' luxurious condo.

In addition to getting the necessary documents to investigate the Crandells' financial records, Scott would ask the DA's staff to evaluate Pamela Case's written testimony as evidence, but there was no reason to wait for the experts' consensus before confronting Dale Crandell. The art of investigative interviewing was similar to playing poker—the first round didn't require any particular strategy; its only purpose was to check out your opponent. Only later was it necessary to decide whether to stand, bluff, or fold.

The downside to this approach was that if Dale Crandell continued to claim that he didn't know or remember Pamela Case, Alvarez had no fall-back strategies. But fortunately for him and every other investigator, people didn't tend to stick to their initial, simple denials of any and all knowledge. There was always that human inclination to add just a little embellishment, to feed the interrogator some small piece of information in the hope of placating him. Sometimes that small embellishment, whatever it might be, would point the way to other answers.

Alvarez didn't know who he expected to answer the Crandells' door, maybe a butler, a maid, or one of the Crandells themselves. He certainly wasn't prepared for the tall, striking, twenty-something female who stood before him, her eyes very nearly on a level with his. She was attired in a lavender dress-for-success suit with a very abbreviated skirt, had coal-black hair fashioned into a braid that adorned one shoulder, and wore very red lipstick. And these were details he noticed even before the second look.

"Hi. I'm looking for Dale Crandell."

"Do you have an appointment?"

"No, I don't." He fished out his badge. "I'm a homicide detective, working on a case, and I'd like to ask Mr. Crandell some questions." He gave her his very best smile. "It would be real helpful to be able to talk to him, miss."

She stared at his badge wordlessly for a moment; his was obviously not a request she heard every day. "Uh, usually Mr. Crandell only sees people with appointments. But let me check, maybe he'll make an exception for you."

"And you would be?" asked Alvarez.

"Me? I'm Tamara Tomlinson. I'm Mr. Crandell's private secretary."

"I thought Mr. Crandell was retired."

"He is. But he's a very busy man. Mr. Crandell has lots of social engagements, he has investments to manage, and then there's his fund-raising work."

"Would that include raising funds for political campaigns?"

"Oh, yes. As a matter of fact, right now I'm—" Tamara caught herself and gave Alvarez a stern look. "I'm sorry. That's really something you should be discussing with Mr. Crandell, not me."

"Tamara's a pretty name," Alvarez said by way of atonement. "Unusual, too."

She graced him with a smile. "Thank you. It's not my real name—I picked it out myself. I only do this job part time—the rest of the time I—" She stopped herself mid-sentence for the second time. "Wait, since you're a detective, you tell me."

"Hmmm," said Alvarez. "It's just a wild guess, but are you

a model?'' Tamara shook her head, but the smile didn't diminish. "Then you must be an actress."

The smile increased by a few hundred watts. "You got it," she said, pleased. "I'll see if Mr. Crandell will talk to you."

ALVAREZ GAINED entrance to the Crandell house in stages. First he waited on the porch while Tamara went to consult with her employer. Then he was asked to wait in the entrance hall, and he wondered if Dale Crandell was evaluating the psychological implications of various rooms in which to hold court. In any case, it was another ten minutes before Tamara returned and ushered him into a formal living room, striking in its illusion of ultimate openness.

Structurally, the room jutted out from the house, with floor-to-ceiling windows comprising much of three of the walls. Suspended along the fourth wall was a full-length interior balcony, affording a view of the living room from the second floor, where Alvarez assumed the bedrooms were located. From the chair he was offered he could see the front walk through sheer curtains. Mr. and Mrs. Crandell sat across from him, presenting a unified front by anchoring opposite ends of a couch.

"Thank you for seeing me," Alvarez said.

"Don't be too thankful," replied Crandell. "Keaton claims you're a friend, which isn't always a good reference, but it's the only thing that got you in this house today. Let me tell you right from the get go, I'm not cooperating with any fishing expedition for obscure facts. You say this dead woman's husband followed her to my house? That was what, fifteen years ago? And how reliable is this fellow, anyway? You know what kind of morning we've been through. These questions are in damn poor taste, and I want them to stop."

Alvarez refrained from pointing out that he hadn't asked any questions yet. "There's been some developments since I spoke to you this morning—other things tying you to Pamela Case besides her ex-husband's story."

Crandell drew back slightly while his wife leaned forward just a tad. It was a Tao-like movement of almost perfect balance;

Alvarez wondered if they sat in the living room and practiced when no one was there.

"What kind of development?" asked Mrs. Crandell with her pleasant drawl, as though she were offering cookies and tea.

Alvarez tried to look slightly uncomfortable. "I don't mean any offense, Mrs. Crandell, but it might be better if I discussed this with your husband alone."

She waved her hand in immediate dismissal. "That's quite unnecessary. Dale has no secrets from me."

This was such a loaded statement after their earlier conversation that Alvarez almost expected her to wink at him, but she didn't. "We have a letter written by Mrs. Case," he told Crandell, "claiming that fifteen years ago, you encouraged her to falsify test results for permitting the Monte Vista Heights project."

"Why in God's name would I want to do something like that?" asked Crandell. Alvarez thought Crandell had missed the operative question, which was why Pamela Case would make such a claim in the first place, but he was more than willing to reply to what was asked.

"Mrs. Case claims you and she were both upset by the favoritism showed to Craig Diaz under affirmative action programs."

"Who is Craig Diaz?" inquired Crandell immediately. Alvarez thought that was a nice touch.

"I told you this morning," he said patiently. "Craig Diaz is the contractor who ran against Harry Montoya for a City Commission seat about fifteen years ago, with a campaign platform of implementing more minority set-asides."

"Oh. Right."

"Mrs. Case claimed that falsifying the test results was intended to cause financial problems for Diaz, maybe make him withdraw from the race. It worked too well. After Monte Vista Heights was condemned and Diaz had to declare bankruptcy, he committed suicide. That was pretty effective in putting him out of the running for city commissioner."

"I don't see what this woman's ridiculous claims have to do with me." Crandell's voice had just the right tone of frost to it.

"Why do you think she would go to the trouble to write all this down, send it to her son?"

"I have no idea."

"Mrs. Case was afraid of losing her job. Her letter says she was planning to blackmail you." Alvarez let the silence lengthen for a while. "I want you to think carefully about what you told me this morning, Mr. Crandell. Are you going to go on claiming that you don't know Pamela Case, that you don't even remember who she is?" Alvarez upped the ante. "If I ask you to call Tamara in here, will she tell me that she's never heard the name, that you've never received a single phone call from a Pamela Case?"

Crandell looked more irritated than worried, while Mrs. Crandell continued to look as calm and collected as a porcelain Buddha. This was disappointing, as these were usually not the signs preceding a murder confession. "This is a stupid tempest in a teapot," said Crandell grudgingly. "Yes, I knew Pamela Case. I didn't tell you this morning, because I didn't want to go through the inconvenience of getting sucked into this mess."

"You may call that avoiding an inconvenience. Another term would be impeding a homicide investigation."

"Are you threatening me?"

"I just want to make sure I get straight answers to my questions. What was the nature of your relationship with Pamela Case?"

Crandell glared at Alvarez. "We were casual acquaintances when she worked in Permitting, back before I retired. We had the occasional conversation, a few lunches. After she left Permitting, we didn't cross paths much, and we lost touch."

"When was the last time you heard from her?"

"A couple weeks ago. She called me up and made some of the same ridiculous claims you mentioned. The woman was mentally unbalanced."

"Did she try to blackmail you?"

"She alluded to something about needing money."

"Did you agree to pay the blackmail?"

Crandell looked affronted by Alvarez's repeated use of the "B" word. "Of course not. I simply agreed to meet with her, talk to her. I wanted to see whether she would listen to reason before I decided what to do next."

Alvarez wondered if Crandell realized how ominous that statement sounded. "When were you supposed to meet with her?"

"This past Sunday afternoon, at two o'clock."

"Sunday? Not Saturday?"

"Sunday, that's what I said. Are you hard of hearing?"

"Where?"

"Ascarate Park. Tamara made the arrangements, you can ask her."

"Your secretary made the arrangements for you to meet with a blackmailer?" Alvarez was reminded of one of Scott's quotes, which went something along the lines of "the rich are very different from you and me."

"I didn't view her as a blackmailer," said Crandell with disdain. "Tamara makes all my appointments for me. What do you think she gets paid for?"

Alvarez wasn't going to touch that question with a ten-foot pole. "It would have been simple enough to call Mrs. Case after Tamara did, move the appointment up a day."

"Believe what you want. I was supposed to meet her Sunday afternoon. I went, she never showed up, and now I know why. I won't claim not to be relieved."

"Did you kill her, Mr. Crandell?"

"Of course not," Crandell sounded appropriately outraged. "What do you think I am, one of the petty criminals you deal with on a day-to-day basis? Why in God's name would I want to kill the woman?"

Alvarez held up one finger. "Because she wanted money from you."

"Rubbish," said Crandell. "Pure rubbish. I'm a wealthy man. Why would I kill someone over such a paltry amount?"

So the discussion between Pamela Case and Crandell must

have progressed to a point where a particular sum of money had been mentioned. Alvarez left that for later, and held up a second finger. "Her ex-husband claims you had an affair with her, broke up their marriage. Things like that can turn nasty."

Crandell snorted. "Any affair between the two of us was in Pamela's mind only. Maybe you should ask yourself why this man is telling you these things."

Undaunted, Alvarez held up a third finger. "She implicated you in falsifying documents."

"That's ridiculous. People go to trial for doctoring documents to embezzle millions of dollars, not for falsifying some insignificant permitting test."

"It didn't turn out to be insignificant for Craig Diaz. Are you admitting that you were involved in falsifying the test results?"

"Of course not. Don't go putting words in my mouth. I'm just saying that even if it were true, who would care?"

Alvarez decided to switch topics. "Do you have an alibi for last Saturday, between the hours of three and seven p.m.?"

"I don't know," said Crandell with disdain. "I'd have to check."

"He certainly does have an alibi," said Mrs. Crandell. "You were with Tamara, dear." Her husband looked at her in a good imitation of horrified surprise. "It was one of those afternoons you spent working over at her apartment, remember, hon?"

"You spent Saturday afternoon working at your secretary's apartment?" asked Alvarez, thinking he was doing a good job in keeping a straight face while he asked the question.

Mrs. Crandell had obviously taken over speaking for her husband, which was a good thing, as Crandell was sucking air. "Oh yes," she drawled. "They often have work that carries over into the weekend or the evenings, don't you, Dale?"

Crandell started to say something, but no words came out. He cleared his throat. "Yes, we do," he croaked. He regarded his wife as though she were a coiled rattlesnake.

Alvarez was really beginning to enjoy himself. "I suppose Tamara would verify your whereabouts on Saturday afternoon?" he asked.

"Of course she would," said Mrs. Crandell. "Why wouldn't she? Especially after she knows that I'm the one who told you about it. Besides, Detective, your suspicions that Dale would be paying a blackmailer are totally unfounded. There's just no way that could occur."

"And why is that?" asked Alvarez, fascinated.

"Because, you see, I keep all the financial records. Oh, Dale makes all the decisions, manages our investments, all of that," said Mrs. Crandell modestly. "But I keep all the books, write all the checks, always have, since we were first married. It would be very unusual for Dale to write a check for anything himself, and then he'd have to tell me about it, you see."

"She's right," chimed in Crandell, recovering his power of speech. "We're both perfectionists about that sort of thing, so we divided it out early in our relationship. I always kept the business books—"

"Meticulously, I might add," drawled Mrs. Crandell, smiling at her husband as though he had accomplished some wonderful feat. "Recordkeeping is something Dale is good at, almost to a fault. Isn't that right?" Interrupted in mid-sentence, her husband looked at her as though she might have lost her mind.

"Yes, well, anyhow." Crandell cleared his throat again. "Barbara is right. She kept our personal financial records all the years I was in business, and after I retired, we didn't see any reason for that to change."

"So you see, Detective," said Mrs. Crandell, "there's really no way my husband could have been involved in any of this, no matter what kind of letters this woman wrote."

"I'm sure you're very loyal to your husband," replied Alvarez. "There's no reason why you couldn't have written a check for him, to pay off a blackmailer, Mrs. Crandell."

"But I didn't," Mrs. Crandell smiled. "Next, you'll be asking where I was on Saturday afternoon."

There was no time like the present. "Since you brought it up, why don't you tell me?"

"Well, I'm sorry to say that I was right where I usually am when Dale has to go off and work with someone like Tamara.

At home, by myself, just puttering around the house. I'm just sorry I don't have anyone to verify that, the way Dale has Tamara.'' Her polite smile never faltered. Alvarez wondered if she could possibly mean everything she was saying at face value, the subtext was so blatant. If he were Dale Crandell, he would seriously consider hiring someone to taste his food. Immediately.

"How about Sunday evening?"

"Why?" asked Crandell at the same time that Mrs. Crandell said, "Dale didn't need to work with Tamara on Sunday. Or maybe he did, and she wasn't available. Anyhow, we were home together Sunday evening, weren't we, dear? I cooked chicken for dinner, and then we watched TV. A very uneventful evening, isn't that how you remember it, hon?''

Crandell was looking at his wife with undisguised astonishment. "Yes," he said as though in a trance. "If you say so." Alvarez could have sworn this was the first time Crandell had heard this version of how he had spent Sunday evening.

"Your memory of Saturday and Sunday is remarkable," Alvarez told Mrs. Crandell. "Usually when I interview people, they have no idea what they were doing on a certain day until they think about it for a while, or look it up."

"Then you should be grateful for my good memory. Now that you've ruled out my husband as a suspect, you can use your time more constructively. There was no blackmail and there was no meeting, so I think this conversation is at an end."

"Not exactly," said Alvarez, trying to maintain his focus. Keaton was coming up the ornately landscaped path in the company of a tall, distinguished-looking older man. If Alvarez was a good enough detective to figure out Tamara Tomlinson was an actress, he could certainly surmise that this man was Tory's father. Keaton had obviously seen Alvarez's car in the drive; she was pointing at it and seemingly trying to convince the man to come inside.

Alvarez couldn't help it, he was distracted. The thought of Keaton, of all people, being the one to introduce him to Tory's father at the Crandells' residence while he tried to wrest a confession of murder from her father-in-law, was beyond bizarre.

He was vastly relieved to see Tory's father shake his head, give Keaton a quick embrace, and start back down the walk as Alvarez refocused on the conversation at hand. "There were other allegations in Mrs. Case's letter," he said, grateful not to be stuttering.

"What, that I abused children and small animals?" asked Crandell. Other than dealing with his wife, he must have decided that he was home free.

"No, having to do with Pinnacle Development. Mrs. Case claims that you paid Harry Montoya for political favors while he was in office." Alvarez completed this statement just as Keaton rushed into the room like a breath of fresh air. She no longer looked pale and drawn. Alvarez stood up and she gave him an exuberant hug.

"David," she said, keeping her arms around his waist in an intimate embrace. "How wonderful to see you. Hero's going to be okay, for sure now. They just want to keep her one more day for observation."

Alvarez gently but firmly removed her arms from his waist. "I'm really glad to hear that. How are you doing?"

"I'm fine, just fine. Gary was an asshole, got the doctors to agree to let him sit with Hero this afternoon. I'm going to take a nap, go back this evening. I really want to thank you for coming to the hospital, helping me out."

Alvarez refrained from pointing out he wouldn't be much help if CSU turned up evidence implicating Keaton in Hero's drug overdose. "You're welcome," he said instead.

"What are you doing here? Did you come to see me?"

"No, I came to talk to your in-laws about a case I'm working on. I need some information about Pinnacle, back before your husband and brother took the firm over. Then I'll be on my way."

"If you're talking about Pinnacle, I want to hear. After all, it was my father's firm, too," said Keaton.

"Keaton, dear, this is none of your business," drawled Barbara Crandell, but there was a definite undertone of steel. "You go on upstairs and get yourself a nap, that's a good girl. You need to keep up your strength so you can take good care of Hero when she comes home.''

Keaton turned her pale gaze on her mother-in-law. ''I'd like to stay and hear what you're talking about,'' she said. ''Maybe I can help.''

''And I'm telling you, hon, there's no reason for you to take part in this conversation,'' said Mrs. Crandell. There was a pause, pregnant with an unstated clash of wills, then Keaton turned back to Alvarez.

''Will you be in touch?'' she asked.

''Count on it,'' he said. The Crandells were silent as Keaton climbed the circular staircase leading to the second-floor balcony. Halfway across, she leaned over and wiggled her fingers in a wave to Alvarez. She disappeared down the hall until she was just out of sight of her in-laws seated on the couch. Then she sank to the floor, clasped her knees to her chest like a child listening in on the grown-ups, and put a finger to her lips to make Alvarez her co-conspirator. He ignored her presence, eavesdropping in the hallway. If Mrs. Crandell suddenly snapped, stood up, pulled a gun from her pocket and shot her husband, at least he would have a witness.

''As I was saying, there were other allegations in Mrs. Case's letter,'' he continued. ''She said that you, Mr. Crandell, through your company, made payments to Montoya for political favors.''

''That's absolutely not true,'' said Crandell.

''Are you willing to turn over your business account records for evaluation?''

''Of course not. That's over fifteen years ago; we're not required to keep records going back that far.''

''But did you?''

''I'm not going to answer that. As a matter of fact, I'm not going to answer anything else without my attorney present. And furthermore, if you come here again, I'll sue you for harassment.''

''You'll have to get in line. That's the kind of threat that gives the EPPD's attorneys job security.''

Crandell had found a mode that felt comfortable, that of outraged citizen. "I've tried to be polite, but you have absolutely no idea who you're dealing with," he continued, his voice rising. "I've seen your type before—you come here with some kind of chip on your shoulder. You resent the fact that I've accomplished more than you could ever dream of. Did you really think that you could come into my house, make these flimsy accusations, and have me confess to a crime I didn't commit?"

"What I think doesn't matter that much," said Alvarez mildly. "but since you asked, I'll tell you. I think something's going on here, I'm not sure exactly what. Maybe you didn't kill Pamela Case, I don't know, but you can count on me checking out your alibi. I think you use and manipulate people, Mr. Crandell. I think you're a womanizer and an opportunist. I think you had an affair with Pamela Case and used her to further your personal business interests, which included being in bed with Harry Montoya."

"How dare you make accusations like that?" Crandell's voice had risen to a shout. He had obviously forgotten about asking Alvarez what he thought. "You government employees, you're all alike. Small minds, small thoughts. You have no idea what it takes to run a successful business, take something that's nothing and build it from the ground up. Here's something you can use your meager mental powers to contemplate—even if I did have an affair with Pamela Case, even if I did call in some favors from Harry Montoya, you'll never prove it. You're wasting your time."

"That remains to be seen," said Alvarez, fascinated by Mrs. Crandell's calm demeanor. She sat, following the conversation as though they were discussing the outcome of the latest UTEP football game.

"There're always small-minded people trying to hold you back," ranted Crandell. He was obviously on a roll. "You remind me of my first business partner, always focusing on the details, never able to see the big picture. I've never done anything any other businessman with a vision wouldn't do. You have no concept of what's involved in building a successful firm, that's your problem."

This was interesting, this reference to Keaton's father out of the blue. Maybe it was the little bit of embellishment Alvarez had been looking for. "Did Harold Hinson have a concept of what was involved?" he asked Crandell. "It's interesting, isn't it, all these things happening fifteen years ago. Pamela Case's ex-husband claims you were having an affair with his wife. Craig Diaz's project gets submarined, he kills himself, and Montoya gets elected. Fifteen years ago, wasn't that about the time your business partner had a fatal heart attack? Craig Diaz, Pamela Case, Harold Hinson. They all have something in common, don't they? They all stood between you and something you wanted, and they're all dead." Alvarez was spinning this out of thin air, going for broke. He wanted to see if Crandell's temper would result in one more slip before Alvarez got thrown out. He certainly wasn't prepared for what happened next.

Keaton was on her feet and charging down the hall, headed for the staircase. "It was you, wasn't it? It was you all the time," she shouted at Dale Crandell. "You killed my father."

TWENTY

CONVERGING LINES

MRS. CRANDELL WAS on her feet instantly in a vain attempt to intercept Keaton at the bottom of the stairs. "I won't have hysterics in this house," she snapped like a drill sergeant who just happened to have a Southern accent, "not after everything you've put us through. You have no idea what's going on, and for the last time, I'm telling you, it's none of your business."

"I sat in your hallway and listened to every word, so don't tell me what I know and what I don't. Get out of my way." Keaton shoved past Mrs. Crandell and crossed the room to tower over her seated father-in-law.

Alvarez stood up and closed the space between them.

"Barbara's right," said Crandell hastily. "You don't know what's going on, you're overwrought. Go back upstairs and we'll forget this ever happened."

"The fuck we will," said Keaton. "All these years I thought my father was having an affair and you were covering for him. But it wasn't him, was it? It was you. I should have known. You've always screwed everything in sight."

"I won't have language like that in my house," said Mrs. Crandell, but no one was paying much attention.

Alvarez took Keaton's arm and turned her to face him. "What do you mean?" he asked.

"Do I have to spell it out? I'm disappointed in you, David. My illustrious father-in-law chases everything in skirts. He can't keep his prick in his pants, he—"

Alvarez cut her off before she could come up with yet another description. "What do you mean, you thought your father was having an affair?"

"I'll always remember it, I even dream about it. Ryan stayed at college that summer, so it was just the three of us at home. One Thursday night, Daddy said he was going out to the office. My mother wasn't happy about it, but he told her there were some accounting irregularities he wanted to check out."

Crandell stood up then, too, facing Keaton, his eyes narrowed. "You're making this up to fit what you want to believe."

Keaton ignored him. "It didn't seem like he'd been gone hardly at all when we got the telephone call," she told Alvarez. "It was him"—she pointed at Crandell—"calling to tell us that Daddy had collapsed. I rode with my mother out to the office. She took one look at my father and called the ambulance, but he died on the way to the hospital." She turned back to Crandell. "That really played into your hand, didn't it? I always wondered, if you'd called the ambulance first instead of my mother, whether he might be alive today."

"I didn't know," said Crandell. "I didn't know what was wrong with him."

Keaton turned back to Alvarez. "They had this waiting room with a big leather couch. My father was on the floor beside it, turning blue, but there are two other things I'll always remember. There was a woman's gold earring on the couch. I can close my eyes and still see it today."

"You're making this up to suit your own purposes," said Crandell. "It was a terrible thing for a little girl to have to go through, but that's no reason—"

"What was the second thing?" Alvarez asked Keaton.

"The whole room reeked of sex. So strong it about knocked me over. I kept wondering how my mother could go on acting like she didn't notice. All these years, I thought my father had a heart attack in the middle of screwing someone out at the office."

"This is ridiculous," said Mrs. Crandell flatly, "and it needs to stop. We've all made allowances for you, Keaton, but this is too much. You were what, thirteen when Harold died? God knows you've always shown a proclivity toward promiscuity, but you're not going to stand there and tell us that a thirteen-year-old walked into a room and sniffed out an episode of sexual intercourse.''

Keaton turned her pale gaze on her mother-in-law. "Oh yes, Barbara, I knew very well what sex smelled like. Your darling son Dale taught me. Remember all those nice family dinners we had together? My mother was hatching her little schemes even then, telling me to be nice to Dale, so I played every dirty little game he knew. But it was for a good cause, wasn't it? Isn't that how family dynasties are built, one fuck at a time?"

"You little slut," said Mrs. Crandell.

Keaton gave her a feral-looking smile. "Why, because I did what your son wanted? Or because I used what he taught me later on?"

"This has gone far enough," said Crandell, trying for an authoritative tone and failing miserably.

"Not nearly," Keaton replied. "You made me think my father was a sleaze like the rest of you. I'll bet you were screwing Pamela Case's socks off and he walked in on you, threatened to blow the whistle. So you had to tell him why screwing this poor unfortunate woman was such a good investment of your time, why it would reap such wonderful dividends for Pinnacle. The more he argued with you, the more you told him. When he realized what was really going on, he had a heart attack. Then you called my mother instead of an ambulance, to give you time to hustle Pamela out of there."

Crandell paled. "You don't know what you're talking about," he croaked, pulling at his collar like he couldn't get enough air.

His wife crossed over to him and pushed him down on the couch. "Sit down," she said, "and don't say another word. There's no call to defend yourself against these ridiculous accusations. She's probably high on something again." She turned her attention to Keaton. "I hope you're through making a spectacle of yourself," she said as though talking to a child. "Heaven knows where you'd be right now if we hadn't assumed responsibility for you. I owe it to my son to make sure you're taken care of, no matter how delusional you get, so go back up to your room and stay there until it's time to go back to the hospital. I'd better drive you there myself, that's for sure.''

Keaton looked only at Alvarez. "What should I do?"

"What do you want to do?" Alvarez asked. "You should be able to go back to your own house by tomorrow at the latest.''

"I guess I'll stay here," said Keaton. "This is where I told the hospital to call if they need to get in touch with me." She turned to look at her mother-in-law. "Besides, after I'm rested, maybe I can spend some time visiting with Tamara. She seems like such an interesting girl.'' Keaton gave Alvarez a peck on the cheek, and once more made the trek upstairs and along the suspended hallway. This time, there was the sound of a door slamming after she disappeared from view.

"Poor Keaton has been unbalanced for a long time," Mrs. Crandell said. "She was very close to her father, and I think it was his death that started to unhinge her, poor child." She looked at Alvarez. "I'm sure that anything she thinks she remembers could be discounted, knowing her background.''

"Perhaps," said Alvarez. Maybe Keaton was manipulating facts to form a scenario more palatable than the reality of what had transpired fifteen years ago, or maybe she had in her own crazy canniness adroitly intuited what had really happened. After Crandell's reaction, Alvarez wasn't ready to discount the second possibility.

Crandell was breathing a little more evenly now. "I want you to leave my house," he said, and Alvarez couldn't think of a reason to argue.

"Don't get up, dear," said Mrs. Crandell. "I'll see him out." True to her word, she graciously led the way to the entry hall, but before Alvarez could reach for the door, she laid a hand on his arm. "I certainly hope you aren't going to let a little drama distract you from your primary purpose," she told him.

"And that would be?"

"Why, to catch a murderer, of course," she told him with a touch of disappointment, as though he were rather dense.

"With all due respect," said Alvarez, "if your husband has some kind of relationship going with his secretary, it wouldn't be impossible for her to lie for him. It kind of goes with the job description, if you know what I mean.''

"I was afraid you might think something like that," said Mrs. Crandell. "But you see, Dale really does have an alibi, and I can prove it." For one horrible moment Alvarez thought Mrs. Crandell was going to confess to being part of a threesome. "Reliance Security Consortium," she said cryptically.

"I beg your pardon?"

"Reliance Security Consortium," she repeated. "A private detective agency. They how shall I put this? They help me keep an eye on Dale, help me keep him out of trouble.''

"You mean you've hired a private detective to keep track of your husband's extramarital affairs?''

"I would never put it like that. You call Reliance up, ask for Simon Stiller. He'll tell you where Dale was Saturday afternoon.''

"How long have you known about your husband's affairs?''

"His relationships, Detective. I'm not saying he has affairs. All I'm saying is that I keep track of the women he spends time with. That way, I can keep these things from getting out of hand.''

"You mean you pay them off or something?''

She frowned at him. "You have a murder investigation to conduct," she told him. "That's the only reason we're having this conversation, and that's the only thing that should be of interest to you. Wasn't it Senator Hart's wife who said something along the lines of 'if I don't care about it, why should anyone else?' Those would be good words for you to remember. You concentrate on this—if Dale was somewhere else Saturday afternoon, he couldn't be the one who killed your Pamela Case.''

"He could have paid someone else to do it.''

"You think my husband would engage a hired assassin? You've been watching too many movies.''

Alvarez studied her a moment. "You could have killed Pamela Case," he said. "You don't have an alibi.''

This time she laughed as though he had said something terribly witty. "No, I don't have an alibi, but what would be my motive?"

"To prevent your husband from being blackmailed."

"Like Dale told you, we're wealthy people. I would have just written her a check."

"Maybe you killed her out of jealousy."

"But why would I wait so long? Why would I kill someone over something that might have happened fifteen years ago?" She opened the door for him as she posed her parting question. "Doesn't Tamara look like she's in good health to you?"

As he walked to the Corvette, three marked patrol cars pulled up to the curb as if on cue. He was glad Keaton had decided to stay with her in-laws. She was bound to get a kick out of watching them serve a search warrant on Mr. and Mrs. Dale Crandell, Senior.

ALVAREZ SAT in his car outside the Crandells' condo, pondering the next move and wondering what his general feeling of unease was telling him. He decided it had to do with Keaton, the fact that he didn't know what evidence CSU would turn up at her house, what Cabrioni's accusations would amount to, or if she could spend the night under lock and key of her in-laws without further confrontation. Alvarez had about decided that Keaton could take care of herself for the short-term when the words "lock and key" stuck in his mind.

If you moved into your in-laws' house, did you get the locks changed? Did you even think to ask for all the sets of keys? It was a common thing for relatives to have keys to each other's houses. If the keys weren't often used, would the relatives come to mind when identifying people who had access to the house?

An outlandish idea was starting to form in Alvarez's mind. It was almost too bizarre to contemplate, yet it tied together several disparate threads that had been plaguing him for the last few days. Pamela Case's written testimony implied that there were crimes other than the one she had been party to. Mrs. Crandell had referred to her husband as a meticulous recordkeeper, and they had lived in the house Keaton now occupied. Wasn't it the overly-analytical Tory herself who gave credence to Keaton's tales of nocturnal visitors? And wouldn't any nocturnal search of a residence be infinitely easier if the inhabitants were drugged?

Alvarez tried phrasing the story in his mind as though he were relating it to Scott. Dale Crandell killed Pamela Case to avoid paying her blackmail, but not before she threatened to expose his bribe payments to Harry Montoya. Then Crandell burned down Saul Case's house, reasoning that if Pamela sent documentation to anyone, it would be to her favorite son. Thinking about records, Crandell recalled other evidence left behind in his former residence. Alvarez tried to remember if Keaton mentioned calling her in-laws when she was trying to get someone, anyone, to believe her claims about nocturnal visitors. Anyone knowing Keaton would realize that there were substances at hand with which to drug her and her daughter.

But this story posed its own questions. Where did Mrs. Crandell fit in? Was she helping her husband? Did she kill for him, cover for him, commit arson for him, help him search Keaton's house? Although Alvarez suspected that Mrs. Crandell's cultured Southern-belle demeanor disguised a ruthless will, he thought her husband had been genuinely surprised to find that she knew about his afternoon tryst with Tamara. Hypothesizing Barbara Crandell eliminating her husband's former lover while he met with a current one was a little far-fetched.

Then there was the problem with the concept of the Crandells, either individually or as a couple, searching their past residence. If evidence was left behind, wouldn't they, of all people, know where it was? And if it was something obvious, why didn't Keaton know about it? In any case, Alvarez would bet that if he had asked about last night, Mrs. Crandell would produce an alibi for both of them identical to the one for Sunday evening.

His thoughts were interrupted by his cell phone. It was Tory. "*Cara,*" he said. "I was just thinking about you." It was almost true.

"I know why the water-tightness test is turning out the way it is," she said triumphantly, getting right to the point.

It took him a moment to remember what she was talking about, and why he had been interested. "*Que sí?* Good for you, but it doesn't impact my investigation anymore. We found out you were right about what went down with the permitting originally, so I'm not concerned about the current test."

"You're so fickle."

"Never about things that matter."

"Well, see if this piques your interest. Irma Lujan and Tommy Diaz were harassing Pamela Case. They papered her house, threw stink bombs."

Alvarez thought it over. Was it possible he was on the wrong trail? He didn't think so. "That's interesting," he said, "but I think I know who killed her."

"Tell me," Tory said immediately, so he did, starting with his visit to Saul Case, describing Pamela's letter and its contents, and finishing with the conversations at the Crandells' condo. The only thing he left out was the part about seeing Tory's father. Any mention of her family always made Tory edgy, and he wanted her attention on other things.

"Why are you sitting around talking to me?" she asked when he was done. "Why aren't you busy arresting him?"

"Because of one small detail," said Alvarez.

"What?"

"He's got an alibi."

"Oh." There was a pause. "Details are killers sometimes."

He winced at her unintentional pun. "But I don't give up easily," he told her.

"Yeah," she said. "I've noticed that."

"I'm glad. I hoped you had. I have an idea."

"What idea?"

"Meet me at Keaton's house, and I'll tell you." He added the magic words sure to suck her in. "I need your professional help."

"Keaton's house? You told those officers this morning to treat her house like a crime scene, so it's bound to be off-limits."

"I'm a detective."

"So what? That doesn't mean you can open locked doors."

"I have a key," he told her.

There was another pause. "I'd be happier not asking why you happen to have a key to Keaton Crandell's house, right?"

He smiled. "I've always admired your intelligence, *cara*. It was the second thing I noticed about you."

"You've used that line before."

"Think of it this way—I'm like the Boy Scouts, I like to be prepared. Keaton offered me a key to her house, and I took it, thinking it might come in handy some day. Looks like I was right. So are you in, or do I need to look for some other consulting engineer willing to assist in fighting crime?"

"It sounds more like trespassing to me."

"Yes or no?" he insisted.

"Twenty minutes," she said, businesslike. "And this idea of yours, it better be good. I don't like to waste time." She hung up.

"Neither do I," he said to himself. "Neither do I."

TWENTY-ONE

HOUSE INSPECTION

WHEN TORY DROVE UP, Alvarez was sitting in a rocking chair on Keaton's porch, his legs stretched out in front of him as though he had all the time in the world to sit and rock and contemplate the panoramic view from Rim Road. Not for the first time, Tory wondered why she was responding to this man's beck-and-call instead of hightailing it downtown to tell Cal Cortez about her discovery.

She reviewed her justifications: Alvarez was good-looking. Tory immediately heard Sylvia in her head, correcting her: he was *very* good-looking. And the time she spent with him was never boring. Then there was the fact that he had once rescued her from being held at gunpoint. That alone surely rated a few minutes before turning her attention to other things. She parked her car beside his and walked up to join him on Keaton's porch.

"So what's your idea?" she said in way of greeting.

"Good to see you, too. Sit down. It's been a long day, and me still on medical leave."

She glanced at him curiously as she perched in the rocker next to his. "Are you okay?"

"I'm conserving my energy for things to come. You should do the same."

"Why, what do you have in mind?"

"That depends."

"Depends on what?"

"What you want to do about us."

Her stomach dropped six inches. She hadn't come prepared for this. "There is no us," she said automatically, studiously observing the view in front of her.

Alvarez gave a mighty sigh. "Don't act stupid, Tory. It doesn't become you, not to mention you don't do it very well. I've been very clear about my intentions toward you."

"So?" It sounded lame, but it was the best she could come up with.

"So," he repeated, sounding thoughtful. "In my job, I have a talent for forcing people's hands. I'm really good at it, but it's not a talent that I like to carry over into my personal life."

"Then why are we having this conversation?"

"Because I get the impression that to get your attention, to get you into bed with me, I have to hit you over the head with a two-by-four."

"That's an attractive way of putting it. Unlike you, I don't happen to believe in irresponsible sex."

"Well, that's a relief. I was beginning to think you didn't believe in sex at all. Look at me, Tory."

She had never considered herself a coward, but turning to look at him, sitting in a rocking chair on Keaton's porch in the late afternoon sun, was one of the hardest things she'd ever done.

"You can't claim to know what I believe in, until you've asked me. Are you saying that you need some kind of commitment in order to go to bed with me?"

Was that what she was saying? If it was, it sounded hopelessly un-cool. And what was she going to do if he started talking about commitments? "I don't remember saying anything at all about going to bed with you," she told him, back to studying the horizon.

He refused to be distracted from his original question. "Have you ever thought about getting married again?"

Then she did turn to look at him again, hoping her mouth wasn't gaping open. "Is this supposed to be some kind of joke? You're the poster child for living without commitments. You about had a fit when you found yourself stuck with a dog. You don't even like to answer questions. If I ask you three things in a row you start bristling."

Instead of getting angry he grinned at her. "Depends on the questions, *cara*. I've spent a good deal of my life as a need-to-know kind of guy, but people change. I'm not saying it wasn't a shock, getting you stuck in my head, no matter what I did about it. But I'm a realist—I call it like I see it.''

"No one is more of a realist than I am."

"Doesn't take much to bring out your competitive edge, does it? If you're such a realist, then what about you? Carl must have seemed like a miracle to you, coming from your background, but then he up and died on you. Looks like you've done a pretty good job yourself of avoiding commitments ever since. Does it seem like the safe thing to do?"

Tory was tempted to make a big deal about him including Carl's name in this conversation, but even in her dire need for a distraction, that seemed like hitting below the belt. "I have a son and a business," she said instead.

"I have a sister who will always be dependent on me, and a career every bit as demanding as yours," he countered.

She was starting to get angry, which was infinitely preferable to being embarrassed. "Don't you have any idea how absolutely wrong we are for each other?" she asked, glaring at him.

"Why? Because we come from different backgrounds, live in different places? Or because I actually make you feel something, and you're too damned scared to deal with it?"

She looked back out at the view in front of them, and rocked in silence for a while. "I didn't expect this conversation," she said finally. "Or I wouldn't have come."

"I know. I didn't expect this conversation, either. But every time I see you, wherever it is, when you come sauntering up in those jeans—"

"They aren't tight," she said immediately, "they're just work jeans."

He ignored her. "When you come sauntering up, all intent on finding answers, thinking you know everything, not giving up, not backing down, I want to put my hands on you. Sometimes I want to strangle you, but mostly I want to take you home with me, call you mine."

Tory wondered what she could possibly say to all that, but

then she realized she didn't need to worry about it, he wasn't finished.

"When that car bomb went off, when I got caught in the second explosion, it was all I could think about—that I might not have a chance to tell you these things."

Tory took a deep breath. "And now that you have, what do you want me to do about it?"

"Get in your car, follow me home, come inside, tear my clothes off and make mad passionate love with me."

She supposed she could have paused longer to give the impression she was considering his suggestion, but she was long past such subtleties. "And what would be your second choice?"

Another man might have cursed in exasperation or gotten up and walked off in disgust. But Alvarez wasn't another man, which was a big part of the problem. He laughed. Who could help but admire a man who had just dramatically propositioned a woman, got turned down flat, and laughed about it?

"My second choice would be for you to go inside this house and see if you can figure out somewhere the Crandells might have left something they can't get to now."

"What?"

"I'm looking for someplace they might have stored documents, but can't access now." Just like that, Alvarez dropped the previous conversation and went on to explain what he was looking for, and why. Tory tried to concentrate on the subject at hand and not on what he'd said before.

"You want me to look for someplace they might have installed a safe, or something?"

He shook his head. "I don't think so. If there were things left behind in a safe, they'd know where it was, how to retrieve the stuff. I don't know exactly what I'm looking for, that's part of the problem. Keaton and her husband have lived in this house more than seven years. Maybe they've made changes, renovations. Maybe they changed something so that Crandell can't get to the original hiding place."

Problem-solving was a great distraction. Tory looked at Alvarez, thinking. "Like the Crandells had a wine cellar, stored documents in it where no one could see, and then Keaton and her husband came along and walled it up?'' She shook her head at the improbability of what she'd just said. Someone else had already written that story. "Why not ask Keaton?"

"I plan to, but not until she's out of their house. I get the feeling that telephone conversations over there don't stay real private."

"I don't know what you think I could tell you."

"It's not like I have anything to lose. Just take a quick look, see if anything looks like recent construction, or looks funny to you."

"It's a crime scene," Tory hedged.

"CSU finished a few hours ago—I checked. They won't be coming back unless there're other developments."

Tory was reluctant to go inside. "The whole thing seems like a reach to me."

Alvarez grinned. "What can I say? I've already pleaded guilty to wanting to see you."

"Let's not go there."

"All right. Then let's go inside, do something constructive."

Since he put it that way, how could she refuse?

IT WAS STRANGE, walking around in someone's house while she wasn't there and feeling like you had a justification in doing so. Tory wondered if this was how voyeurs got started.

The access doors to both Keaton's attic and basement were so dusty that Tory ruled both areas out immediately. Then she started looking around on the second floor to see if anything appeared to be recent renovation, or if the room configurations seemed to indicate hidden space somewhere. She diligently stuck her head in every closet, tapped on the walls for an unexpected hollow sound. She didn't find anything. She didn't expect to.

She thought she would take a quick look around the ground floor and then make her exit. If she was quick about it, there would even be time to drive downtown and talk to Cal. At the very least, she reflected as she walked through Keaton's immense sitting room, she might pick up some nifty decorating ideas. Alvarez wasn't saying anything, just tagging along behind her, watching her, so she started talking to fill the silence as she walked into the kitchen.

"I don't see anything that looks like a recent renovation, and I don't see anything like what you're looking for, although it's hard to say since I'm not exactly sure what it is you're looking for." She made an effort to stop herself from prattling. She was a trained professional, the least she could do was act like one. "Two-story houses are more likely to have strange little storage places than single-story houses, on the whole," she told him. "I'll give you that." She paused by the back staircase, much more utilitarian than the formal one at the front of the house. This staircase led up to the second floor from the kitchen.

"See," she said as though teaching a course in house inspection, "there's this closed-off space under the stairs. It's not big enough, or the right shape for a proper closet, but by walling it in, whoever built the house provided another storage space." She bent down to unlatch the access, which was a cabinet-sized door at ground level. "Let me take a look," she said.

She sank to her knees by the staircase, then lay down on her back on the kitchen tiles and scooted herself partway in so she could look up into the walled-in space under the staircase. "I can't see very well without a flashlight, but it just looks like some brooms and mops in here," she said, her voice sounding muffled in the enclosed space. She started to wriggle out the way she'd come. "I'm sorry, but I don't see a point to this."

Alvarez squatted on his heels beside her. "I do. It got you where I wanted you, on your back," he said coarsely, his voice changing timbre to one she remembered from not very long ago.

She looked up in shock at the vulgarity of what he'd just said, suddenly aware that her shirt was bunched under her, exposing a few inches of naked stomach above her jeans. That hesitation gave him all the time he needed. He leaned over, put his good hand on her exposed stomach as though to keep her in place, and started kissing her. The first article of clothing to be discarded was his sling.

"Your arm—" she managed to exhale.

"I was getting really sick of that thing," he said as he kissed his way down her neck. "How will I know if my arm is healed if I don't try putting it to good use?"

She couldn't answer that, because he was kissing her again. She was sure she could stop him, she just couldn't figure out a good time to do it. Unlike her one episode of love-making after Carl died, when Lonnie considerately stopped at every juncture and asked if she was okay until she wanted to scream with her lack of conviction, Alvarez was a man intent on a goal, apparently with enough conviction for both of them.

No sooner had she managed to frame this distracted observation than Alvarez paused. Without opening her eyes Tory knew he was studying her. She could feel him getting ready to say something, and that would be that. He'd ask about her consent to all of this, and then she'd have to analyze whether this was really okay. Whether a thirty-five-year-old widow, a mother, a business owner, should be lying on a stranger's kitchen floor, rapidly losing articles of clothing.

Well, Keaton wasn't exactly a stranger... Tory could go catatonic over all the variables in this analysis.

Tory should have learned by now never to discount Alvarez's ability to surprise her in any calculations—he didn't ask anything, he made a flat statement instead. "If you have a problem with this, you'll let me know."

She must have scrunched up her face with the effort to get through the moment, for she heard Alvarez give an incongruous laugh. "This will not," he said, his voice now filled with the conviction of his earlier actions, "be like going to the dentist."

About the time her shirt was discarded, she managed to come up for air long enough to blither something about being responsible. He hushed her with whispered reassurances. He hadn't lied when he'd said he believed in being like a Boy Scout. There went the last insurmountable objection to what was happening; he had come prepared.

Later, when it was no longer feasible to change her mind, she shattered in a panic, losing every remaining vestige of self-confidence. She pulled free long enough to say clearly, "I haven't done this for a long time. I mean a really long time. I'm afraid I'm not going to be any good at it."

He stopped and looked directly into her eyes, his face inches from hers. "I'm a trained detective, *cara*," he said huskily. "You should know better than to lie to me." And then it was too late for truths or lies or anything else spoken.

ONCE, IN A RESTAURANT, when Alvarez had said something scandalous to her, she had told him that he was bad. He had deliberately paused, looked at her, and told her that she was wrong. He was very, very good, he told her. He hadn't lied about that, either.

TORY-LIVING-IN-THE-PRESENT was warm and safe and tingling, lying in David's arms. Tory-living-in-the-future wanted to die. She couldn't even claim the cover of darkness. At some point she was going to have to sit up, search for her clothes, face what had just happened. Maybe it was the effect of being in Keaton's house. Maybe she could claim temporary insanity by reason of environmental surroundings.

She opened her eyes just a tad, experimentally. She wasn't prepared for the sight of dark brown eyes staring intently into hers. So much for any hopes that maybe her companion had nodded off and she could extricate herself and be on her way with no further interaction.

"That was okay for starters," he told her. "Now let's go find a bed and get serious."

"You can't mean that."

"Well, you're right, I don't mean here. CSU may be done, but taking you to bed at a crime scene before it's been released, that might be pushing it, even for me." He laughed. "I might have a hard time talking my way out of that one."

"How can you laugh at a time like this?"

"Why not? I feel great. And I could have sworn you were doing pretty good, too." He started to pull away to get a better look at her, and she clutched at him.

"Don't move," she said tersely. "I don't have much on."

He laughed again, dropping back down to hold her. "Are you getting shy on me, *cara?* How about this—I close my eyes, you put your clothes on, we drive back to my house, and I take them off again." Instead of responding, Tory clenched her eyes closed again, which obviously concerned him. "What?" he demanded.

"I didn't say anything," she replied, keeping her eyes resolutely closed.

"You didn't have to. You think louder than any woman I've ever known. What are you thinking?"

"That you can't be serious." This time the misery in her voice got through to him.

"Of course I'm serious," he said immediately. "What did you think was going to happen—that I'd jump up, put another notch in my gun, and be out of here?" It was ridiculous, but it was so near to her unspoken thoughts that she nodded wordlessly against his chest. "Well, that's not going to happen," he said firmly. "Maybe I should have asked this before—if it was in your file, I missed it. You raised Catholic or something?"

"Episcopalian."

"That's not so bad. You can get past it."

"Using you as my example?" Somehow the words came out as an accusation. "This will never work. Never, never, never." It sounded like a chant. Maybe it would make him disappear.

Undaunted, he kissed her nose. "To decide that a relationship won't work, first you have to have the relationship. I would never have guessed what a moralistic little pessimist you would turn out to be. Give me the chance to convince you you're wrong. Tell me you'll come back to my house with me."

Tory believed in living her life according to priorities. "Promise you'll close your eyes while I get dressed," she insisted, refusing to think about the lack of logic in her demand.

"I promise. So will you come home with me?"

"I don't know."

"Works for me." In spite of her best efforts, Alvarez insisted on being disgustingly good-natured about everything. He rolled away from her and sat up, grabbing pieces of her clothing and handing them over his shoulder to her. True to his word, he kept his back to her while they got dressed, never glancing in her direction. She couldn't say the same for herself. After all, it had been a long time.

When she was finally dressed she stood up, and he immediately stood too and turned to face her. She took a step back, bumping up against the staircase storage space that had been her undoing, and he leaned forward, putting one hand on either side of her to keep her there. "So what's the answer?"

Before she could frame a response, there was the sound of someone coming into Keaton's house. It would have been shocking, but not quite so frightening, if it was merely the sound of a door opening, but it wasn't. From the other side of the staircase, it was unmistakably the sound of someone breaking the large window over the kitchen sink, opening it and climbing inside.

TWENTY-TWO

REINSPECTION

ALVAREZ SUDDENLY had gun in hand. He motioned for Tory to be quiet, then pushed down hard on her shoulder. She slid into a sitting position; satisfied, Alvarez moved silently out of her line of vision around the staircase into the kitchen.

Tory watched him go, having a hard time gearing up to produce the prerequisite rush of fear. All she could think of was that this was just what she needed—seduction and dragon-slaying in the same afternoon.

She was considering whether or not to grab a broom as a weapon when she heard a crash and a scream, then a woman cursing like a sailor. When Tory heard Alvarez cut into the tirade with a shouted "What the hell are you doing here?" she figured it was safe to check out the action in the kitchen.

Keaton, still dressed in the gray sweats she had been wearing at the hospital, sat ignominiously in the sink, legs dangling over the kitchen counter. Broken crockery and white powder adorned the tile beneath her dangling legs, so Tory assumed a flour canister had been the only casualty.

"I could have shot you," Alvarez yelled at Keaton.

"For what, being in my own house?" she yelled back at him.

There were no flirtatious undertones in this exchange. Alvarez looked furious as he reholstered his gun. "What the hell are you doing, breaking a window to get into your house?"

"I forgot my keys," Keaton said, glaring at him. "Is that a crime?"

"We need to talk," he said tersely, looking as though he wanted to wring her neck.

"No shit, Sherlock," replied Keaton. "You're a public ser-

vant, right? Then help me get my ass out of the kitchen sink."
Alvarez grabbed one of Keaton's hands, and with no small
amount of struggling on her part, helped her extricate herself
from the sink and jump down off the counter.

She noticed Tory. "What are you doing here?" she asked. It
took all Tory's will power not to reach up and straighten her
hair. "You look like someone who just—" Keaton broke off
and turned her pale gaze on Alvarez. "Nah, I must be imagining
things," she said after a moment.

"We need to talk," repeated Alvarez.

"In a minute," said Keaton. She grabbed a glass from the
counter, then bent down and opened the cabinet under the sink.
She straightened triumphantly with an economy-sized bottle of
white vinegar in hand, the same type Tory kept in her kitchen
for cleaning purposes. Keaton poured a half glass from the bottle
and downed it in a few gulps.

"You drink vinegar?" asked Tory blankly.

"No," said Alvarez flatly. "It's vodka."

Keaton smiled at him, lifting her empty glass in a parody of
a toast. "And why is that, Detective Alvarez?"

"Because drinkers think you can't smell vodka on their
breath," he answered.

"These little games aren't really necessary with Dale gone,
but I'd hate to lose my touch." She poured another half glass
of the clear liquid and gestured at the kitchen table. "Wherever
are my manners, as my dear departed mother would say. Please,
sit down."

Alvarez yanked out a chair for Tory, who sat. "You still
haven't told me why you're breaking into your own house," he
shot at Keaton.

She sat down at the table and waved her hand dismissively.
"Cut me some slack. I had to climb down a tree to get out of
in-law prison. I had money for a taxi, but I forgot my keys."

"Didn't you see our cars out front?" demanded Alvarez,
standing over Keaton. Tory hoped it was the adrenalin high of
drawing his gun that was making him surly, not the possibility
of Keaton arriving fifteen minutes earlier.

"No, I didn't see your cars out front," snapped Keaton. "Or I would have rung the doorbell like a good little Girl Scout selling cookies. I had the taxi drop me at the bottom of the hill in the back. You're not supposed to break into the front of a house in the middle of the day—shit, why am I telling you this?"

"So why are you here? Decide you'd left behind your supply of pharmaceuticals?" asked Alvarez in what Tory had come to think of as his cop voice.

Just like that, Keaton discarded her belligerent attitude. "Shit, David, don't be mad at me." She patted the chair next to her. "I'm trying to figure some things out for myself, and I could use your help, instead of you giving me grief. I only got part of the story back there, walking into a conversation that was already underway."

"You mean eavesdropping on a conversation that was already underway," Alvarez said, but he sat down and told Keaton the whole story about the discovery of Pamela Case's letter, its contents, and why it had taken so long to come to light.

"Two sons, and one was the favorite," mused Keaton. "Sounds like Dale and his brother."

"Yeah, I've been wondering about the brother ever since you mentioned sex games when you were thirteen," replied Alvarez.

Tory had been willing to ask about drinking from a vinegar bottle; she was not willing to ask about a brother and sex games at thirteen. But that was okay; Alvarez and Keaton seemed perfectly content to go on having the conversation without her.

"Jonnie?" asked Keaton and laughed. "No, there were no sex games with Jonnie. In high school, his parents caught him naked, in bed with a classmate."

"It happens," said Tory before she knew the words were out of her mouth. Why in God's name did she feel a compunction to defend this person named Jonnie? Alvarez looked at her as though she had just said something very strange.

"Yeah, it happens," agreed Keaton. "But it's not so often that it happens the classmate's name is Hector. Daddy Crandell flipped his lid, then he shipped Jonnie off with orders to go to college and to go straight. Jonnie declined to do either. His parents disowned him, and told him to never darken the doorway again, all that dramatic stuff."

"What happened to him?" Alvarez asked.

"We're not supposed to talk about it, but I think he's out in California somewhere, has been for years."

"California," said Alvarez. "That's where Pamela Case's unfavored son used to work. Saul works with Craig Diaz's son. If I find out Jonnie Crandell worked with Paul Case Junior out in California, I'm turning myself in to the coincidence police."

"Well, it's not the sons, prodigal or otherwise, who I'm concerned with," said Keaton. "After I got over the entertainment value of watching your guys go through everything in my inlaws' condo, I cooled down a little, started thinking about my own situation. If your guys find evidence that Hero's water was spiked with tranquilizers, that's not going to do much for me, is it? In fact, it could play into Gary's hand."

"Maybe," said Alvarez, not sugar-coating it.

"So I started thinking about what you were saying, about looking for evidence that my father-in-law paid political bribes, and I started thinking about them living in this house for twenty-five years."

"That's what we were thinking," said Alvarez. "That maybe he left something behind, something he can't get to now. So I asked Tory to come over and take a look."

Keaton looked at Tory. "That's pretty lame," she said.

"That's what I said," chimed in Tory.

"You have a better idea?" Alvarez asked Keaton.

"Yeah," said Keaton. "I do. There's an old safe in this house. Dale didn't want to use it, said it was too old and small for his purposes, so he had a new one installed upstairs in our bedroom."

"Just where is this safe?" asked Alvarez. He reminded Tory of a bird-dog coming to point. It was contagious; she found herself leaning forward, waiting for Keaton's reply.

"In the floor of the storage space under the stairs over there," said Keaton. "We tiled over it when we moved into the house."

"The storage space under the stairs?" Alvarez asked incredulously. Tory refused to look at him she was busy taking an inventory of all her articles of clothing. "Tory just finished looking in there, and she didn't notice a thing."

"Want me to show you?" asked Keaton.

"Yeah," said Alvarez. He turned to Tory. "I think that particular place bears revisiting, don't you?" She wondered if she were quick enough, if she could lunge across the table, grab Alvarez's gun out of his shoulder holster, and shoot him. But then he stood up and the moment passed.

Tory trailed behind the two of them to the storage area under the stairs. When Keaton dropped to her knees to open the access door, Alvarez ran his hand up and down Tory's back affectionately. She was just about to jab an elbow into his ribs when Keaton looked up at them, a tile in hand, exposing the top of a recessed safe. Alvarez abandoned Tory to drop down beside Keaton.

"Your in-laws tell you the combination?" he asked.

"No," she said. "They never mentioned anything about this safe."

"Your husband have an electric drill?"

"Yeah, but I don't think that would be a good idea. This is one of those old-time safes, with vials of nitric acid behind a false front in the door. The idea is that if you drill through the dial, the acid drips onto the lock mechanism and makes it impossible to open." By this time, both Alvarez and Tory were staring at Keaton. "And sometimes the stuff decomposes into nitroglycerin, which is highly explosive," she added.

"That possible?" Alvarez asked Tory, who was trying to remember what she had learned in freshman chemistry.

"I don't know," said Tory. "Engineering students only took one semester of chemistry. We never got to the good stuff like stink bombs and explosives."

But Alvarez wasn't listening any more. "Keaton," he said, his voice ominous, "how do you know all this?"

"The locksmith told me," she said as though he were dense

not to know this all along, "when I had him come open the safe for me. I figured it would be a good place to keep things."

"So then you had him change the combination." Alvarez didn't make it a question; Tory knew he was thinking that would be the only reason a former occupant of the house couldn't access the safe, since it was obviously simple enough to pry up the tile now covering it.

Keaton shook her head. "Why would I do that, when he could tell me the combination? Just because I have a lot of money doesn't mean I go throwing it away." She made a few deft turns of the dial and opened the safe. Apparently forgetting his previous concerns about an explosion, Alvarez leaned closer to look into the interior of the safe.

"These boxes," he said. "Were they here when you moved in?"

"Yeah. They held all kinds of old records, going back years and years."

"Held?" asked Alvarez, opening one of the boxes. Tory, peering over his shoulder, saw what appeared to be numerous vials of prescription drugs.

"I moved the stuff that was in here originally," said Keaton, "to make room so I could store supplies, for when Dale gets going on one of his search-and-destroy campaigns."

Tory blinked. "Search and destroy?"

"He already keeps the liquor under lock and key, which is why I use the vinegar bottle. Every once in a while he decides I should throw out all my pills, so this is where I keep my emergency supply."

"Keaton," said Alvarez, back to using his cop voice, "where are the records that were in these boxes?"

Keaton looked at him and grinned. "Where do you think?"

"Keaton—" said Alvarez in that ominous tone, but Tory laid a hand on his arm.

"They're in the liquor cabinet, right?" Keaton nodded and Alvarez looked at Tory in amazement. She shrugged. "You have to adopt a certain mind set," she told Alvarez, who didn't look at all reassured by her explanation.

"Dale is so compulsive," explained Keaton. "He always replaces his beloved bottle of Jack Daniel's before he breaks into the extra case he keeps in the liquor cabinet. So I liberated the bottles in there, which made space for the records. Ingenious, don't you think?"

"Show us," Tory said.

Keaton retrieved the key to the liquor cabinet from its hiding place behind an encyclopedia on the bookshelf. "He hides it behind the 'L' volume," she sighed. She opened the cabinet and handed Alvarez the case of Jack Daniel's.

"Why didn't you tell me about this in the beginning?" he asked, still using his cop voice.

"You're a detective. I thought you liked detecting." Alvarez shot her a serious frown, then turned his attention to the contents of the Jack Daniel's box. Keaton and Tory sat silently on the couch like obedient children while Alvarez sifted through papers.

"There's all kinds of stuff here, all jumbled together."

"Well, it was hard to move it from the safe, cram it into the Jack Daniel's box and keep it in perfect order," replied Keaton.

They sat a while longer, Tory trying to figure out what she was still doing there. "I've found something that looks like a business ledger," Alvarez said finally, "from a long time ago. It shows some kind of payments to Harry Montoya."

"Perfect," said Keaton. "You think this is what my nightly visitor was looking for?"

"Maybe," said Alvarez. Tory wondered why he wasn't dancing around the living room, it all seemed to fit so nicely. "I sure as hell don't think it would have occurred to your father-in-law to look behind the 'L' encyclopedia to get to the case of Jack Daniel's," he added.

"Finding pills where I'd left documents would certainly pique my interest," contributed Tory.

"So let's arrest him," said Keaton gleefully. "I might not be able to prove that he brought on my father's heart attack, but if he poisoned my little girl, I'd like to see him burn in hell."

"It's a ways from here to proving he was in your house without your knowledge, much less that he drugged Hero," cautioned Alvarez.

"What about fingerprints?" asked Keaton. "What if his fingerprints are on Hero's water pitcher?"

Alvarez looked at her, not saying anything. "Keaton," said Tory gently, "don't Hero's grandparents ever come to visit? Maybe even tuck her in goodnight?"

Keaton looked at Tory, comprehension dawning. "Shit. What are we going to do?"

"Give us time to work with what we've got, build a case," said Alvarez.

"Yeah," said Tory. "You've done enough. You need to leave it up to the police now—they'll get right on it. David will take these documents straight downtown, no going home, no passing Go, no collecting two hundred dollars—"

Keaton looked at Tory as though she were the crazy one. "What do I do in the meantime?" she asked.

"Nothing," said Alvarez flatly. "No discussion of what you think went down with your dad or what we found here. Most especially, no more accusations."

"Yeah, right," said Keaton. "Like I'm going to go back to that house with that murdering, kid-drugging sleazeball and not say anything."

"You need to be out of there," said Alvarez, which Tory thought was the understatement of the year.

"Where can I go?" asked Keaton.

A motel was the obvious answer, but Tory couldn't leave it alone. "You could stay with David," she said helpfully. "He could give you his house key, then you'd be even."

Alvarez ignored her. "Let me make a phone call," he said. "I think I know a place where you can stay."

"Where?" asked Keaton. "I refuse to stay with Ryan and Marshay, and it's not like I have a lot of friends to choose from."

"That Episcopal priest, Father Sanchez," said Alvarez. "I have his card here somewhere. He'll help me out, probably make me promise to attend Mass in return."

"Communion," said Tory automatically.

"Communion," repeated Alvarez. "That's right, Communion. No confession required beforehand, right? How convenient."

"You two are acting strange," said Keaton. "Is there something going on I should know about?" She transferred her pale gaze to Alvarez. "I keep thinking there's something different about you." She cocked her head and Tory found herself holding her breath. "You're not wearing your sling," Keaton concluded.

"I decided to try life without it," he told her. "I wanted to avoid being stereotyped as handicapped." This time, Keaton was the one who blinked.

"The only thing that's strange is why I'm still here," said Tory, standing up. "It looks to me like you've solved the mystery of the nocturnal visitor. There's nothing else for me to do here."

"Doesn't mean you can't be useful other places," said Alvarez.

"That remains to be seen," she replied.

"On what?"

"On what you can do for me."

"Name it," he said immediately.

"Fax a copy of Pamela Case's letter over to Cal Cortez," said Tory. "That way, maybe he'll approve our original engineering report, and we can get paid." She was pretty proud of an exit line that put things back on a business basis.

It wasn't that simple, though. With Alvarez, it never was. He followed her out to the porch, taking her arm and turning her to look at him. "You okay?"

"Of course I'm okay." If she wasn't okay, she certainly didn't want to discuss it with him out here on Keaton's porch.

"I really do have to go downtown, turn this stuff over, see what we have," he said. "But there's no notch in my gun."

"I don't know what you mean."

"I mean things aren't finished between you and me."

"There is no you and me," she said. It sounded juvenile and

petulant even to her; she didn't like to think how it sounded to him.

He shook his head at her. "Let me get Keaton settled and try to wrap up this case. You concentrate on the things you need to do."

What was he talking about? Was he really so arrogant as to tell her how to do her job at a time like this? "You mean explaining the upgradient connection to Cal?"

"No," he said. "I mean thinking about when you're going to introduce me to your father and your son."

Tory turned on her heel and left, her stomach churning at the thought of what he'd just said. She didn't realize until later that he'd effectively distracted her from having her stomach churn over anything else.

TWENTY-THREE

COMPUTER APPLICATIONS

ALVAREZ PERCHED on the corner of the computer desk where Scott was working. He was not in a good mood; he had tried calling Tory up until midnight, getting nothing for his efforts but a busy signal. He didn't want to think she'd sunk so low as to take her phone off the hook, but he didn't know what else to conclude, and now, in the advent of morning, no one was giving him the answers he wanted.

"Que crees, ese?" asked Alvarez. It was the same question he had asked at least five times that morning. Scott responded with little stuttering, but spoke so deliberately that Alvarez felt as though they were conversing in slow motion.

"It's too early to tell," said Scott. It was the same answer he gave each time, as various developments occurred at a tortoise's pace. If something exciting didn't turn up pretty soon, Alvarez would have to start thinking about resisting the urge to call Tory at work.

"At least now we can document that Pinnacle made regular payments to Montoya, right?"

"Right," replied Scott. "But we have to prove that the p-payments weren't for legitimate services rendered."

"What legitimate services would a city commissioner render to a development company?" Scott just shrugged. Alvarez knew as well as he did that the burden of proof depended heavily upon answering all the potential "what if's." "So now someone has to analyze business transactions back then, try to tie the payments to unwarranted favors, approvals, awards."

"Right," said Scott.

"Sounds like a full-time job, trying to reconstruct nebulous things that went down fifteen years ago. Guess it would be too much to hope that Montoya's family would want to cooperate."

Scott didn't bother to try to frame a stutter-free reply to that. Alvarez cocked his head, thinking. "I know who would be a good person to dig into this—Irma Lujan."

"Assuming we don't like her as a suspect."

"I think it's worth a go, as long as all she's chasing is political bribery."

"Even if we p-prove bribery, it's a long way from p-p-pinning P-Pamela's murder on Crandell," Scott reminded his partner.

Alvarez didn't need to be reminded. Just the financial investigation could take weeks, even months, particularly when the subjects refused to cooperate. It was slow going, tediously sorting through documents gleaned from the Crandells' house, matching accounts with local banks, serving papers, then sorting through endless computer records of various transactions, 99% of which would probably be of no interest whatsoever.

In addition to the documents obtained from the Crandells, the search had turned up three safe deposit box keys. Alvarez was interested to hear that one was discovered in Barbara Crandell's purse. Since both Crandells steadfastly refused to impart any information, Scott had a rookie calling local institutions to see whether they showed a record of the Crandells renting a safe deposit box. Alvarez sometimes thought that the criminals would eventually take over the world, based merely on the fact that they were not required to document everything in triplicate.

He shook himself out of his reverie. "Those p's sneak up on you, don't they? Maybe we need to work at this tangentially."

"Tangentially," Scott repeated, not sounding convinced, but not stuttering, either.

"Yeah, hanging out with an engineer has done a lot for my vocabulary."

"Just how much hanging out with this engineer are you doing these days?" Alvarez noted that this was the first exchange in quite a while that had gotten Scott's attention away from the computer screen.

"Not enough," Alvarez said shortly. "To break Crandell's

alibi for the afternoon Pamela Case was murdered, we have to discredit Crandell himself, the lovely Miss Tamara Tomlinson, and Reliance Security Consortium."

"I think the Reliance verification is bogus," said Scott.

"Tell me."

"Barbara Crandell made pretty regular p-payments to Reliance up until about four years ago, then they dwindle out. I can't find any during the last two years or so."

Alvarez thought this over. "Pretty coincidental for Reliance to be tailing Crandell this particular Saturday afternoon after two years of doing nothing. You think maybe Barbara Crandell was such a good client that Reliance fabricated a de facto surveillance report for her?"

Scott nodded. "Not that my opinion is going to do us any good. I called the guy and hassled him some, but he wouldn't b-budge off his story."

"What'd he say about the pattern of dwindling payments?"

"He had an answer to that, too. Said some of the last work he did for Mrs. Crandell was installing do-it-yourself devices, like mini-recorders on the phones."

"How cozy. Maybe that's what they got each other for their fortieth wedding anniversary. Isn't there supposed to be some kind of list for that kind of thing? Maybe the fortieth is domestic listening devices."

"I think it was something she bought for herself." Scott paused. "My p-parents didn't get listening devices for their fortieth."

Alvarez couldn't help himself. "What did they get?"

"Dad got Mom a week at a spa, by herself."

"What did she get him?"

"A week at a spa, by herself."

Alvarez nodded at the wisdom of this arrangement. "Using a tangential approach, let's put the Saturday night alibi aside. If we're right about Crandell, Sunday night he torched Saul Case's place. Monday night he was over at Keaton's drugging her daughter and creeping around her house. If we can place him at either of those, maybe the original alibi will start to unravel."

"Yeah, and p-p-pigs can fly," said Scott glumly.

"Pigs can fly," repeated Alvarez. "If that's the best quote you can come up with, you must be more depressed than I thought. Not to mention that it has one of those sneaky p's in it."

"I have a feeling we're working this case uphill," replied Scott. "It won't take a lot to send it rolling back down the other side."

"You've been staring at computer screens too long. If you've done all the digging you can do with the Pinnacle records, why are you still messing around?"

"I'm trying to make sense out of the p-personal accounts."

"Why? There's nothing that looks like bribe payments to Montoya, is there?"

"Nothing goes back that far."

"Wouldn't be likely to come out of personal accounts anyhow. Both Crandells said that the missus keeps the household books, and I believe them. Otherwise, how could she make all those payments to Reliance without her husband asking about it? Little indulgences are one thing, but Reliance Security Consortium doesn't sound a bit like Victoria's Secret." Alvarez went with the flow of that line of thought. "You see anything looks like payments to other women? Large checks made out to people with names like Delila Delight, Misty Midnight, or even Modesty Blaise?"

Scott shook his head. "Back before you told me who kept the books, I thought maybe I'd find monetary evidence of other affairs. 'Money cannot buy the fuel of love but it is excellent kindling,'" he said solemnly. "W. H. Auden."

"Yeah, well, try this on for size," replied Alvarez. "'The most sensitive part of a man is not his skin but his wallet.'"

"Who said that?" Scott asked with interest. "Will Rogers?"

"Adolph Hitler." *The Dictionary of Cynical Quotations* had been worth every penny Alvarez paid for it. "So there's nothing to indicate that Mrs. Crandell might be paying off women in her husband's life?"

"Nothing, except for a decade of checks made out to Mary

Masters," said Scott, back to sounding glum. "That's a cleaning service," he continued before Alvarez could ask. "Donna uses them."

"How about checks to Tamara Tomlinson?"

Scott shook his head. "She's paid through a secretarial agency. Of course, there's no way to know how much cash Crandell spends, and on what."

"Then why are you still in front of that damn screen?"

"I can't find the money."

"What do you mean, you can't find the money? You've been staring at account records for the past two days, while I've been out doing all the dirty work, gathering evidence."

"Keaton found the evidence, not you," said Scott without rancor.

"Yeah, well, you wouldn't believe how hard I had to work for it. So what do you mean, you can't find the money?"

"These accounts don't show anything like the amounts I'd expect the Crandells to keep in local banks." Scott sighed. There was nothing that bothered him more than not being able to follow a monetary trail. "Without their cooperation, there's no foolproof way to identify every p-place they have accounts."

"What a concept," said Alvarez. "Having so many accounts you have to keep track of them."

"If I could find a loan application," continued Scott as though Alvarez hadn't said anything, "I could pull up a financial statement. But I'll bet they haven't taken out a loan for years."

"Must be nice. Researching my finances would be a piece of cake," said Alvarez. "Cotton, though, that's another story. She likes to keep her funds invested in animal-friendly businesses. Things like Seeing Eye dogs for dogs whose eyes you can't see."

"I can't access IRS returns without a federal court order," Scott continued, "and even then, they're notoriously slow to respond."

"That's because the IRS is not a cop's best friend," said Alvarez philosophically. It was true. The IRS wanted to collect as much money as possible; they didn't care whether the source was legal or not. Loan sharks and drug dealers could safely report their income and never fear that the IRS would send cops to get them, as long as they paid the required taxes. The only time the IRS was friendly with law enforcement was when the case worked the other way—the agency made it easier to get longer sentences for felons busted with unrelated evidence, because the IRS was always eager to add on time for tax evasion.

"Even a copy of their tax return isn't guaranteed to give me a complete picture." Scott said. "The Crandells could have a Swiss bank account for all I know."

"A wealthy couple where the wife keeps all the books, and somehow they don't appear to have much money," mused Alvarez. While Scott continued to stare at the screen in front of him, Alvarez had the glimmer of an idea. "Computers aren't everything," he told his partner. "You know what I always say about Artificial Intelligence."

"No," said Scott, not sounding the least bit interested. "What do you always say about Artificial Intelligence?"

"That it's no match for natural stupidity. Listen, what if we're missing the message with the discontinued payments to Reliance? What if it's like the Dog in the Night-Time?"

Scott looked up at Alvarez, puzzled. "I don't get it. Why do you keep bringing up your dog?"

Alvarez shook his head in exasperation. He could never understand how Scott had managed to get an Ivy League education and yet remain so abysmally ignorant of certain important things. "The Dog in the Night-Time," he repeated. "Not my dog. It's famous—a major clue in one of Sherlock Holmes's cases. The point was that the dog in question didn't bark."

Scott looked at him blankly. "I think you've been spending too much time with Keaton."

Alvarez persisted. "What if the dwindling payments to Reliance and the installation of do-it-yourself devices simply mean the obvious thing that—Mrs. Crandell is running out of money?"

Scott looked aghast. Alvarez had to admit it was quite a reach to think of misplacing funds equivalent to the estate of Cotton's previous mistress. "No way," Scott said.

"You've been looking for particular kinds of payouts, right? Ones that would indicate mistresses or bribes or blackmail."

"And to Reliance," added the ever detail-oriented Scott.

"Let's try something else. Try looking for large sums of money moving through the account, regardless of who it's paid to."

Scott typed instructions into the keyboard, then sat back to study the information assembling itself on the screen in front of him. "Holy sh-sh-shit," he said, his stutter control momentarily forgotten.

"What?"

"Hundreds of thousands of dollars, no, more than that, transferred to USB-CIA over the last five years."

"USB-CIA?" Alvarez asked incredulously. "That's it, Scott, we've finally hit the big time. The Crandells are part of a conspiracy to take over the government."

Scott never took his eyes off the screen. "That would be the US CIA, or maybe even the USA CIA. And I doubt they take direct deposits, would ruin their reputation as a covert operation. USB, it sounds familiar." He brightened. "I'll bet it's United Service Bank."

"What's that?"

Scott gave Alvarez a pitying look. "One of the largest privately held banks in the Southwest."

"The Crandells could have an account there?"

"I'd bet my next paycheck they have an account there." For Scott to bet anything like a paycheck was a serious matter. "USB has a local office here, otherwise, we'd be SOL." Physically serving papers on out-of-town institutions could take days, weeks. Scott was really perking up. "More than that, one of Donna's brothers works there."

"Does that rate a discount? Should I move Cotton's funds to USB, take advantage of some home-grown nepotism?"

Scott ignored him. "Let me make a call. Get ready to serve another set of papers. They're just down the street."

This was a new development. Usually Alvarez made the calls and Scott did the paperwork. Alvarez could only hope that Donna Faulkner had come up with an appropriate reward system for Scott's reduction in stuttering. He made a mental note to be sure to suggest some things the next time he saw her.

It took ten minutes for Scott to get put through to Donna's brother, another thirty minutes to get the papers served, another five minutes to talk Donna's brother into putting them on-line instead of printing out records and sending them over. Scott finally hung up the phone and turned to look at Alvarez.

"Consolidated Investment Account," he said, looking as satisfied as someone who had just been served a large hot fudge sundae.

"That's what CIA stands for?"

Scott nodded. "It's a special type of brokerage account where you can hold investments, like stocks, bonds, mutual funds, in addition to cash. They're calling to verify my badge number, then they'll put me on-line with their system. They already told me something interesting—the account is in the name of Barbara Crandell only."

Alvarez felt they were definitely onto something, he just wished he knew what. Why was Barbara Crandell moving joint assets into an account in her name only? Was she preparing to leave her husband? If so, why would she cover for him, getting Reliance to provide an alibi for Saturday, and providing him one herself for Sunday? This new information was tantalizing; he hadn't thought about trying to call Tory for the last thirty minutes or so.

The computer made some interesting grinding noises and Scott turned his attention back to the screen, rapidly typing instructions. "Good God," he said tersely.

"You can tell where the money went?"

"I haven't gotten to that—I'm just looking at deposits. In addition to cash deposits, hundreds of shares of stock have been transferred into this account and liquidated." Scott's fingers danced over the keyboard. "Top five entities for p-payouts in the last year—J. Davis, California Cancer Control and Cure Center, Los Angeles Good Samaritan Hospital, Diablo Digestive Disease Associates—''

"Diablo Digestive Disease Associates?" asked Alvarez. "Sure you didn't read that wrong?"

"Nope," said Scott without looking up from the screen. "P-probably located in California, what do you expect? Number five is Janet Wettig, PA," he added.

"Janet Wettig, PA, doesn't sound like a girlfriend to me."

"No," agreed Scott. "Probably some type of medical practitioner, maybe a therapist of some kind."

"Didn't you tell me the older Crandell son was named Davis before he was adopted?"

Scott nodded. "Must have gone back to using his original name after his stepfather disowned him."

"But it doesn't look like his mother disowned him, does it? You're thinking stereotypical thoughts like California, prodigal son, homosexual lifestyle, AIDS, medical bills."

Scott nodded. "Yeah, well the comforting thing about stereotypes is sometimes they're true."

"Don't try saying that around Irma Lujan."

Scott ignored him. "I just read an article about the leading causes of lost family fortunes. Catastrophic illness of an uninsured family member made the list."

"Makes sense, with all the new high-tech medical procedures," said Alvarez. "What were the others?" he asked curiously.

"Gambling, addiction, bad investments, and acrimonious divorce," recited Scott.

"In the last case, you just transfer the money to the attorneys, save everyone a lot of trouble." Alvarez thought a moment. "I don't suppose death of a dog made the list?" Scott just shook his head, refusing to dignify that question with an answer. "So what does this tell us?" Alvarez asked.

Scott apparently considered this a question worth answering. "Barbara Crandell has been spending vast sums of money for the last five years," he said without hesitation. "And her husband probably doesn't know about it."

"Could be a motive for murder, if she thought Pamela Case was going to pressure her husband into paying her money," said Alvarez thoughtfully. "Think what would happen if you wrote a check for blackmail and it bounced. Would be damn embarrassing."

"It would also tend to make you look at your personal accounts real close," observed Scott soberly.

"But that reasoning only holds if our hypothesis about the disappearing money is right," continued Alvarez. "What if the Crandells have lots of money somewhere else, like you were talking about? I think we're on the right track, but I'd hate to tip our hand prematurely."

Scott thought for a moment. "Life insurance," he said.

"What does life insurance have to do with the Crandells' finances?"

"The Crandells have their life insurance with a local firm—I came across those p-payments when I was looking for other stuff. Life insurance p-policies are usually the last things people cash in."

"Let's send over the papers. At the rate we're going, the few financial institutions in El Paso that don't get a court order from us are going to feel left out," said Alvarez. "Meanwhile, I'll see what I can do about tracking down medical records for Jonnie Crandell-now-Davis."

"We don't have any authorization for that."

"Since managed health care became such a buzzword, doctors have gotten really friendly with insurance companies."

"You don't work for an insurance company."

"You know that, they don't."

FORTY-FIVE MINUTES LATER, Scott and Alvarez finished simultaneous phone calls. Alvarez said, "I got through to three out of four on your list. They all confirmed Jonathan Davis as a patient, and one sounded pretty crabby, asking when they could expect payment on an overdue bill. Sounds to me like Barbara Crandell is starting to get strapped for cash."

"Her policies were cashed in about a year ago, but her husband's haven't been touched."

"Makes sense to me. Probably can't cash in her husband's life insurance policies without him knowing about it."

"She's the owner of her husband's policies," said Scott. "I asked."

"Maybe she hasn't gotten that desperate yet, or maybe there's some kind of notification procedure if the policy is cashed in, regardless of who owns it."

"Maybe," said Scott, "but I still think it's strange. Initially, the insurance guy didn't want to give me the time of day. Then he changed his tune, kept asking if there was anything else I wanted to know. Sounded like he was waiting for me to ask something I didn't."

Alvarez gave a mock shudder. "Hate it when that happens, but let's drop it for now. I think it's time to sweat one of the Crandells."

"Which one?"

"Dale—I think he's the weak link. If his wife did Pamela and all the stuff afterward, she's got nerves of steel. Imagine showing up at the hospital cool as a cucumber, knowing you'd poisoned your own granddaughter."

"Step-granddaughter."

"Still."

"What's the plan?"

"Barbara Crandell told us she doesn't have an alibi for Saturday, and I think her story about the two of them spending Sunday evening together is bogus. If we can get the husband to give us her whereabouts Sunday night, tell us she lied about them being together, it would be a start. Then maybe if we're lucky, he'll tell us he woke up Monday night and found her missing."

"I bet they don't share a bedroom."

"Stop being a pessimist. I think we can get Dale Crandell to give up his wife; we just have to play it right."

"How?"

"Get him by himself, tell him his wife is draining off assets for payments to the prodigal son."

"He'll want to check that for himself."

"Let him. But before he can do that, we hit him with an emotional appeal."

"And that would be?"

"The cold-blooded murder of Pamela Case. If Crandell had an affair with Pamela, he must have cared about her at some point. We hit him with the financial information, then take him out to where she was killed, recount what the last minutes of her life must have been like. We play it right, he'll be begging to give up his wife." Scott didn't say anything. "Well?" Alvarez asked.

"The first part sounds okay. The second p-p-part sounds kind of lame."

Alvarez grinned. "Lame has worked before."

TWENTY-FOUR

LAMINAR FLOW

CAL CORTEZ glanced up when Tory entered his office; he looked about as friendly as a pit bull defending a favorite patch of turf. "Don't mess with me today," he growled before Tory could formulate a greeting, then pointedly turned his attention back to the papers on his desk. She walked into his office anyway.

"I'm not here to 'mess with you,' Cal. I'm here to help you."

He looked up again. "I'm a government employee—that's my line. And when we say that, we don't mean it anyhow." He frowned. "You look different. What is it, did you cut your hair or something?"

"I don't look different," Tory said. She'd had this conversation earlier in her own office with Sylvia. "I have some information for you." She sat, uninvited, in one of the chairs she and Alvarez had occupied a few days ago.

"I already got it," Cal said curtly. "Your friend from the EPPD faxed over that little jewel of a letter. Just when you think modern civilization can't get any worse, it does. Who would have thought someone would stoop so low as to sabotage a water-tightness test?" Cal changed from looking surly to looking indignant.

"It's been done before, rigging construction tests," Tory pointed out. "It's just that in all the instances we know of, people fudged on the side of passing, not the other way around."

Cal glared at her. "I don't know about you, but I'd like to think that water-tightness tests would remain beyond the reaches of the amoralism that permeates other aspects of our daily life." Tory was still trying to digest that statement when he hit her

with another question. "And don't you know better than to contradict someone who owes you money?"

Phrasing like that put her on automatic pilot. "Which reminds
me—"

"Don't start with me. I'll deal with the information in that
letter when the time comes, which isn't now. I've got bigger
problems than the status of your engineering report. I've still got
that damn system filled with water, EPPD still wanting to poke
around, and the city commissioners dying to schedule a PR shoot
of them accepting the grant check on that godforsaken site." Cal
shook his head at the unfairness of it all. "I should have stayed
in traffic," he muttered.

"Things go wrong in traffic, too," Tory said before she remembered Cal's advice about contradicting people who owed
you money. She quickly switched topics. "When I said I had
information for you, I didn't mean the stuff in Pamela Case's
letter."

Cal looked at her balefully. "You have more information for
me? Why is it I don't think that's good news? I don't know
whether to listen to you or have you thrown out of my office.
You're like a walking, talking technical disaster waiting to happen, you know that?"

"That's not fair," Tory protested.

"Who cares about fair?" he replied. "Let's talk about statistics, probabilities. You inspect a construction project that turns
out to have a structural member with vertebrae. Then you inspect
a collapsed room that happens to have two bodies in it. What
are the probabilities that would happen to any engineer in one
lifetime? I should have known better than to let you near one
of my projects."

"Those aren't my fault," Tory said, genuinely insulted. "In
every case, the dead bodies showed up without my help."

"Now you walk into my office," continued Cal as though
she hadn't spoken, "acting like it's good news, that you have
information for me. What are you here to tell me, that someone's
taken our surveying crew hostage and is holding them for ransom? Well, if that's the case, I don't care, they haven't done

shit for me lately, and the ransom will have to come out of someone else's department budget." Cal frowned at her again. "There is something different about you," he said accusingly. "What is it?"

"There's nothing different about me," she said sharply. "You're under too much stress. Now that you've blamed me for everything, do you feel better?"

"Yeah," said Cal, looking surprised. "I do."

"Good," said Tory. "Then listen to me. The best thing you could do right now is figure out what's going on with the storm-sewer system. Then you could drain the pipes, answer everyone's questions, and let the commissioners shoot PR pictures out there to their heart's content."

"Yeah," said Cal, sounding surly again. "Then things might halfway go back to normal, but I'm not holding my breath. With my luck, this will be the first storm-sewer system in the country to be featured on Oprah."

"Probably Jenny Jones," said Tory without thinking, "or maybe Jerry Springer—" Cal's face started to turn splotchy. "I can tell you why the storm-sewer system won't fill," she said quickly.

"So can I," Cal snapped. "Here's a news flash—I passed hydraulics, too. Either we've tapped into some type of huge aquifer draining the system, unheard of in our topography, or there's an upgradient connection somewhere. Or wait, I left out a possibility. Maybe we've been time-warped into some southwestern version of the Bermuda Triangle."

"I know where the upgradient connection is," said Tory.

Cal regarded her in silence for a full beat, then leaned forward. "Where?" he demanded.

"Desert Ridge," she said.

The room was silent while Cal thought this over. Tory could almost see him sorting through various conclusions in his head. "It can't be," he said finally.

"It is."

"No."

"Yes," replied Tory.

"Well, it's possible location-wise," said Cal hesitantly, "but—"

"But it's an Eldon Carver development," Tory finished for him. "That's what you were going to say, right?"

"Right." They sat and looked at each other for a while. "How do you know this?" he asked finally.

"I can't say."

Cal groaned. "I knew you were going to say that." He stood up, went to his files and started pulling out papers. "Show me," he said.

"I can't," she replied. "I know that the upgradient connection is in Desert Ridge, but I don't know where. My source didn't know exactly where the tap-in was located."

"Your source," Cal muttered to himself. He stopped searching through his files and turned to look at her. "What am I supposed to do, take your word for it?"

"No," said Tory slowly. "I'm pretty sure about this, but not a hundred percent. I could go looking myself, but I don't have access to plans of Desert Ridge, like you do, and besides, it's not really safe for me to go on my own."

Cal was back to frowning. "You're not suggesting—"

"Now would be a great time to do it," Tory continued, "because it would be easier to identify the connecting line—we'll see water off in the distance since you've got the downgradient portion of the system filled." She was warming to her proposed scheme. "We can take the plans for both developments, go out there together, just you and me, real low-key, and see if we can locate the connection."

"You must be joking," Cal said. "Do I look like I'm dressed to go out into the field?"

"Would you rather explain to the city commissioners why they have to postpone their picture shoot?" Tory countered.

Cal turned away from her and started yanking plans out of the files. "I have a bad feeling about this," he said.

"Come on, Cal," Tory cajoled, "it could be fun. You could turn out to be the hero of the hour."

"Hour is about right," muttered Cal. "I hate crawling around in pipes. I should have stayed in traffic."

"It'll be okay."

"If anything goes wrong, I'm holding you personally responsible," he shot back at her.

"This will work out, I know it," Tory said soothingly. "You'll get your answers and get this project out of your hair. There might even be some other benefits."

"Like what?" he demanded, reaching over from the file cabinet to pull his jacket off the back of his chair.

"You might get to be on Jen—I mean Oprah." Cal threw his jacket across the room at her, but Tory didn't care. He'd agreed to do what she wanted, and she hadn't had to mention hair transplants, not once.

TWENTY-FIVE

SITE VISIT

THE LOVELY Miss Tamara Tomlinson wore a garnet-colored, dress-for-success suit, which Alvarez thought made a nice change from the pale lavender of yesterday. However spiffy her outfit, she looked none too happy to see him at the Crandells' front door again, this time with company.

"It's you," she said dubiously, blinking as though he might morph himself into the visage of some more welcome person if she just squinted hard enough. Alvarez didn't bother to reply; he had never figured out an appropriate response to the greeting, "It's you." What did she expect him to do, contradict her? "I don't suppose you have an appointment this time, either," Tamara continued in an accusing tone. "Not that it would do any good, probably, after all the trouble you caused yesterday."

There was that regrettable phenomenon of guilt by association. Alvarez hadn't been part of the team executing the search warrant served on the Crandells yesterday. He'd been busy doing important detecting work at Keaton's house. "No," Alvarez admitted, "we don't have an appointment. This is my partner, Scott Faulkner." Scott gave Tamara his All American Boy grin, and Tamara responded with a dazzling smile. "He's married," Alvarez added; the things he did for Donna Faulkner. "But we'd like to speak with Mr. Crandell anyway."

Tamara blinked again, and Alvarez had to admit that he had covered three topics in one exchange—their lack of an appointment, Scott's marital status, and their desire to see Mr. Crandell. He decided to go for broke, adding a fourth. "Is Mrs. Crandell here?" he asked.

"No," said Tamara importantly, happily latching onto something for which she had a concrete response. "She had an appointment with her insurance agent." Alvarez resisted the urge to glance in Scott's direction. "She should be back in an hour or so," Tamara added helpfully.

"We'd like to talk to Mr. Crandell, please," repeated Alvarez.

"I don't know about him talking to you. He was awfully upset yesterday." She stared at Alvarez. "I stayed to help straighten up, and he was talking about phasing out some things, maybe even eliminating the need for a secretary altogether."

Alvarez didn't plan on holding his breath until Crandell found the resolve to eliminate Tamara's job. "Tell your boss we're not here to ask him any questions. Tell him we're here to give him some information."

"And that would be regarding?" asked Tamara, adopting her official personal secretary persona again.

"Tell him we have some information about Jonathan Davis, information that would be of interest to him," said Alvarez.

"Who is Jonathan Davis?" asked Tamara blankly.

Alvarez shrugged. "It's something we need to discuss with Mr. Crandell. Tell him we're here as a courtesy—we want to make some information available to him before we act on it."

Five minutes later, he and Scott were shown into the same room where Alvarez had met with the Crandells before.

Dale Crandell waved Tamara off and made a show of closing the ornate French doors behind her. As Keaton had so ably demonstrated, this room was not ideal for private conversations, but Alvarez figured that unless you were on the second floor it would be difficult to eavesdrop. He would have to take Tamara's word that Mrs. Crandell was out of the house—this opportunity was too good to pass up.

Dale Crandell didn't invite them to sit down. Instead, he pointed to a phone sitting on an elegant antique writing desk. "See that phone sitting there?" he asked.

"Yes sir," Alvarez said smartly.

"The minute you say one single thing out of line," said Crandell, "I'm picking up that phone, calling my attorney. You got that, mister?"

"Yes sir," said Alvarez again.

"Tamara said some nonsense about you having information for me—something to do with Jonathan Davis. Are you threatening to get another search warrant on some flimsy excuse having to do with my stepson? If you think I'm just going to stand by and go through that humiliation again, you're wrong."

"No sir," said Alvarez. He refrained from pointing out that if they did get another search warrant, standing by was exactly what Dale Crandell would be doing. What did he think he could do, charge the police with breaking and entering?

"If you're digging into my personal affairs," continued Crandell, "wasting more taxpayer money, let me save you some time. That boy is my wife's son from a sorry first marriage, and a sorry kid he is, too. If you're here to tell me anything about how he lives his life, what he's like, then I'm here to tell you that it won't be a surprise to me, and furthermore, I don't give a damn. I kicked him out years ago, haven't heard from him since."

"M-m-may we sit down, Mr. Crandell?" asked Scott. "What we have to tell you, it may take a while. We'd be more comfortable if we could sit down, I think."

Yeah, thought Alvarez, and it might save having to pick you up off the floor when you find out where all your money has gone in the last five years. "Okay, but don't get the wrong message," said Crandell gruffly, sitting down himself, perching on the edge of his seat like he didn't plan to stay there long. "You say one thing out of line, I'm on the phone."

"We've been investigating your financial affairs since the allegations in Pamela Case's letter came to light," said Alvarez by way of introduction.

"Some allegations," snorted Crandell. "A poor unfortunate unbalanced woman gets killed, and just because I knew her in a business capacity years ago, you think this means I murdered her."

"No," said Alvarez, "we no longer think you murdered her." Crandell looked at him sharply. "But to go back to what I was saying, we looked for evidence of blackmail payments in your personal accounts, and evidence of bribing a city commissioner in your business accounts, back before you turned the business over to your son and his partner.''

"Waste of taxpayers' money," repeated Crandell emphatically, obviously emboldened by Alvarez's statement that he was no longer viewed as a murder suspect. "Even if you do turn up something, what's the big deal? Montoya is dead, Pinnacle belongs to someone else, and I'm retired. If I were running for President, it might be another story, but I'm not, so who's going to care?''

Alvarez was afraid Crandell was right, and he was glad that he could sidestep those questions for the moment. "What we did discover," he told Crandell, "was a surprising lack of monetary assets.''

Crandell stared at him, taking a moment to process what he'd just been told. "Ha," he responded finally. "No surprise to find my financial affairs are over your head—you're probably the kind of person who lives paycheck to paycheck." Alvarez thought another good insult would be "You're the kind of person who lives off your dog's income," but he didn't want to interrupt Crandell's train of thought by suggesting it. "You don't think I'm fool enough to keep my money sitting around in banks, do you?" Crandell continued. "I keep most of our assets invested in stocks.''

"Your wife set up a special account at United Services Bank," said Alvarez. "It's special in that it's in her name only. During the last five years, she's moved hundreds of shares of stock into that account, liquidated them, and paid out the proceeds.''

"You're crazy," said Crandell bluntly.

"No, we're not," said Alvarez. "You'll have the opportunity to check out everything I'm telling you, but first, let me finish. Your wife has liquidated hundreds of thousands of dollars of stocks, bonds, and mutual funds.''

Crandell looked at him blankly. "Why on earth would she do that?''

"She's been paying the money to a J. Davis, and to various medical practitioners and facilities, all located in California.''

"She wouldn't, she couldn't," said Crandell, the color draining from his face. "I gave her a choice years ago, that sorry excuse of a son, or our marriage."

"Looks like she chose none of the above," said Alvarez.

"But why—why all the stocks? Even if she's been sending him money, how in God's name could he need that much?"

"You have a very low opinion of your stepson," said Alvarez. "Is it possible he might be involved with alcohol addiction, maybe other drugs?"

"Yes," said Crandell slowly.

"Rehabilitation clinics can be very expensive. Also, Keaton led us to believe your stepson may lead a homosexual lifestyle."

"That little slut should keep her mouth shut. Why we ever gave into Lenora's wishes and let Dale Junior marry her, I don't know. She's been a problem from day one, and now she's made a laughing stock—"

"In any case," continued Alvarez doggedly, "if drugs and alcohol are involved, it's unlikely that your stepson is in a monogamous relationship. Large medical bills may indicate that he's contracted AIDS. High-tech medical procedures can be very costly." Alvarez had to tread carefully here; confirmation of Jonathan Davis's status as patient was, by strict definition, information illegally obtained. As Alvarez saw it, his phone efforts had merely been confirming a hunch with information that could be gathered through proper channels later, if needed. However, the courts might see it differently, which was why he intended that the subject of his calls to various medical institutions should never arise.

Crandell was staring at Alvarez in horror. He had obviously made the connection between his stepson's lifestyle and staggering medical bills with no further hinting required on Alvarez's part. The man made an effort to pull himself together. "Even if it's true, why are you telling me this?" he croaked out.

"Because we think your financial status provided your wife with a motive to murder Pamela Case," said Alvarez bluntly, cutting to the chase.

"How—why—?" Crandell was reduced to gasping out his words.

"We think your liquid assets were insufficient to pay Pamela's request for a sum equal to her retirement benefits with the city," said Scott.

"The sum you previously referred to as paltry, when I talked to you yesterday," added Alvarez for clarification, just in case Crandell didn't get it. "We don't think your accounts had money to cover the amount she was asking for. At least, not without liquidating something that would take some time and noticeable effort." He glanced around the room. "Probably take a house like this at least two, three months to sell on the open market, and your wife might be afraid you'd ask about the For Sale sign out in front. If you weren't too distracted by other matters, that is." Alvarez smiled at Crandell pleasantly.

"I don't believe you," said Crandell flatly, regaining some of his composure. "And even if I did, what's the point in telling me all this?"

"Because if your wife killed Pamela Case," said Alvarez, "and you weren't involved, it means that she also torched Saul Case's house and tried to drug Hero and her mother so she could wander around Keaton's house, looking for financial records that you left behind."

Crandell looked as though he was putting together the pieces of a puzzle and not getting a picture he liked. "What is it you want?" he rasped out.

"We know you weren't home on Saturday, when Pamela was killed, so you can't help us there. But your wife said that the two of you spent Sunday evening together. We want you to tell us if that's a lie, and we want to know where she was Monday night."

Crandell clenched his eyes shut. "I need to think about this, talk to Barbara—"

That was the last thing Alvarez wanted him to do right now. "Fine, but first we want to show you something."

"What?"

"A little show and tell. We want you to take a ride with us."

"I don't have to go with you," Crandell said.

"No, you don't," agreed Alvarez. "But this may be your last chance to get out from under, help us out, convince us that you weren't part of it."

"None of this makes sense anyhow. Pamela was killed the day before she agreed to meet with me."

"Right," said Alvarez, standing up. "Let me show you something." He picked up the phone that Crandell had repeatedly pointed out, pulled a pocketknife out of his pocket and started to pry off the bottom plate.

"What are you doing?" Crandell demanded. Alvarez wondered if he could possibly have such a low opinion of police detectives that he thought this was their strategy to keep him from contacting his attorney.

"Calm down," he told Crandell. "This phone will still work just fine when I'm done with it." The bottom plate came away from the phone unit, and a microcassette with thin wires, disappearing into the internal mechanisms, was visible. Alvarez was relieved; visual demonstrations were really effective in an interview situation, but they could make you look like an idiot if they didn't work out. "Reliance Security Consortium," said Alvarez.

"What?" asked Crandell.

"Reliance Security Consortium," repeated Alvarez. Was it only yesterday that he and Mrs. Crandell had had much the same conversation? "They're a detective agency your wife hired to keep tabs on you, starting years ago. When she decided to stop paying for their services, she had them install some do-it-yourself devices." He held the phone up so Crandell could get a closer look. "If your wife monitors your phone conversations, then she knew what was going down with Pamela Case."

"But still—" protested Crandell.

Alvarez continued, talking over him. "And if she listens in on your conversations, you can bet she listens in on Tamara's. All she had to do was call Pamela up, say she was your secretary calling back with a change in plans, and move the meeting up a day. Poor Pamela was such a failure as a blackmailer that she let the arrangements be made by a go-between. What an amateur." Alvarez shook his head regretfully. He looked up at Crandell. "Does your wife own a gun?" he asked suddenly. "Do you?"

"I don't have to say anything," said Crandell desperately. "I don't have to answer any of your questions."

"No, you don't," Alvarez agreed. "We're not telling you to come with us, we're asking. Believe me, we've seen a lot of these situations, and you need to arm yourself with as much information as possible. So we're asking you to give us a few minutes of your time and accompany us on a little trip. On the drive, you can ask Scott as many questions about the financial stuff as you want. When we're done, we'll bring you back here and then we'll leave. It will be up to you to decide what you want to do with the information we provide. But I can tell you this, Mr. Crandell: This is a one-time offer, and if I were in your shoes, I'd jump at it."

Crandell kept looking back and forth between Alvarez's face and the phone he was holding. "If I go with you, it doesn't mean I have to answer any questions," he said.

"No sir," Alvarez assured him again.

"And it doesn't mean I'm committing myself to anything."

"Not a thing. All we're asking is that you take a ride with us, let us answer any questions you might have, and get you to listen to what we have to say. Then we bring you back here, we walk away, and that's it."

"That's it," Crandell repeated to himself, staring off into space. After a moment, he slowly stood up. "Okay, I'll do it. But I'm not just going off with you willy-nilly."

Alvarez had to work to keep the pleasant smile on his face. Willy-nilly? This from a man who had set in motion the events that resulted in a suicide, a blackmail attempt, and a murder? "What do you want us to do, sir?" he asked evenly.

"You tell me where you're taking me," Crandell demanded, "and how long we'll be gone, so I can let Tamara know. If I'm not back, she can take the appropriate steps."

Scott must have known that the words "Then what do you expect her to do, call the cops?" were on the tip of Alvarez's tongue, because he answered for him. "We want to d-drive out to Monte Vista Heights," said Scott. "It shouldn't take more than an hour, hour and fifteen minutes."

"Monte Vista Heights." Crandell spat the words out like they left a bad taste in his mouth. "I wish I'd never heard that name."

Alvarez thought for sure then that the jig was up and Crandell would balk, but he didn't. Crandell walked to the French doors, threw them open and told Tamara to fetch his coat. Then he told her where he was going and for how long. Holding his head high, as befitted his position in society, he walked away from the house toward the car waiting at the curb without once looking behind him to see if Scott and Alvarez were following.

THE WIND WAS kicking up. Tory helped Cal spread the plans across the hood of the city pickup. Cal ran his hand nervously through nonexistent strands of hair while the plans tried to blow away. "I don't know," he said for probably the hundredth time. "I have a real bad feeling about this." He squinted up at the sky. "Looks like it might rain."

Without bothering to look up, Tory replied, "Nah, not a chance. Look, I think there're three places where Carver might have made the connection." She pointed to the downgradient portion of the Desert Ridge sewer system closest to the series of ridges that visually separated the neighborhood from the vacant property composing Monte Vista Heights.

Cal stroked his head a couple more times, not looking at her. "Didn't ever say that I agreed it was Eldon Carver made the connection," he muttered.

"Okay," said Tory impatiently, "just because he has an elementary school named after him. I'm sure that has nothing to do with your reluctance to invoke his name in connection with what we're doing."

"Told you I had a bad feeling about this," Cal repeated. "Maybe we should just head back to the office, shelve this outing."

"No," said Tory firmly. "That's not a good idea. Look, if there're only three possibilities, it means that we might find what we're looking for with the first line we walk."

"Sixty-six-point-six percent chance we won't," said Cal dismally. "And when I do find this supposed connection, what am I supposed to do about it?"

Tory didn't have a politically correct answer to that one, so she opted for the technical approach. "What are you going to do if you don't have any answers to why the system works the way it does?" she countered. Cal didn't reply, and Tory decided to press her point. "How will all those deserving grant recipients ever live happily ever after out here if the city's Engineering Department can't figure out how to make the storm sewers work? How will—"

"Okay, okay," said Cal, holding up a hand as though to fend her off. One corner of the plans flew up in the air and Tory had to lunge across the hood to wrestle it back down flat. "You've convinced me, for the simple fact that I don't have any other good choices. Let's get this done, Travers. I swear to God it's gonna rain, and then I'm gonna have to wring your neck."

"It's great, working on something like this with someone I really feel good about, and trust," she replied. "You pick. Which one do you want to try first?"

Cal closed his eyes and let his finger come to rest on the plans. It wasn't the most technical approach, but it was the best Tory could get out of him. She resolved that if Cal Cortez ever needed a hair transplant donor, he'd need to look further than her head of hair.

AN HOUR LATER, two much grubbier people looked at the same set of plans, spread out on the hood of the same pickup truck. "Okay, so there must be another possible point of connection," Tory said desperately, studying the plans.

Cal had long given up even pretending to refer to them; his attention was once again riveted on the sky. "I know it's going to rain," he said. He sniffed the air like a hound dog. "Can't you smell it?'' What Tory smelled wasn't rain, and she felt sure the musty odors were emanating from her as well as Cal.

"So, where do you think we should try next?'' she asked.

"Madam,'' said Cal with a flourish, "you're acting like I give a damn. You know something, traffic engineering is looking better and better to me. You pick out one more damned line, and I'll walk it with you. If it doesn't pan out, that's it, that's the shooting show, the whole tamale, I'm out of here.''

"The whole tamale?''

"What now? You ridiculing my Hispanic roots?''

"Yeah, sure, Cal. Everyone has an angle.''

"Like you don't? Why are you so hot to figure this thing out, anyway?''

"I want to get paid for the work we've done.''

"That's not it,'' said Cal belligerently. "That damn letter from Pamela Case lets you off the hook for the engineering report, but you're still out here. What's it to you? Upgradient connection or not, it's no skin off your nose, *chica*.''

So now Cal was calling her the Spanish equivalent of chickie. How soon they regressed out in the field under a little pressure. Tory knew she was letting Irma Lujan down by not taking Cal to task for his language, but everything was relative, and she had other priorities. "I want to know the answer,'' she said doggedly.

"Shit,'' said Cal, grabbing the plans, bunching them together and throwing them inside the cab of the truck. "I want to know the answer, too, but not enough to spend the rest of my life duck-walking storm sewers.'' He strode purposefully to a manhole a hundred feet from Tory, knelt down and started prying off the cover. "Here,'' he said, "this one. We try this one, it doesn't work out, we go back.''

"Why this one?'' asked Tory, walking over to help.

He looked up at her and she wondered if her face could possibly be as dirty as his. "You know, your reputation is exaggerated. You really aren't that bright, are you?''

She stared at him, her mouth hanging open. "What?''

"This was the manhole closest to the truck, Sherlock.''

TWENTY-SIX

TURBULENT FLOW

ALVAREZ WASN'T PLEASED about the wind kicking up. He would have preferred a still afternoon with no breeze stirring for Dale Crandell to contemplate the things they were telling him, but sometimes you had to work with what you had. They had just pulled up at Monte Vista Heights, Scott driving, Crandell in the passenger seat and Alvarez in the back, providing the narration for this particular sight-seeing trip.

The isolated barren tract of land was as deserted as it had been the first time Alvarez set foot on it. The only evidence of yesterday's testing activities was the fact that all the manholes still stood uncovered, pocking the earth like giant, regularly spaced gopher holes.

"So they may have talked some at Ascarate Park, your wife and Pamela Case, or maybe not," Alvarez said, continuing his running commentary, "we'll probably never know for sure. What we do know is that at some point, your wife forced Pamela to get into her car and drive out here."

"You don't know that," said Crandell, but his tone was far from confident. "Everything you're saying is supposition."

"If she didn't think it out too clearly," continued Alvarez as though Crandell hadn't spoken, "she sat in the passenger seat next to Pamela, holding a gun on her. If she's seen enough cop shows and movies, she sat in the back—it gives you more control when the car comes to a stop and you get out."

In response to Alvarez's imagery, Crandell leaned forward, placed his forearms on the dash and put his head down. His words were muffled; Alvarez had to listen carefully to make out what he was saying. "All you can prove is that Barbara paid money to my stepson, paid his medical bills. I can't believe the woman I've been married to for forty-one years is a killer. Hell, she's never even gotten a traffic ticket.''

Alvarez was unconvinced. ''We've got means, we've got opportunity, and if you don't think we've got motive, you're kidding yourself. Living dishonestly takes a toll on a person. How many years has your wife been sneaking around, keeping tabs on you behind your back? How many years has she secretly kept in touch with her son? How long has she been finessing your finances while she kept you totally in the dark? Hell, I know professional embezzlers didn't do half as good a job as she did.''

''Still doesn't make her a murderer,'' mumbled Crandell, not lifting up his head.

''Remember when I was talking to the two of you at the hospital, telling you about Craig Diaz's affirmative action politics? Your wife told me that her idea of affirmative action was to raise your own kids. Kids, plural. You may have thought you disowned Jonathan, got him out of your life, but it didn't work that way for her. I'll bet if you could ask her, she'd say she had no other choice.''

''That's ludicrous. Of course she had other choices.''

''Really? If she would have come to you, talked about it, asked you to soften your stand on the kid, would you have listened?''

''You don't understand,'' said Crandell, lifting his head, but still not turning around to look at Alvarez. ''I tried to be a father, exert some positive influence, but there was nothing worthwhile in that kid to salvage,'' Crandell fervently told the windshield. ''He lied, stole, did drugs, defied me, you name it, he did it. Then on top of it all, he turned out to be a pervert.''

''And that was the last straw, wasn't it?'' Alvarez asked. ''The ultimate subgroup, the one that obscures any race or gender considerations.''

''It's different now,'' said Crandell, ''with all these gay pride groups, legislation to ensure freedom of sexual orientation, all that crap. Back then, such things weren't acceptable in polite society. I was a respected businessman, I couldn't have that kid going around town, acting like a goddamn fairy. You don't know what he was like—there was nothing in him to love.''

"Your wife didn't agree. You know," continued Alvarez thoughtfully, "this whole sorry business has its roots in maternal love. Pamela Case got bitter over things that happened after she moved here—her kids getting beaten up at school, her husband getting passed over for a promotion. Seeing how those things affected her kids was part of the reason she turned into the kind of person willing to falsify documents for you. She thought she was serving some greater good, tipping the political scales to make life fairer for her offspring. Everybody has an angle, Mr. Crandell, and looking out for her son has been your wife's major goal in life for years. You still think she wouldn't kill to make sure she could keep achieving her goal?''

"I want to go home," said Crandell. "Are we done here?''

"Not quite," said Alvarez. "I'd like you to step out of the car, sir.''

"Then will we be done?''

"Not more than ten minutes, and we'll be done.''

Alvarez, Scott and Crandell all opened their doors and climbed out of the car. "Your wife had to keep Pamela under control at all times," Alvarez continued. "So even if they talked for a while after they got out of the car, before your wife shot her, she probably stood behind her, holding a gun to Pamela's head. Like this.'' Alvarez stepped behind Crandell, trying to decide whether he should pull his gun and hold it to Crandell's head to make the narration more realistic. He was saved from having to decide when his cell phone rang.

He had the damn thing blocked for incoming calls except for headquarters and the three numbers with emergency status priority. Alvarez's sister had never had an emergency in all the years she had lived at Horizon House, Scott was standing next to him, and if Tory wouldn't answer her phone all evening, Alvarez doubted she was trying to get in touch with him now.

That left only headquarters, and as soon as he answered the phone, his guess was confirmed.

"Can it wait?" he immediately asked the person on the other end of the line. "I'm kind of in the middle of something."

"No, it can't wait." The voice on the other end, though trained to be dispassionate, crackled with a distinct undercurrent of urgency. "We have an emergency situation developing and we've been requested to notify you."

Just what he needed in the middle of a dramatic demonstration designed to push Crandell's emotional buttons. "What?" he demanded.

"A Dr. Gary Cabrioni is on another line, talking to us on his cell phone. He wants us to tell you that he's tailing a Mrs. Crandell. He says she abducted a young woman at gunpoint from the parking lot of Providence Hospital, made her get in a car with her and drive off."

Alvarez had an immediate sickening hunch about the identity of the abducted woman. "What the hell is Cabrioni doing, tailing them?" Scott stared at him from the other side of the parked car.

"He says the Crandell woman told him to wait five minutes before he did anything, or she would shoot the hostage. Cabrioni says he waited until her car was out of sight, then got in his car and drove until he caught up with her."

"What's he doing now?"

"Continuing to tail her. He doesn't think she's noticed."

"So where the hell is he?" Alvarez held up a time-out hand toward Scott and Crandell while he concentrated on the phone conversation, trying to decide what to do next. Sending in patrol units with lights flashing was not always the brightest thing in a hostage situation. Alternatively, hoping an unmarked car was in the vicinity was a slim shot.

"Sir," said the dispatcher, sounding apologetic, "he says he doesn't know where the hell he is, he'll let us know when he gets there. Uh, would you like to speak to him directly? I can patch him through."

"Goddamn it," Alvarez snarled into the phone. "Don't put

him through to me—I won't be responsible for the results if you do. Tell him this isn't some kind of game—we need to know where the fuck he is. We need cross streets, neighborhoods, any kind of reference point. Tell me exactly what he says."

There was a pause and then the dispatcher was back, sounding even more apologetic. "Cabrioni says fuck you, sir. I mean, he said fuck you, I added the 'sir.' He doesn't know where he is, and he says he doesn't have time to look for street names. He says he's never been held at gunpoint, tailed a car, and talked on a cell phone at the same time, and he's doing the fucking best he can."

In the distance, Alvarez saw Keaton's car appear over the ridge which was bisected by the entrance road to Monte Vista Heights. "Never mind," he said. "They just pulled into view. We have a hostage situation developing out here at Monte Vista Heights. Tell Cabrioni to stop following. We've got everything under control, tell him to stay away."

There was another short delay before the dispatcher was back. "Dr. Cabrioni just said fuck you again," the dispatcher informed Alvarez. "Actually, what he said was fuck you, asshole. Then he hung up." There was a pause. "Uh, I can't find Monte Vista Heights on our map. Can you give me a street name?"

"Yeah," said Alvarez, keeping one eye on the car as it pulled up to within a hundred feet of where they stood. "The street names are A, B, and C. Let me tell you what we're near." Scott already had his gun out; Alvarez stepped in front of Crandell while he continued to give detailed directions to the dispatcher. He'd just had a previous question answered—Mrs. Crandell was in the back seat, professionally holding a gun to Keaton's head.

IT WAS A SIGHT as rewarding as finding water in the desert—that moist sheen visible in the distant end of the pipe that Tory and Cal were walking.

"See," said Tory, pointing ahead with her flashlight. "There it is. There's the answer to all your design questions. Now, aren't you glad you came?"

"You never know enough to stop when you're ahead," replied Cal. "My back is going to be killing me for months. So now we've found the upgradient connection. Let's head back to where we can see the sun and stand up straight."

"It's not quite that simple," said Tory.

Cal whirled around to look at her, not an easy task in a storm-sewer pipe. "What the hell do you mean, it's not that simple?" His voice echoed in her ears.

"We need to know where the line ties into the Monte Vista Heights system," she said quickly, resisting the urge to put her hands over her ears before he could answer.

The city engineer just stared at her for a moment. "You're telling me we have to walk to the end of this line? Are you crazy? You realize that at the end, it's partially full of water?"

"Yeah," she said.

"And you realize it's January?"

"Yeah," she said again.

"But you're still standing there and—no, I take that back. You're still crouching there and telling me that we have to walk to the end of this line."

"That's the only way we'll be able to pinpoint the exact location of the tie-in to the other system," Tory explained. "Locating this line just gives us half the answer. Besides, I checked water levels last thing yesterday, on my way home, after everyone else left." She didn't feel the need to mention that she'd needed some time alone after the various inspection activities at Keaton's house. "There shouldn't be more than two to three feet of water in any of the inlet boxes." She did her best to make that last piece of information sound cheery.

"Just two or three?" Cal asked, his tone ominously quiet.

"Yeah," she said again.

"Well then, what are we waiting for?"

She looked at him, surprised. "I know what I'm waiting for. You're ahead of me, so you have to go first."

"Before we proceed any farther," said Cal formally, "let's get something straight. You're the consultant, right?"

"Right," said Tory, wondering where this was going.

"And I'm the client, right?"

"Right," said Tory again.

"So that means you, as the consultant, are supposed to provide me, the client, with required services. Right?"

"Right," said Tory for the third time, cautiously.

"Good, I'm glad we got that straightened out. Here's the plan. When we get to the end of this goddamn line, I'm climbing out. Then you go back through this goddamn pipe, get the truck, and come pick me up."

Tory glared at him, wondering if he would notice in the dimly lit pipe. "Boy, is chivalry dead, or what?"

"I'm assuming that when you said boy, you didn't mean it as a personal insult," replied Cal. This, from the man who had called her *chica* earlier. "Listen, you wanted equal opportunity, you got it," he continued. "I'm not treating you any different than I would if your name was Tony."

"Right," said Tory through clenched teeth, and Cal turned away from her. "Hope it rains," she said under her breath.

Sound must have carried well, for Cal did a pretty good job of whirling around again. "What?" he demanded.

"Nothing," said Tory, then added, as one would say to a horse, "Walk on."

TWENTY-SEVEN

THE HERO TRAFFIC ENGINEER

"WHAT'S HAPPENING." Dale Crandell grabbed Alvarez's shoulder from behind; Alvarez shook him off, never taking his eyes from the car that had come to a stop in front of them, easing his gun out of his shoulder holster and training it on Barbara Crandell as she slowly emerged from the back seat, gun in hand, pointed all the while at Keaton.

"Get in the car," Alvarez said.

"The hell you say—" Crandell responded, and Alvarez decided that as long as the old man didn't get in the way, he would just ignore him. He needed to focus on the scene unfolding in front of him.

Mrs. Crandell completed exiting the car, carefully keeping the gun in her hand trained on Keaton's head.

"David," Scott said softly.

"Yeah?"

"We haven't g-g-gotten to hostage negotiations yet."

"What?"

"In my stuttering class, we haven't g-gotten to hostage negotiations."

"No problemo, *ese*," said Alvarez quietly, his eyes never moving from Barbara Crandell. "As long as she doesn't shoot me, I'll do the talking." Before he had even finished his response, Scott melted away, somehow putting distance between him and their car without appearing to move.

Keaton emerged from the driver's seat of the other car and then Mrs. Crandell was almost completely hidden behind her. Alvarez, lover of tall women, was desperately wishing that Keaton were five feet two and wondering if it would go against all known negotiation procedures if he just up and volunteered to give Mrs. Crandell her husband, no strings attached. Even if he and Scott were somehow wrong in their assumptions, even if the Crandells were both in this together, Keaton's life seemed a horrible price to pay for bringing them to justice. Maybe it would be punishment enough for the two Crandells to live out their lives in each other's company, bereft of the funds that had enabled them to engage in their separate practices of duplicity.

As it turned out, worrying about who would make the first overture was unnecessary, since the very next thing Alvarez heard was the deafening sound of a shot rending the air.

TORY AND CAL were approximately twenty feet away from the inlet box that was their destination, slogging through about a foot of water, when they heard the shot.

Cal froze. "What the hell was that?" he hissed.

"Shhhh," said Tory immediately. Then after a moment, she added in a low voice, "It was a gunshot." Somehow, saying it out loud made it seem more real, not that that was necessarily a good thing.

"Holy Mother of God," said Cal, rapidly backing up until he bumped into Tory. "Have you got your cell phone?"

She shook her head. "I left it in the truck," she whispered.

"Let's get the hell out of here."

One part of Tory's mind actually wanted to ask Cal if he still planned to wait while she fetched the truck, but she suppressed the urge. "Something's going on," she whispered furiously. "Someone might need help."

"And if someone does," hissed Cal, "what do you expect me to do? Dodge bullets while I beat the bad guy into submission with my hardhat?"

"If we go all the way back through this line, get the truck, it will take too long," Tory hissed back. "If we go on to the inlet box, we can take a peek, see what's happening—no one knows we're in here."

"Yeah," said Cal, "and I want to keep it that way."

"You can just take one look," Tory insisted. "If someone sees you, you can duck back into the pipe."

"Yeah," Cal whispered back. "And if someone comes down in here after us, then what's your brilliant plan? It's a straight shot through these pipes, in case you haven't noticed, and I don't run real fast as a hunchback. You ever hear the phrase, like shooting fish in a barrel?"

Tory didn't have an answer to what he was saying. "Somebody might need help," she said stubbornly. There was a long moment while they glared at each other. Somehow a standoff didn't seem nearly so dignified when both parties were in a crouching position.

"Fine," said Tory finally, trying to convey anger without raising her voice. "Get around me, go back. I'm going up there to take a look."

Cal glared at her for more long moments, and Tory had to concentrate very hard on standing still. Every muscle in her body was itching to take some kind of action, even if a good percentage agreed with Cal's suggestion. For every moment that went by, she felt as though a clock were running out, the silence shrieking a demand to be broken by another gunshot.

"The hell with it," Cal whispered finally. "I try to get around you in this pipe, you'll probably sue my ass for sexual harassment." He turned back around and started slowly toward the inlet box in front of them.

"Be quiet," Tory admonished him, hard on his heels. "And when you get there, go up the side rungs real quietly, just ease your head up and take a quick look."

"Shut up, Travers," Cal shot back at her in an angry whisper. "If there's one thing I can't stand, it's a goddamn backseat driver."

THE FIRST THING a gunshot inspired was an overwhelming urge to return fire, especially if one already had gun in hand. It took all Alvarez's will power to wait until Keaton's body dropped so he could get a clear shot at Barbara Crandell. He went on waiting, and since everything seemed to be happening in slow motion, it seemed like forever before the realization struck him that Mrs. Crandell had discharged her gun into the air.

"I want you to know I'm serious," she called, still mostly invisible behind Keaton. "Scotty, don't try that—you move back where you were. I want all of you close together so I can keep an eye on you." Alvarez felt, rather than saw, Scott return to his original position on the other side of their car.

"My God, you were right," Alvarez heard Crandell gasp behind him. "You were right—she killed Pamela. Oh my God oh my God, what do you think she wants?"

"I don't know," said Alvarez through clenched teeth, "but it would be a good idea for you to get in the car."

He heard the car door open behind him, but then Mrs. Crandell called out again, "Dale, you stay right where you are. Don't make me shoot someone."

Behind Keaton and Mrs. Crandell, Alvarez saw another car crest the ridge and head toward them. It was not a police car. "Jesus H. fucking Christ," he said under his breath.

He heard Scott mutter, "And Donna wonders why I won't watch soap operas with her."

The new vehicle made a wide berth around Keaton and Mrs. Crandell and pulled slowly up next to Alvarez. There were long moments of silence, broken only by the sounds Gary Cabrioni made as he cautiously emerged from his car, dramatically clasping his hands behind his neck without even being asked to do so as he came to stand next to Alvarez. Alvarez resisted the urge to turn and shoot him in the foot just to teach him to follow instructions.

"You all stand there, close together, just like that," called Mrs. Crandell from behind Keaton. "Detective Alvarez?"

"Yes ma'am." Alvarez's deceased mother would be proud of his manners.

"You were on your cell phone when we drove up."

"Yes, ma'am."

"You were talking to the police department."

"Yes, ma'am."

"You told them to send officers out here."

"Yes, ma'am."

"Well, you call them right back and tell them not to send anyone."

Alvarez decided this warranted a different response. "Mrs. Crandell, drop the gun," he said sternly. "You're under arrest."

"Don't be ridiculous," she replied immediately. "If you don't do what I say, I'm going to shoot Keaton. Now, everybody stand real still while we come closer. Then I want you to talk real loud, Detective Alvarez, so I can hear what you say when you make that phone call. And you better make it quick, because if I see any other cars anywhere near here, I'll shoot Keaton. I'm very disappointed in you, Dr. Cabrioni," she added, almost as an aside.

"Sorry," he yelled.

"You just shut up," Alvarez said to Cabrioni. He was struggling to get his cell phone out and make the call with one hand. He was loath to surrender having his gun trained on Mrs. Crandell, even if in truth it was mainly trained on Keaton.

Alvarez watched grimly as Mrs. Crandell walked Keaton to within a stone's throw of where they were standing. Alvarez's only other hostage experience had been when a teenaged kid's robbery of a convenience store went bad and he grabbed the middle-aged man behind the counter, holding him at gunpoint to try to negotiate his escape. In the forty-five minutes it took to talk the kid down, the unfortunate cashier had whimpered, hyperventilated, and urinated on himself. In contrast, Keaton had never looked better than as Barbara Crandell's hostage.

She stood tall as she walked toward them, stumbling a little when Mrs. Crandell steered her around one of the open manholes in their path. No longer dressed in the gray sweats of yesterday, Keaton wore black pants, black high heels, and a plum-colored tunic sweater which set off her reddish golden curls to every advantage. There was color high in her cheeks, and her pale eyes were wide with what looked to be outrage rather than fear.

When Mrs. Crandell jerked her to a stop, Keaton immediately called out to Alvarez. "Shoot her, David. Go ahead and shoot her, I don't care. She's the fucking bitch who drugged Hero, and I want her dead."

"Shut up," snapped Mrs. Crandell, savagely jerking Keaton from behind.

"Be quiet, Keaton," said Alvarez firmly, raising his voice so it would carry over the wind. "Let me make this phone call so we'll have time to work everything out."

"No," called Keaton insistently. "I don't want to wait. Shoot her now."

"No," shouted Cabrioni. "Don't do it. Let Keaton go, Mrs. Crandell, I'll take her place."

"Shut up," yelled Keaton, simultaneously with Alvarez and Mrs. Crandell. Keaton ignored the both of them. "You're an asshole," she yelled at Cabrioni, "and if you think this is going to get you in my good graces, you're crazier than I am."

"This is way more dramatic than hospital linen closets," muttered Scott.

Alvarez wondered if he dared shoot into the air like Mrs. Crandell, just to bring a little order to the proceedings. Instead, he held his cell phone aloft, careful to make slow, deliberate movements. "I'm making the call now," he said, and managed the feat of punching the speed dial one-handed. "Alvarez," he told the dispatcher loudly enough that Mrs. Crandell could hear. "I'm calling from Monte Vista Heights. Do not, repeat, do not send any patrol units. We have a hostage situation, and the subject has threatened to shoot the hostage if any vehicles appear. Block all access roads to this area."

The dispatcher on the other end of the line was well-trained, taking in Alvarez's request without comment, waiting for her one chance to get more information. "Copy that," she said dispassionately. "One subject, one gun?"

"That's right," said Alvarez.

"Hang up," commanded Mrs. Crandell, and Alvarez did. "Okay," she said. "You did good. Now, all you have to do is step away from Dale."

"Shoot her, shoot her," chanted Keaton, breaking her temporary silence. Then her head jerked back, hard.

"Shut up," said Mrs. Crandell, "or I'll rip a piece of your scalp out, and don't think I won't." Tears coursed from the corners of Keaton's eyes, but the outrage didn't die. The fact that the tears appeared to be due to pain rather than fear somehow made it easier for Alvarez to keep looking straight into Keaton's face while a gun was pointed at the back of her head.

"You know we can't do that," said Alvarez, trying to sound firm and reasonable at the same time. "We can't trade one hostage for another." He was desperately trying to think ahead, to anticipate the next request.

"Don't toy with me. You know as well as I do what I want."

Jesus, didn't most hostage-takers come right out and articulate their demands? On top of everything else, he was going to have to negotiate with someone who wanted to play guessing games? "Right," said Alvarez, trying to sound a lot more certain than he felt. "You want your husband, then you want us to let the two of you go. It's not going to work that way."

"Are you really that stupid, or are you just acting?"

"We're not stupid, Mrs. Crandell. We know that you killed Pamela Case, torched her son's house, drugged Hero."

"And do you know why?"

"Yes. We know about your son. We know that's he's ill, that he needs money."

There was a silence that seemed to stretch on forever. "I made sure no one was in the house when I set fire to it," said Barbara Crandell finally, "and I didn't mean any harm to Hero. I just wanted to make sure she didn't wake up. The night before, I thought for sure she'd seen me."

"You must have started going through Keaton's house before you ever met with Pamela," Alvarez said, his detective's curiosity coming to the rescue, providing him with the next thing to say.

"When that woman first called Dale, mentioned other evidence, he told her those records were someplace where no one would ever put their hands on them. But I knew different, and I knew that if Keaton ever got wind of what was going on, she would turn them over. My son Dale would have given them to me in a heartbeat, but he's not where anyone can reach him."

"Why'd you kill Pamela?" asked Alvarez. "Couldn't you reason with her, work something out? She wasn't asking for that much money. Maybe you could have—I don't know." Words, stuttered or not, failed him for a moment. "Couldn't you have worked out some kind of blackmail installment plan?"

"Jesus," Alvarez heard Scott exhale to the side of him. Well, did he want to take over talking to this homicidal society matron? Alvarez was trying to buy time, although for what, he didn't know. The more Barbara Crandell talked, the more it sounded like she was in this by herself. If that was the case, why did she feel the need to liberate her husband?

"I brought her out here. It was isolated, and it seemed the right thing to do, somehow," said Mrs. Crandell. "But she wouldn't listen to reason, she wouldn't promise to leave us alone. She was insistent and whiny." Mrs. Crandell sounded almost surprised at her own observation, and Alvarez wasn't terribly shocked to hear that Pamela Case hadn't crumpled into immediate submission. "If she would have listened, things would have turned out differently. She was rude to me," Mrs Crandell added. There was a pause. "And she was the first one, the one who got Dale started on other women."

"That must have been hard to handle," Alvarez said, then grimaced at himself. Clichés R Us couldn't outdo that one.

Mrs. Crandell didn't seem to mind the lack of originality. "And she knew about Jonathan," she continued, her voice losing its composure for the first time. "Dale had told her about Jonathan, and she taunted me about it. I won't even repeat to you the things she said." There was another pause. "So I shot her." Alvarez thought it one of the saddest statements he had ever heard. Beyond the threats, beyond the blackmail, he felt certain that if Pamela Case had simply refrained from insulting Mrs. Crandell's first-born son, there was a good chance she'd still be alive.

"Well," he said, trying to introduce just the right tone of briskness, "that's all in the past. It stops here."

"You know that's not true," Barbara Crandell replied immediately, her voice sounding strong again.

"Why not?"

"You know why not."

Alvarez felt sure other hostage negotiators had loftier, more intellectual exchanges. "I don't know what you're talking about," he said, feeling like an idiot.

"I was just at our life insurance agent's office," she replied, "before I went home and Tamara told me where you'd taken Dale. I knew you were probably onto me, and even if you weren't, if you still thought that Dale murdered that woman, it didn't matter."

"Why didn't it matter?" asked Alvarez, genuinely confused.

"I'm getting a really bad feeling about this," he heard Scott say quietly.

"Because you were going to cost us lots of money, one way or another, money we didn't have. Dale would either end up defending himself against bribery charges or against murder charges, it didn't matter which. Attorneys cost the same, it doesn't matter what they're defending you against."

"If you thought we were onto you, why didn't you just take off?" asked Alvarez, getting to the heart of what had been bothering him all along.

"Because I need to kill my husband before you arrest me," said Barbara Crandell calmly, as though it were the most obvious conclusion in the world, and Alvarez felt a shiver run down his spine.

"Oh my God oh my God," he heard Crandell start chanting behind him.

"You can't hope to collect on his life insurance," Alvarez said.

Barbara Crandell laughed, which was almost as scary as listening to her explanations. "Do I look like someone who expects to walk away? Think I can shoot Dale right now and no one will guess who did it? I know that you talked to that insurance agent. He told me the police had called. Now is not the time to be coy."

"You're right. We talked to him. We wanted to see if you'd cashed in your life insurance policies."

"You mean he didn't tell you?" There was surprise in her voice, then irony. "You mean I could have waited, taken care of this in my own sweet time?"

"What was it that the insurance agent didn't tell us, Mrs. Crandell?" asked Alvarez, trying his best to sound authoritative.

"That I changed the beneficiary on Dale's policy to Jonathan. That's why I went there, that's why I waited to kill my husband. I needed to make sure that the change was in effect. Dale's policies will see toward Jonnie's needs nicely—it won't really matter that much what happens to the rest of our estate."

"Does this make sense to you?" Alvarez asked Scott quietly, never taking his eyes off the women in front of them. Crandell continued his endless chant from behind Alvarez.

"What m-matters is, it seems to make p-p-perfect sense to her," Scott replied in the same quiet tone.

"Now, Detective Alvarez, I need you to step aside," continued Barbara Crandell, "or I'm going to shoot Keaton. It may not achieve what I'm after, but you might have a hard time living with the knowledge that you sacrificed her life for someone like my husband."

Three things happened simultaneously as Alvarez had the sickening realization that his training was making the decision for him; he simply could not step aside and allow someone to shoot the man behind him in cold blood.

"Noooooooo," wailed Cabrioni.

"Don't you move," shouted Crandell from behind Alvarez. "It's your job to protect me, so don't you move a step."

Alvarez wanted to remind Crandell that he thought Alvarez merely a paycheck-to-paycheck kind of guy, as he saw movement at ground level. A hardhat, then a forehead, then Cal Cortez's eyes emerged from a manhole directly behind the two women, stared at him in horrified recognition, then disappeared as quickly as a rabbit down a hole. Alvarez wondered if he had imagined the whole thing while he fervently hoped that neither

Cabrioni nor Crandell would give any indication that human life was emerging from the storm sewers beneath them.

"I'm going to count to five," said Mrs. Crandell. "And if you don't step aside by the time I get through, I'm going to blow Keaton's brains all over the place, just like I did with Pamela Case. And don't think I won't. It's easier the second time, and I have nothing left to lose. One, two..."

CAL WAS CLINGING to the metal rungs on the side of the inlet box, looking down at Tory. They didn't need to engage in any discussion, they had heard most of the conversation on Mrs. Crandell's end just fine, more than enough to fully grasp what was going down above them.

"Do something," Tory hissed, trying to be quiet and at the same time galvanize Cal into action. He looked at her blankly for a moment, as though his mind had gone elsewhere.

Mrs. Crandell began her countdown. Cal turned away from looking at Tory and began an agonizingly slow movement back up the metal rungs. "Do something," Tory hissed again, louder this time.

"Two, three..." Tory heard.

Cal paused at the opening, then hunched his shoulders and projected himself out of the manhole, using muscles and reflexes that hadn't been called into action since he made a name for himself in basketball in the Bowie High School gym three decades before.

Tory heard a gunshot, then Cal yelled "Oh shit," and then she was frantically climbing up the metal rungs.

ALVAREZ ALWAYS THOUGHT it was damned unfair when people cheated, especially when they did it to your face.

He had decided to shoot on the count of four, hoping he could graze Keaton's side and hit Barbara Crandell, hoping that if Keaton crumpled she would take the woman down with her. He never got the chance, because Mrs. Crandell never uttered the word four. On the count of three, Cal Cortez propelled himself out from the manhole behind the two women, embracing them both about the knees and bringing them to the ground.

As Alvarez watched Keaton, Barbara Crandell, and Cal Cortez fall to the ground in a tumble of arms and legs, a huge force struck him, seemed to lift him up for a moment, then dropped him on the ground beside the car, hard.

TWENTY-EIGHT

POINT OF DISCHARGE

SCOTT WAS ALREADY standing over Barbara Crandell by the time Tory climbed out of the manhole, kicking the gun away and reaching for his handcuffs. Cal was off to the side, curled into a ball, rocking back and forth, nursing a hand that stuck out from his wrist at a strange angle. He was chanting "Oh shit oh shit oh shit," but no one seemed to be paying him much attention.

Keaton scrambled to her feet, her eyes riveted where Tory's were, on Alvarez crumpled at the side of the car, bright red blood blossoming from his left side like a rose blooming in relief against the bleak winter desert landscape behind him. Dale Crandell stood leaning against the car, breathing as though he was having a heart attack. Then Keaton was up and running, closing the space between her and Alvarez, and Tory was right beside her.

By the time they reached him, Cabrioni was bending over him, stripping off his jacket, using one of the sleeves as a tourniquet. "Arterial blood," he said as though to himself. "Not a good sign."

"Do something do something do something," Keaton screamed at him, falling to her knees next to Alvarez. Alvarez looked very white, and he hadn't opened his eyes. Tory stood frozen over the three of them, not knowing what to do, not wanting to get in Cabrioni's way.

"Goddamn it Keaton, I am doing something," Cabrioni shouted without looking up. "Somebody get a car phone, call nine-one-one."

"Got it," Tory heard Scott yell. She glanced back at him.

Sure enough, he had Mrs. Crandell handcuffed and a cell phone already in hand.

"Let's get him flat," Cabrioni said, looking up at Tory. She helped him lay Alvarez down, then she sat on the ground and cradled his head in her lap. Keaton used the opportunity to shuck her sweater, shrugging it off over her head, then covering Alvarez with it. Tory was not surprised to note that Keaton's bra was color-coordinated with the plum-colored sweater.

"What do we do now?" Tory asked Cabrioni. She could already hear sirens in the distance.

"We wait," said Cabrioni. "Shouldn't be long, if he doesn't lose too much blood, he should make it. Looks like the bullet hit an artery, but his arm took most of it; it just grazed his side, I think."

Alvarez opened his eyes, looking sleepy, and focused on Keaton kneeling beside him in her lacy plum-colored bra and tight black pants. "I must have died and gone to heaven," he said.

Tory was so relieved to hear him speak that she didn't care what he was saying. "David," she asked frantically, "are you all right?"

"*Querida,*" said Alvarez, turning his head slightly to look up at her, "you are a wonderful, intelligent woman. An unpredictable woman. I love the fact that you crawl through storm sewers at the most unexpected times. But I am not all right. In case you haven't noticed, I have just been shot in the line of duty." Tory surprised herself by starting to cry. "You okay?" asked Alvarez, losing a little bit of his sleepy look.

"No, I'm not. I'm as close to having hysterics as I've ever been in my life," she said. It was true. She'd lived through demonstrations, arrests, the scandal of being a teenager romantically linked with her father's campaign manager, childbirth, her husband's horrible lingering death from cancer, being shot at, an attack by a madman sitting behind a crane, and being held at gunpoint. But she had never, ever seen this much blood. She didn't know how one person could have that much blood in him.

"Think about something else," Alvarez said.

"Like what? What should I think about at a time like this?" Tory tried to keep the hysteria out of her voice; she could see blood continue to course from under the tourniquet, pulsing out with every beat of his heart. Cabrioni knelt on the other side of Alvarez, holding his wrist, monitoring his pulse. He hadn't said anything in a long time. Tory didn't know if that was a good sign or a bad sign.

"Keaton's underwear works for me," Alvarez said. When she didn't reply, he added, "I couldn't get through to you last night, *cara*. Why did you have to run and hide, take your phone off the hook?"

"Why did I what?" asked Tory blankly, then she understood. "I didn't take the phone off the hook," she told him. "For a detective, you're not very good at figuring things out." The sirens were getting really loud now, but she didn't look up.

"Tell me."

"I don't have to take the phone off the hook. I have a teenager at home. A teenager in love."

Alvarez looked thoughtful. "You're right," he said. "I should have thought of that." There was the sound of vehicles pulling up and then people in uniforms were suddenly everywhere, some of them telling her to move out of the way. "Don't worry, I'm not going to die." Alvarez raised his voice to be heard as he disappeared from view behind the emergency medical technicians. "I would never make things that easy for you."

Tory stood up, wiping her hands on her jeans. They felt sticky. She looked down and saw that she was covered with blood.

"I'll put on a shirt when I goddamn feel like it, you pissant excuse for a human being," she heard Keaton say. "Take care of him first, get your hands off me, you little pervert—"

A lot of people were talking at once, and all the sounds seemed to run together. Tory felt as though she was going to throw up, then Scott was suddenly next to her, holding her up. "It's going to be all right," he said. "You need to sit down, put your head between your knees."

"Over here," she heard one of the ambulance drivers call. "We've got one going into cardiac arrest."

"What the hell does it take to get some medical attention around here?" yelled Cal, still curled in a ball, still rocking back and forth.

Then Tory didn't hear anything else, because the ground came up to meet the sky and everything turned black.

EPILOGUE

IT WAS LATE in the afternoon, the last Friday in January, and Tory should be on her way home, not taking one last look at a prospective job. But she was nervous, and work, as always, was a good distraction.

Tory kept trying not to count up the number of people who were coming to her house for dinner. The very thought made her queasy. It hadn't taken Cody a lot of effort to convince her to have the food catered; all she had to do now was get home, take a shower, get dressed, and go pick up dinner. It seemed simple enough, all she had to do was those few things, and avoid having a nervous breakdown while doing them.

The dinner was ostensibly for her father, who was leaving on Sunday, finally, to return to his home in Florida. But it was also the first time Alvarez would be meeting her father and son.

For a while, it had been touch and go whether Alvarez would be discharged from the hospital before Tory's father departed. Not only had he lost copious amounts of blood, he'd contracted a devastating fever afterward. It had complicated his condition and lengthened his stay in the hospital, but he had finally been discharged two days earlier. Alvarez was thinner and weaker than after his previous injury, but sporting a whole new set of slings for his left arm.

Scott told Tory that there had been significant muscle and ligament damage, and that physical therapy would take longer and be more extensive this time, with the results less certain. Alvarez refused to discuss the matter with Tory when she visited him in the hospital, always changing the subject to something else. Instead, they played endless rounds of gin rummy and discussed past cases. She didn't know if he was in denial, or if that was simply his way of coping with uncertainty.

When the medics had temporarily abandoned Alvarez to rush to Barbara Crandell's side, he had seen Tory keel over in Scott's arms in a dead faint, which he took as a sign of her undying devotion. She refused to discuss the matter with him, always changing the subject to something else. She didn't know if she was in denial, or if that was simply her way of coping with uncertainty.

Barbara Crandell had been rushed to the hospital along with Alvarez, but she never regained consciousness, and died two days later from heart failure with no family member at her side. Her husband, in spite of his gasping and wheezing, was pronounced to be in fine health. Alvarez told Tory that no one had decided whether to press charges against Dale Crandell Senior, but he doubted that the matter would ever go to trial. Tory wondered who would notify Jonathan Davis of what had transpired, but Alvarez didn't say, and she didn't ask.

Tory's father had asked her to invite Keaton and Hero to dinner, and when Tory issued the invitation, Keaton asked if she could bring Dr. Cabrioni. She quickly added that she was keeping her options open, but for now, Cabrioni had dropped the discussion of a custody suit, and that rated a dinner invitation in Keaton's opinion.

If Tory hadn't been so nervous about the whole idea of dinner, she might actually have gotten some enjoyment out of the thought of Keaton meeting Sylvia. Tory had already warned Sylvia that Alvarez was recently discharged from the hospital, and to keep that in mind when choosing her outfit for the dinner party.

Jazz would be there, and Lonnie, which was something else that Tory was carefully not thinking about. She had invited Cal Cortez, still sporting a cast, and his wife, in addition to Kohli and her parents. Fifteen people, her mind counted them up without her permission. In order not to panic, she resolved to concentrate on the benefits of having so many people at her house at one time—it was relatively unlikely Cody and Kohli would end up in a room by themselves. And, she might even be able to work a conversation with Cal around to the subject of how soon the city could be expected to pay for services rendered to date.

She walked to her car, taking one last look around Monte Vista Heights. Cal had told her that the city wanted to hire an engineering firm to design the site improvements required to move ahead with the project. Travers Testing and Engineering Company would certainly be submitting a proposal for that work, and Tory thought they should have a definite edge over the competition, having nothing to do with affirmative action programs. She felt beyond familiar with the project, she felt intimately acquainted with it. And she felt that if the ghost of Craig Diaz somehow still haunted this place, he would be proud of what it would be turned into.

As Tory got in her car, it began to sprinkle. She drove out of Monte Vista Heights and in a matter of minutes, the sprinkle turned into a hard, driving rain. As Tory headed for the interstate, the water wet the asphalt streets, then started to run off the gravity-graded surfaces, gathering into little rivulets as it did so. All over El Paso, rainwater started running through inlets into the storm sewers. Gradually, the storm sewers began running with water, small pipes leading to larger pipes, small streams combining to create a rushing flow of water, finally exiting the last pipe in a rushing flow of storm water, discharged into drainage structures, surface waters, or irrigation canals.

All throughout the city, motorists drove through the rain, making their way home after a full work week, mindful of slippery streets, but never giving any thought to the subterranean systems keeping the streets from being flooded.

Except for Tory, heading home, reviewing the dinner menu in her mind, wondering what she could possibly wear to gain Sylvia's approval. Except for Cal Cortez, walking out of the City Engineering Building, running for his car to head home and get dressed for dinner. Except for Tommy Diaz, staying late at school to meet with students entering the Science Fair, watching the rain dance on the school parking lot from the window in his classroom. Except for a gaunt man wearing a sling, scratching the head of a white, fluffy dog, looking out the window and thinking over his first words to a teenaged boy he'd never met.

And in Monte Vista Heights, the streets were deserted, devoid of any human traffic.

But the storm sewers functioned just fine.